Abigail Padgett grew up in Indiana. She has worked in teaching, vocational counselling and as a child abuse investigator. She now works as an advocate in the field of mental health.

Abigail Padgett lives and writes in San Diego, California.

ABIGAIL PADGETT

Moonbird Boy

a Bo Bradley thriller

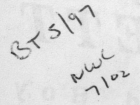

Published in Great Britain by The Women's Press Ltd, 1997
A member of the Namara Group
34 Great Sutton Street, London EC1V 0DX

First published in the United States of America by Mysterious Press,
Warner Books, Inc, 1996   07062032

British Library Cataloguing-in-Publication Data
A catalogue record for this book is available from the British Library

ISBN 0 7043 4513 7

Printed and bound in Great Britain by
BPC Paperbacks Ltd

To Nora

ACKNOWLEDGMENTS

To Mary Daly for dis-covering in *Gyn/Ecology* the dark history that gives this book its lurking viper.

To Michael Burleigh, Reader in International History, London School of Economics and Political Science, for the inspiration of his scholarship.

To Laurie Weir, Principal with Arkhos-Tekton, Inc. of Los Angeles, for technical advice on the architecture of rammed-earth dwellings.

To anthropologist Florence Connolly Shipek for sharing information amassed during her lifelong commitment to the Kumeyaay.

To the Kumeyaay, for surviving.

Author's note: While numerous bands of Kumeyaay Indians survive and even thrive on reservation lands within San Diego County, the Neji Band and their beloved Ghost Flower Lodge are entirely fictional.

Moonbird Boy

Prologue

The shark was old. Forty-two years had passed since she writhed from the body of her mother in the same shallow coastal waters where she now lazily observed a young California sea lion playing too far from the offshore rocks. At birth the shark had been only four feet long and weighed less than fifty pounds. Now she approached seventeen feet in length and weighed two tons. Her milky underside had prompted another, equally predatory species to name her *grand requin blanc, grande squalo bianco, Weisshai*. The great white shark.

Her ancestors had roamed Paleozoic seas nearly four hundred fifty million years before that other species, a landlocked ape, saw its own opposable thumb, grabbed a stick, and quickly assumed its place at the top of the terrestrial food chain. The human.

Its sweetish, fatty meat held little culinary interest for the great white. Like all sharks she preferred the more familiar taste of aquatic flesh. Only the blood of the little ape, its chemical composition similar to the seawater in which its distant origins lay, could create more than a passing attraction in the huge olfactory bulbs of her brain.

A quarter-mile from the safety of the rocks now, the young sea lion felt something in the water far beneath him. A shadow, moving away and then turning back with terrible purpose. The shadow arched its head toward the sparkling surface of the water and lowered a massive jaw. Three curved rows of triangular, serrated teeth, two rows in the lower jaw and one above, reflected the sun's light. The sea lion felt a consuming fear.

The shark's eyes, the only surface of her body not covered with an armor of overlapping, toothlike denticles, were rolled back in her skull. The sea lion raced through sunlit surface swells toward the impossibly distant rocks, using every resource of his immature body. His terror was a metallic scent in the water as his efforts failed. And then he wasn't in the water but airborne against the blue sky, catapulted above the water's surface by a massive flick of the shark's double-lobed tail as she turned abruptly to the south.

Blood! There was blood in the water less than three miles away. Molecules of hemoglobin and serum albumin, quickly dispersed by ocean currents, wafted through powerfully sensitive nasal sacs inside the shark's nostrils. The scent notified her brain to choreograph a sequence of events five hundred million years in development. All ten of her gills automatically pumped an extra surge of oxygen-laden water and then closed flat against her body, providing near-perfect streamlining as she moved swiftly toward the source of the attraction.

In minutes she was there in a cloud of red, her jaws wide and then clamped with thousands of pounds of pressure on something in the water. Twisting violently, she shook the thing, then released it and swam away to await its death. When it didn't move, she attacked a final time, tore a dangling segment of its body into her mouth, and swallowed. Then she turned away and moved into deeper water.

The sea lion, dazed but safely panting on the wet rocks, watched the surrounding sea for a hurtling shadow. He would watch for it now, forever.

Chapter 1

Bo Bradley adjusted her nest of rumpled blankets at the end of a battered leather sofa and eyed the TV with practiced cynicism. A window containing a digital time and date readout appeared annoyingly on the screen every five minutes. Her disinterest in the fact that it was 5:47 P.M. on a Tuesday in October was boundless. A perfect match for her disinterest in everything else, although she *was* improving. The worst of the depression, she acknowledged, was past, leaving in its wake wide stripes of crankiness and torpor. The newscaster's voice, stripped of regional accent, sounded mechanical and phony in the dim living room of Ghost Flower Lodge.

"Police and experts from the Scripps Institute of Oceanography confirm that the tragic death of San Diego heiress Hopper Mead this afternoon was the result of a shark attack," the man announced. He was trying to sound appropriately somber, but in the slight flare of his nostrils Bo saw another feeling. Fear. Safe in a studio four miles from the nearest saltwater, he could not hide his terror of sharks.

"Wimp," Bo whispered at his profile. The news broadcast made her irritable. But then so did everything else.

On the screen, footage of a tanned, blond woman replaced the image of the newscaster. She was dressed in a tailored gray business suit and appeared to be receiving an award from a gaggle of politicians standing on risers. Bo noticed the young woman surreptitiously glance at her watch as she matched the insincerity of her smile to those of the politicians. Hopper Mead at only twenty-five, Bo thought, had been nobody's fool.

"Mead founded the well-known philanthropic organization called Mead Partnerships," the newsman went on in voice-over, "making significant contributions to numerous San Diego charities. Ms. Mead is seen here only two months ago receiving the Weinerth Award for Outstanding Civic Contribution. Surviving Ms. Mead is a brother, Randolph Mead, Jr., head of the locally based Mead Policy Institute. Mr. Mead has asked that in lieu of other remembrances, donations honoring his sister's life be made to the Mead Institute's charitable trust. The funeral will be held privately."

Bo found the television's remote control wedged in her blankets and pressed the mute button. A thirteenth-century painting of a shark devouring an out-of-proportion sailing vessel filled the screen. The painting carried a message she'd been fighting against for weeks. An awareness that life with its endless, dreary demands possessed no purpose whatever. Clinical depression.

Bo knew her condition's name but retained a suspicion that behind the name it was probably just the truth. Sharks might eat ships or svelte young heiresses with equal aplomb. Everything alive simply chewed its way back to the abyss of meaningless absence from which it had come. The melodramatic ideas were a good sign. They meant she was climbing out of the pit, getting better. In celebration, Bo allowed herself a long, shuddering sigh.

"Oh, Bo," Estrella Benedict said, shifting sideways on the couch to touch her friend's shoulder, "we're right here and whatever you're thinking isn't really the way it is. Dr. Broussard said it would take a while for you to get over this. I don't think you should focus on things that . . . that upset you. So let's turn the TV off, okay?"

Bo looked at the Spanish-speaking investigator with whom she'd shared an office at San Diego County's Child Protective Services for over three years. A friend who knew about Bo's manic-depressive illness but who had never seen this, the hollow shadow that gave the illness half its name. Nor, Bo realized, was Estrella seeing it now. She was just seeing Bo with stringy hair and mismatched clothes, sitting on a couch in a psychiatric facility ostensibly sighing over a bad painting of a fish. Nobody could really "see" what clinical depression entailed except those with the rotten luck to experience it. A fate Bo wouldn't wish on a shark, much less her best friend.

"Hey, are we ever going to eat?" Mort Wagman yelled from the adjacent game room where he was listening to a CD of Tchaikovsky's "1812 Overture" while hustling Estrella's husband, Henry, for pocket change at the lodge pool table. "Television news is a Mideastern plot to eradicate whatever intelligence remains in the Western psyche. You owe it to your nation to resist. Let's go eat!"

Mort was already a patient at Ghost Flower Lodge when Bo's psychiatrist, Dr. Eva Blindhawk Broussard, drove Bo there from the hospital and checked her in. A depression had flattened Bo after the gentle and carefully managed death of Mildred, her faithful old fox terrier, only a month ago. And Mort had understood. Had stayed up nights with Bo reciting poetry and the weird stand-up comic routines he performed in clubs, reassuring Bo that her grief was honorable and sane.

Bo liked Mort Wagman even though he was only twenty-six and prone to an incessant patter that might be a symptom of his schizophrenia or might just be who he was. It didn't matter. They'd become friends.

"A shark ate somebody for lunch today," Bo yelled back as Henry missed a seven-inch sidepocket shot and glared accusingly at his cue. "That's where an obsession with food can lead."

"Everything's relative, Ms. Morose," Mort answered over booming cannon from the stereo, grabbing the chalk cube with short fingers that trembled from the medications he was taking. "Did you know there's an old maritime belief that sharks will eat anything but pilot fish, who are their friends, and birds. To sharks the presence of feathers is sacred. So ask any chicken which species is innocent of murder—the shark or the human?"

As usual, Bo felt the murky cloud of depression in her mind diminish a little at Mort's remarks. His riddles were like flickers of light, points to navigate by in a sea of darkness. Or maybe it was just his caring that pulled her back toward life. Either way, it worked.

As Estrella turned the TV sound back up, Bo imagined a cathedral full of sharks. Above the altar a dazzling stained-glass chicken held sunlight in its feathers. She could do a painting of the scene, she thought. Watercolor, of course.

"Mead was attacked while swimming near her anchored yacht, *Minerva*," the newsman went on. His voice was barely audible over Tchaikovsky's celebration of Napoleon's retreat from Moscow blasting from the game room. "Authorities can only conjecture as to the reasons for this, one of surprisingly few shark-related human deaths on record."

The shark story concluded, the newscaster began an uninspired think-piece on rumors of organized-crime involvement in San Diego's Indian gambling casinos. A fuzzy police surveillance photo of a man with light hair and a dark mustache, reportedly an out-of-state gambling kingpin, filled the screen. But the shark snagged in Bo's brain and sat there. Millions of sharks and people inhabited the planet, she thought. Confrontations between the two nearly always involved the death of the shark from pollution, entrapment, or the deliberate savagery of hunting. Sharks were, in fact, so decimated in number by human predation that the ocean's food chain was dangerously unbalanced. Bo had watched a PBS special on the subject with Mildred only weeks before the little dog's death from an inoperable cancer. Sharks were slaughtered by the thousands, but very few times in the recorded history of human-shark encounters had a human perished. So why would this shark choose to kill this human on an October afternoon off the coast of San Diego, thereby joining a statistically improbable short list of gilled killers? Something about the story, Bo mused, seemed unlikely. The newsman capped his show with a cheerful description of four hundred "Christian family advocates" rallying to terminate public health care for single mothers and anyone else who "chose sin over righteousness."

"Mort's starving. Time to get dressed for dinner," Estrella said, grimacing at the TV. "He says this place we're going to is pretty casual, so just slacks and a top will do."

"I am dressed," Bo said, demonstrating the fact by tugging on a fold of lank T-shirt. "And remind me not to watch the news again this year."

"Well, you're not naked," Estrella agreed fondly, "but you're a mess. Get cleaned up or we'll have to eat in the car."

The predictable standoff between psychiatric outsider and insider over the issue of appearance. Bo glanced at her friend's shining dark hair and the starched white maternity blouse lying in folds over Estrella's expanding middle. The effort necessary to construct a tidy outward appearance, Bo thought, could be overwhelming when all your energy was consumed by arduous tasks like standing up and walking from one piece of furniture to another. She calculated that the achievement of a normal standard for appearance would probably take her about three days.

"I don't mind eating in the car," she said hopefully.

"Dr. Broussard says this is important," Estrella replied with finality. "Come on. I'll help you."

"My psychiatrist harbors a secret desire to sell overpriced makeup in department stores. You should ignore her."

"You're getting out of here in a day or two," Estrella sighed. "You can't come back to work looking like a used shoelace. This is practice. Let's go."

A half-hour later Bo allowed Estrella to blow-dry her freshly washed silver and auburn curls in the bathroom Bo shared with another guest known only as Old Ayma. Crusty Old Ayma, the facility's current albatross.

Bo had tried but couldn't bring herself to like the towering black woman. With her layers of musty shawls and veils and her habit of muttering angrily at invisible antagonists, Old Ayma was a walking stereotype of mental illness. Bad PR. The very image they were all fighting to overcome. Another guest told Bo he'd heard that Old Ayma lived on the street, that she'd been arrested for harassing the guest tenor at one of the Sunday afternoon organ concerts in San Diego's Balboa Park. Since she wasn't really a "danger to herself or others" the county psychiatric hospital wouldn't admit her and the police had phoned Zachary Crooked Owl out of desperation. And Zach's wife, Dura, had driven the sixty miles down into San Diego to get the old woman.

But Bo had seen Ayma "cheeking" her meds, pretending to swallow the pills that might help her and then secretly spitting them out. A lot of the younger people did that, before they'd accepted the truth about what was wrong. Bo had done it herself when she was young. But Ayma was *so* obnoxious . . . Bo shook her head and tried not to think about the old woman. She was glad Estrella hadn't seen Ayma. Too embarrassing.

"You can't tell me you don't feel better, even though you need a haircut," Estrella said as Bo selected a navy poplin blazer from her closet and switched off the light. "It's obvious that you feel better."

"Appearance isn't everything." Bo smiled, suspecting that it probably was. "Let's go eat."

Half an hour later she surveyed the interior of a restaurant that had once been a gas station as Mort Wagman smiled conspiratorially over an O'Doul's. The decorating motif reflected a Western theme featuring framed barbed wire samples orange with rust and an abundance of bovine skulls.

"Maybe we should just have eaten dinner back at the

lodge," Henry said. "This table's sticky and I'm afraid the ceiling fan's going to fall on us."

"Oh, no, this is just great," Bo and Mort insisted in unison.

"Really good for us to get out!" Mort went on.

"And I hear they have great refried beans," Bo added, ignoring Estrella's look of sheer disbelief.

California's child protection laws, exhaustive in their intent to avert harm, were actually responsible for the presence of the Benedicts, Bo, and Mort Wagman in a high desert eatery so desolate a tumbleweed had blown in the door with their arrival. When Estrella heard that Bo's friend Mort would be leaving Ghost Flower the next day, again stabilized on his medications, she had insisted on joining them and the other patients at the lodge for dinner to say good-bye. And that, Bo had explained to Mort, could not be.

"I think I'm technically off the hook as a mandated reporter as long as I'm in a licensed psychiatric facility," she told him the day before. "I'm technically nuts. But Estrella isn't. In California anybody who has regular contact with children is legally mandated to report any suspicion of child abuse, anywhere. Failure to do so can result in fines and a jail sentence. Estrella and I are employed by San Diego County to investigate cases of child abuse. Es will *have* to report that Bird is here with you."

Mort had pushed the mirrored sunglasses he wore day and night up into the long, dense black hair that had prompted the Indians to nickname him Raven, and hugged his son. The wiry little boy pulled away and rolled like a hedgehog under the pool table as his father replied.

"Keeping Bird with me here, where there were several other adults to care for him when I couldn't, isn't child abuse," he said quietly. "What does your system want parents who have psychiatric illness to do, give their kids away?"

"It isn't my system," Bo had answered. "I don't have systems. But if Estrella eats dinner here she'll see Bird and find out he's yours. Red flags will go up. A sick parent can't take care of a kid, and besides, when most people hear 'psychiatric rehab facility' they imagine gaunt, wild-eyed people in rags, chained to stone walls while screaming obscenities. Not exactly something a kid should see."

"There isn't a serviceable stone wall anywhere in Southern California and besides, Bird sees worse things every night on television." Mort laughed without humor. "Some of them are commercials *I* do. And this isn't a hospital emergency room. Everybody except Old Ayma is mellow, just recuperating. But why don't we duck the whole thing by inviting your friends to go out?"

Bo had glanced at the two-foot-thick rammed-earth walls of Ghost Flower Lodge, beyond which lay nothing but five thousand acres of unpopulated high desert—the Neji Indian Reservation.

"Out *where?*" she asked.

"Zach will know of someplace." Mort grinned, gesturing to the lodge's director, Zachary Crooked Owl. "Zach, baby," he'd asked in a flawless mockery of Hollywood patois, "where can Bo and I take some sane people out to dinner around here?"

There was a diner a couple of miles from the reservation, Zach said, but it was a dump. Bo and Mort had been delighted.

As Henry perused a handwritten menu in its cracked plastic slipcase, Bo pondered a framed announcement on the restaurant's wall.

"BEWARE THE DESERT!" it warned in block letters above a black-and-white photo of a dead, mummified body half covered with blown sand. The man's shriveled hands looked like claws emerging from his faded shirt cuffs. Vultures had left only blackened indentations where his eyes had been, and in one sand-filled socket a tiny cholla cactus displayed its murderous spines to the camera. Below a list of desert safety tips was the logo of San Diego County's Backcountry Sheriff's Department.

Bo sighed and tried to distract Estrella from the poster.

"I saw it when we came in," Estrella said. "Don't think about it."

"*You* shouldn't be looking at it," Bo answered, eyeing Estrella's bulging waistline. "It's not good for the baby."

Estrella shook her head and grinned. "Three weeks out here and you think like an Indian, old wives' tales and all."

"Yep," Bo agreed. Zach's wife, Dura, was a fountain of folk wisdom and never tired of telling stories. According to Dura an ancient Kumeyaay woman had spent her entire pregnancy trying not to see anything unpleasant that would mark her baby. "You can't touch guns, either, or the sights will go crooked," Bo went on. "Same for arrows."

"World peace through pregnancy." Estrella nodded. "If only it were true, we could end all wars just by organizing teams of pregnant women to fondle their heat-seeking missiles. I love it!"

"So, Mort," Henry interrupted uncomfortably, "Bo has told us you do TV commercials. What's the most recent one?"

Bo watched Mort Wagman smile his full-lipped smile inside the fashionable stubble of a two-day beard.

"Athletic shoes," he crooned. "The big bucks. The gig I went off my meds for."

"You went off your medications to do a *commercial?*" Estrella gasped. "I thought you had schizophrenia, and—"

"And nobody in his right mind would risk going back into that hell for anything," Mort finished and then took a pull on his nonalcoholic beer. "Except the Raven here. Except for the right money, the really huge money, the fuckin' mother-money of all time, dig? These guys just love insanity. Their market, teenage boys mostly, gets off on it. I'd already done three commercials just *acting* crazy. But this time I sold them the real thing, and they paid for it."

Under the table his right leg was jiggling nervously, a side effect of the medications he was taking again. The side effect would wear off in a few weeks, but meanwhile it gave him a twitchy, Hollywood-killer aura. Bo could see the waitress eyeing him with distaste.

"The next SnakeEye shoe promotion you see," he finished, twitching his ponytail over a shoulder, "will feature a *real* psychotic crawling around under the bleachers chewing on the basketball star's sneakers, not the usual half-baked fake. It's so high-concept the competition will wet themselves, I get rich, and nobody with a grain of human decency will ever buy another pair of SnakeEye shoes. This gig is my gift to posterity."

And a way to assure your son's future, Bo thought, but said nothing. Something in Mort's eyes suggested there might be another reason as well. A look of personal triumph, confidence. She wondered what it meant.

"My God," Henry breathed, "that's horrible!"

"Yeah," Mort said, grinning. "Don't ya love it?"

"That business about the shark was pretty horrible, too," Estrella said, deliberately changing the subject. "It's like *Jaws* right here in San Diego."

Bo glanced out the smudged glass door into desert darkness. "Nice to know it doesn't have anything to do with us," she mused aloud. "That shark isn't our problem at all."

But the words sounded hollow and the blackness against the glass outside seemed to shiver as if it were giggling. Just a spook of the depression, Bo told herself. There could be, after all, no sharks in the desert.

Chapter 2

By nine o'clock Bo was glad to see the reassuring outlines of Ghost Flower Lodge silhouetted against the mountains as the group returned from dinner. Behaving normally, tracking and joining a conversation shared by four people, had been exhausting. So had the effort to disguise the fact that canned-chicken tacos and greasy refried beans held about as much appeal as a plate of pond scum. A serious depressive episode, she acknowledged, could be an effective weight-loss program. Nothing tasted good and what was the point in eating anyway? It only prolonged the inevitable. After hugging Estrella and Henry good-bye she headed for the solace of her room, only to find Zachary Crooked Owl waiting for her.

As was the way with all the Indians who ran the lodge, Zach said nothing but merely sat on the thick window ledge fingering the owl's claw he wore on a leather thong around his neck. His massive body filled the arched opening like a buffalo seen through a keyhole, and his dark skin seemed to absorb the dim light.

"Zach," Bo said. "I'm tired."

He merely nodded without noticeable movement of the wiry braid resting on the back of his denim shirt. He'd say whatever he had to say when it felt right, Bo knew. The Kumeyaay who owned and ran the lodge all did that, a practice eminently suited to the needs of their frazzled guests. Leaving the door open, she settled into the room's only chair to wait.

It was a requirement that doors remain ajar when a man and a woman were alone in a room at Ghost Flower Lodge. One of the many old-fashioned Indian rules designed in a more realistic past when it wasn't politically correct to ignore the danger inherent in the nature of things. Zachary Crooked Owl wasn't dangerous, but Bo approved of the rule. Like the rammed-earth building with its massive walls and courtyard fountain, the rule made her feel safe.

"Ahh," Zach exhaled sadly, apparently lost in his own thoughts. Then he continued to sit in silence.

She'd been a little surprised when Eva Broussard first introduced her to Ghost Flower's Kumeyaay Indian director, who was also black, but at the time her depression had precluded any interest in the anomaly. Later she'd learned that the anomaly existed only in her mind.

"The poor living in city streets aren't so poor that a woman can't trade sex for the protection of a man from other men," Dura explained after Bo had been at Ghost Flower Lodge for a few days. "That's always there when she hasn't got anything else left to sell. Lots of street people are black, lots are Indian. The children they make are black Indians. And no tribe will refuse a home to a child whose mother can claim membership, whether that child has red hair and freckles like you or black skin like my husband. Except that it was his father who was Indian, not his mother. And that is why Zach has his own story."

That afternoon this tag line had pulled children from all over the lodge to Dura as if she'd blown a whistle. Sun-bronzed Indian children of the Neji Band of Kumeyaay, Dura and Zach's darker brood with their curly hair, who were also members of the band, and Mort's pale little boy, Bird, all ran to fling themselves on the floor at Dura's feet. Bo had been reminded of Pavlov's experiments with dogs. Except these weren't dogs, she noted, but people. And the reward for their response would be the ultimate human treat—a story.

"John Crooked Owl," Dura had begun that day many weeks ago, pointing to an amateurish oil painting of an old but bright-eyed Indian man over the lodge's stone fireplace, "once had a brother named Catomka. But something happened to Catomka. Something sad. In the old days the people believed in witches, and they said a witch had put a special stone in a spring that is in our mountains. A very terrible stone."

In the dramatic pause the children's eyes grew somber.

"This stone could hurt people's minds if they drank the water. This stone could make people hear voices that nobody else could hear, and see things that nobody else could see. This stone could make it so people couldn't *think!*"

Bo had thought she was just listening to a children's story, but her eyes filled with tears as she realized what was really being taught. The children, who had obviously heard the story many times, shook their heads sadly.

"But John Crooked Owl's brother, Catomka, drank from that spring," Dura continued. "Which is just a story-way of saying he got an illness in his brain. And Catomka heard voices that nobody else could hear, and saw things that nobody else could see, and couldn't think right anymore. And so his brother, John Crooked Owl, took care of Catomka for a long time until Catomka died. He took care of Catomka right here on his own land, the Neji land. John Crooked Owl cared for his brother, Catomka, until Catomka died and John was very old. Do you want to know what happened next?"

Embarrassed, Bo had caught herself answering, "Yes," along with the children.

"John Crooked Owl was the last of the Neji Band, the last of the Kumeyaay people who lived on this land. He never married because he had to care for his brother, and so he had no children. If he died, there would be no one to inherit the land, and the United States government would take the land and own it. It wouldn't be Kumeyaay land anymore."

"Nooo," the children whispered.

"So John Crooked Owl walked down into San Diego and looked and looked for a wife to love and have his baby even though he was an old man. But the people there just thought he was a stupid old Indian, too silly to talk to."

"Hah!" came a chorus of small voices.

"Finally John Crooked Owl was ready to give up and go home alone, when he found a lovely black lady who was running from a bad man and had no food and no place to sleep. Her name was Bea and she came here with John Crooked Owl to hide from the bad man and they began to take care of other people who were like Catomka. People who had no one to care for them. After a while Bea had a baby boy with John Crooked Owl, and they named him Zachary. He grew up and Bea went away and John Crooked Owl died, but Zachary Crooked Owl stayed. And that is how the Neji Band and the Kumeyaay land were saved. And that is why we care for people who are like Catomka at Ghost Flower Lodge to this very day."

"Wow," Bo breathed as the children whooped and ran back to whatever they'd been doing. She'd enjoyed the story. Now she thought of it again as the man sitting in her window turned to face her.

"What are your thoughts?" Zach asked softly, his words breaking the silence like stones slipping into water.

"I was thinking about your parents, the story Dura tells the children."

"Is there something you want to know?"

Bo stretched in the darkness, no longer quite so tired.

"Who was the bad man Bea was hiding from?" she asked.

"Her pimp," Zach answered, pronouncing the word in a way that made it sound like a balloon full of poison. "He was also her brother."

"Where did she go?"

The big man placed one hand gently against the horizontally banded earthen wall as if touching a face. Then he nodded.

"My father told me she went 'down the hill' as we say, back into San Diego. She had become very strong inside herself after many years in these hills, but there was still a bitterness. My father heard that my mother's brother had been released from prison and had come back to San Diego. He heard that my mother found her brother and killed him with a knife, but no one really knows if that's true or not. We never saw her again."

Bo felt another question leap unexpectedly from the darkness inside her.

"Was it hard for you when she left?" she asked.

"I was ten years old, nearly a man. But I still remember her voice, the way she held me all night in her arms when I had whooping cough, the songs she'd sing. I'm forty now, only a year younger than you are. I still remember. There's no way to stop missing love that's gone, Bo. Which is why I'm here."

"I don't want to talk about it," Bo said, tight-lipped. "I'm doing fine on the meds; I'm almost ready to go back to work. It's a depressive episode. I have to expect that when . . . when these things happen."

Soundlessly the big man slid from the window and placed a hand in Bo's long, tousled hair. "I'm not talking about the part your meds can control," he said. "I'm talking about your heart."

Bo felt a familiar convulsion of grief. What was Zach trying to do, send her over the edge again?

"I've lost my best friend and I have to go on living," she pronounced in a voice that wavered like the bands of earth that comprised the walls. "What else is there to say?"

"That you must grieve or you can't go on living in the right way," Zach answered. "The Kumeyaay, the Yuma, the Cahuilla, the Chemehuevi—all the peoples of this region—have known this and made special ceremonies for grieving.

The details have been lost over the years when we were not allowed to speak our languages or perform our ceremonies, but enough has been passed down. We can do a kind of Kurok, a Kumeyaay grieving ceremony, for you tonight if you will permit it. I decided on tonight so that your friend Raven could be with you before he leaves tomorrow. And your psychiatrist, Blindhawk, is also here."

Bo had no idea how her shrink, a half-Iroquois French-Canadian transplant to Southern California, had learned about Ghost Flower Lodge. But it wasn't surprising. Eva Blindhawk Broussard and Zach Crooked Owl had similar ideas about the proper care and treatment of people with brain disorders. That they continually called each other "Blindhawk" and "Owl" rather than their usual names was a source of amusement to everyone at the lodge.

"So Eva thinks I should do this grieving ceremony?" Bo asked.

Zach was already in the hall before he answered.

"No," he said. "She's just here to offer support in case *you* think you should do it. We'll be outside."

Zach was right, Bo acknowledged with a nod to her own reflection in a mirror over the bureau. The death of Mildred, her companion and closest friend, however predictable, had so shocked Bo's precarious neurochemical balance that she'd plummeted into a clinical depression. That nasty chemical trick that turns joy to loathing and makes daily activity into a marathon of exhausting tasks that can't be done. And while the antidepressant medication had corralled her symptoms, the precipitating reality was still there.

Bo wondered if the Kumeyaay, who'd lived on San Diego County's beaches, deserts, and mountains for thousands of years until their near-disappearance by the end of the early twentieth century, had ever performed a grieving ceremony for a dog. Probably not, she thought. This would be a first.

Squaring her shoulders, she walked through the silent lodge and made her way along a boulder-lined path to an arbor of cottonwoods over a dry creekbed. A natural gathering place, people seemed to gravitate to it at all hours. And a few of the Kumeyaay were always there, telling stories in a traditional allegorical mode that their guests could internalize and ponder without feeling vulnerable. Always easier to hear about a crow who betrays a tortoise than to admit that a trusted co-worker got you fired from your job. Bo had decided that every psychiatric treatment program should employ Indian storytellers and skip group therapy altogether. She hated group therapy.

"Since long ago," Dura said as though continuing a narrative begun before Bo's arrival at the creekbed, "the Kumeyaay knew that any spirit on earth may honor any other spirit with friendship. When this happens, it is important. Once Lizard and Butterfly were friends, and as Butterfly grew weak with the coming of autumn, Lizard would carry him from place to place on her back. One day . . ."

Bo found a seat on the ground near Mort Wagman and fixed her gaze on a granite outcropping half a mile in the distance. No one looked up, but continued to listen as Dura told a story Bo already knew would end in Butterfly's death. Most of the staff and the other guests were present, including Old Ayma in her shawls and veil. Bo wrapped her arms around her knees and let herself cry as the story went on and on, punctuated occasionally by the howl of a distant coyote. One of the Dog People, she thought. A dog singing. Mort Wagman nodded as if he'd thought the same thing.

Ten feet away Eva Broussard's cropped white hair shone in the faint moonlight like something metallic glimpsed under sand. She was humming, keeping time with Dura's voice. But her moccasined feet, Bo noticed, were flat on the ground as if she expected to move. The fact was reassuring to Bo as pictures from the seventeen years she'd shared with a small fox terrier rose in her mind and then were gone.

A young husband named Mark Bradley giving her a puppy for her birthday. The sadness later when they'd known the marriage couldn't work and they'd parted. But Mildred had stayed with Bo and been a link to that other life which was gone, no longer an option. Then the suicide of Bo's sister, Laurie, and shortly after, the accidental deaths of their parents. And the illness, the hospitalizations, the wretched old-fashioned medications, the shame when people whispered "crazy" and tapped their temples. Somehow the loyal little dog had made the losses bearable by providing a sort of continuity. Mildred had simply been there and had loved Bo, no matter what.

Now that continuity and that love were gone, leaving an absence that spiraled from Bo's past into nothingness. It wasn't fair, and it hurt. She sobbed and let herself rock back and forth, her hands knotted in her hair. Zach rose and threw a basket of sage leaves on a small fire in the creekbed, fanning the smoke toward Bo with something that looked like a white pillowcase knotted in four corners. Bo could hear the wooden rattles tied around his feet and wrists, and noticed that the white fabric he was holding had black-circle eyes and painted brown spots.

"A Kurok is a ceremony to tell the spirit that has gone we will never, never forget," Dura explained. "A Kurok says we remember the spirit's image here, how it appeared in life, but know it is now free. We release the spirit to its freedom, even though it hurts to do this."

The rattling sound from Zach's ankles and wrists was like sand blowing in Bo's mind, abrasive and relentless. She didn't want to release Mildred's spirit, she wanted Mildred back, wanted her whole life back, wanted to start over and do everything right. But that wasn't possible. She felt like tearing her hair out.

"In great grief a Kumeyaay woman will go away alone and cut her hair," Dura said softly. "It is a natural thing to do."

Only then did Bo see what Mort held in his hand near her right knee. It was an old Indian knife, its handle made of mahogany-colored manzanita wood and bound in strips of bleached rawhide. He demonstrated the sharpness of the blade by shaving the bark from a cottonwood twig and then turned to her somberly. He'd taken off his sunglasses and Bo could see both the question in his eyes and his pride in helping her. Like a little brother, Bo thought. A brother she'd never had, until now.

When she stood and nodded her answer, he stood as well and followed her away from the group. So did Eva Broussard, her moccasins making no sound on the rocky path. Bo traversed the bare spaces between creosote bushes and cholla cactus for a while, watching for some private niche in the desert rocks. In minutes she found it, just a dim grotto where the sandy ground had washed away over centuries, exposing a cluster of half-buried granite boulders. Inside the enclosure she turned to Mort, who extended the knife to her, handle first. Then he left.

Eva Broussard remained, her eyes hooded and downcast. No shrink on the planet would send a depressed patient off alone into the desert with a knife in the middle of a grieving ceremony, Bo knew. There were enough suicides without urging that option on people. But Eva could make herself unpresent, could withdraw from Bo's awareness and not intrude while remaining physically there. She didn't move and in seconds seemed nothing more than one of the rocks as Bo grabbed the first hunk of her own long red-silver hair in her left hand and with her right, raised the knife.

Afterward Bo stood and watched her hair blowing away in tufts into the high desert. She hoped quail might use some of it for nesting material, or more likely woodrats, since quail wouldn't be building nests in October. She felt tired and hollow, but the knot of despair around her heart had dissolved. After awhile she turned to the motionless form that was her psychiatrist and friend, and said, "How does it look?"

Eva Broussard's black eyes caught a shard of moonlight and twinkled as she battled an obvious impulse to chuckle.

"Appropriate to the situation," she finally answered. "Tomorrow you can go into town and have it styled."

Halfway back to the gathering Mort Wagman sat on a rock, waiting. Bo handed him the knife and smiled. As the three of them walked back toward the lodge a coyote howled far up in the hills, another answered, and then there was silence.

Chapter 3

A choir of Spanish monks filled the darkened Phoenix offices of MedNet, Inc. with a Gregorian chant. The music was amplified from a CD by state-of-the-art speakers to an intensity far surpassing the original human voices. Alexander Morley, his white shirtfront turned a flickering green by the laptop computer monitor glowing before him, listened.

The music, as usual, calmed him. Its monophonic notes defined the only place left where he could remember who he really was. Not the chairman of a medical management consortium that had just lost a four-hundred-and-fifty-million-dollar judgment. Not the husband and father to a wife and now-grown children who had for more than thirty years seemed to him like actors in a tedious play. Certainly not the soulless entrepreneurial predator described on the financial pages of every major paper only three weeks ago. And not a fool.

Rising stiffly from a leather orthopedic chair expensively designed to hide its adjustable lumbar support, vibrators at seven shiatsu points, and heating coils throughout, he stood and gazed through the office's glass wall at Phoenix twinkling twelve stories below. He'd just placed an antiarrythmia medication beneath his tongue to slow an uncomfortable fluttering that seized his heart more often than anyone knew. As the regular beat resumed in his chest, he pondered the situation before him.

MedNet could eat the loss incurred in the judgment by selling off its chain of immensely profitable geriatric centers. Even without final approval from the other three executive board members, he'd leaked the tentative plan to a few key people. And shares in MedNet stock had already jumped two points on the big board. No, Alexander Morley was no fool.

MedNet would keep buying up every little drug company with a patent on *anything* that looked promising for Alzheimer's and every other brain disease, but dump the seventeen GentleCare centers. Bob Thompson was the only board member still opposed to the plan. But Bob Thompson would just have to get used to it. The U.S. departments of Justice and Health and Human Services would get their money. And MedNet would stay in the black. Just as long as Alexander Morley was running the show.

The chanting surged and ebbed, making of the starkly elegant office a stone-floored cloister where a man's soul could stop fighting and soar. Morley imagined his soul alive again in the music. The boy who wanted to be a doctor, who wanted to save people. That was his soul and he kept it secret and apart in ancient chants he shared with no one.

But that boy wouldn't survive ten minutes in the real world, Morley knew. He'd learned the lesson early and never forgotten it. To succeed you had to watch the big picture and be prepared to make a few sacrifices along the way. And in this business those sacrifices were likely to be people. Alexander Morley took pride in having no illusions about life or his role in it. He'd accept the responsibility for those sacrifices, pay up, and get on with business. He hadn't made the rules. He just lived by them.

Turning back to his desk he silenced the music with a slender black remote control, and studied the projections outlined on the laptop screen. He'd long ago seen where medical profit would be made by the twenty-first century, and he'd amassed a fortune pursuing that vision. Now the rest of the world was catching up and would have to pay Alexander Morley for seeing it first.

The brain. Where the quality of every life is determined. He'd seen where the technology was leading even then, when the only computers were monstrous mainframes capable of little more than uninspired mathematical filing. He'd seen it when his fellow med school students were sampling every morphine-based medication they could pilfer, searching for euphoria. Life was uncomfortable and certain chemicals in the brain could make it less so. For some, life was worse than uncomfortable; it was hell. And their loved ones would do anything, *pay* anything to relieve their suffering.

In time, computer technology would explore and map the chemistry of the brain and new drugs would follow. Drugs that would end psychic misery. All Dr. Alexander Morley had to do was track that misery with well-diversified investments.

And now two foreign medical management concerns—one German and one Japanese—had shown him a new track. And a way to recoup all and more of the millions MedNet would pay the government because its chain of private psychiatric hospitals, each called Silvertree, had been a little overzealous in confining people until their insurance ran out. Confining people who in reality had no psychiatric illness at all, and confining them against their will.

It was unfortunate that the Los Angeles Silvertree had overdiagnosed and detained a man whose brother happened to be an attorney. The Silvertree hospitals were deliberately marketed to a lower-class clientele traditionally awed by doctors and unlikely to file lawsuits. The attorney had orchestrated a class-action suit, and the government had caught on. These things happened.

Morley clicked off the laptop and smiled as he buzzed for his car to be brought up from the building's parking area. The Germans and Japanese were bickering openly about a franchise on a unique new psychiatric program. Something put together by an unheard-of tribe of Indians in Southern California. Morley hadn't known there *were* Indians in California, not that it mattered. The Indian craze was just starting in Europe and Japan. He'd buy this place out, then sell individual franchises for whatever it was they did to foreign medical entrepreneurs. At the same time he'd redesign the Silvertree chain along the same lines and sell all fourteen hospitals. The potential profit from the sales of the GentleCare chain now and modified Silvertree chain later could be ten times the money this judgment was costing MedNet. And he'd already hired just the man to negotiate an attractive deal with the Indians.

Alexander Morley brushed the sleeves of his British-tailored suit jacket with arthritic fingers and pushed the button that would open his double office doors. His wife would have been asleep for hours by the time he reached the estate he'd built in Scottsdale. They hadn't talked to each other in years. At sixty-nine, after forty years of marriage, they simply had nothing to say. A tremor of distaste brought a frown beneath his well-groomed silver hair, but he shook it off. Nothing really mattered except what existed in this room. Success. Power. And the memory of his boyish soul.

Chapter 4

During the night Bo awoke sweating from a dream in which the desert sky had cracked. She'd heard it, she was sure. A sound that shattered the dome of stillness outside and sent whining aftershocks to throb in her ears. But the sky beyond her window was as immense and silent as ever when she looked. Nothing moving but a falling star so distant that its brief arc seemed merely an illusion. The night desert. Bo was certain no other living thing had seen the star fall, and the awareness filled her with a familiar, lonely exaltation. And a sense that she was going to make it through.

"Could it be death ye've been courtin'?" asked the voice of her long-dead Irish grandmother from somewhere in her head. "And with no priest in sight, a disgrace it is to think!"

"I cut my hair instead," Bo whispered in the dark. "And besides, there are plenty of priests here, Grandma Bridget. Indian priests. No problem."

Great, Bradley. Now you're talking to dead relatives in the middle of the night. Lying *to dead relatives. What next?*

But in the greater psychic privacy of her bed Bo grinned. Bridget Mairead O'Reilly would be proud that her granddaughter had thwarted the suicidal goblin called depression one more time, even though she'd be horrified at the "pagan" setting in which the battle had been won. Bo made a mental

note to make a donation to something of which her grandmother would have approved, just to even things out. Maybe
sponsor a pennywhistle competition.

In the morning she woke to a silence that seemed odd until
she realized Old Ayma wasn't in the bathroom between their
rooms, muttering noisily as she brushed her teeth. Bo had
grown accustomed to using Ayma as an alarm clock. And the
whole lodge seemed eerily quiet, as if everyone had left during the night.

After pulling on jeans and a clean T-shirt she hurriedly
downed her usual morning pill. The one that would keep her
mood swings in the same arc with everybody else's mood
swings. Hah. That one had clearly fallen on its face. Then she
took the other pill, the antidepressant that would enable her
to remember to wash her hair and smile sweetly when people
said banal things like "good morning." Even when not
depressed Bo found nothing good about morning. Any morning. And this one was weird.

Padding barefooted down the earthen-tiled corridor, she
listened for voices, the clatter of dishes from the dining area,
somebody playing a flute, anything. From a paloverde tree
beyond an open door at the end of the hall came the scratchy
cooing of a white-winged dove.

"Who cooks for you all?" rasped the bird in sounds that
seemed words. "Who cooks for you all, who cooks for you
all?"

The effect was creepy. An empty building and one dove
repeating the same question over and over in the bright
morning air. Bo blinked in the sunlight spilling through the
door and steadied herself by touching the wall. A sculptor had
carved random animal forms in the layered earth walls, and
she noticed that her hand was touching the ear of a jackrabbit
half emerged from a band of red-brown clay. The rabbit
seemed to be listening to the dove. It occurred to Bo that perhaps she'd heard one too many Indian stories. And where in
hell was everybody, anyway?

In the lodge living room the portrait of John Crooked Owl stared out from the fireplace wall. His dark eyes looked through the front wall and into infinity. Bo followed the track of his gaze and hurried through the garden courtyard beyond the front door. What she saw made no sense.

Everybody was outside. All the Neji, the children, and eight of the other guests who were already up. Old Ayma, swathed in what looked like several tablecloths with a flowered blouse over her head, hunched near the door. Only her eyes were visible beneath layers of fabric. Dura stood holding Cunel, the youngest of her and Zach's five children. The little boy was fidgeting in her arms, but making no noise. Zach, Bo noticed, was holding Mort's son, Bird, whose blue eyes looked flat and way too big. She didn't see Mort anywhere.

"What's going on?" she asked.

Dura handed Cunel to her oldest daughter, Juana, and motioned Bo toward the shade of a mission fig tree.

"We're waiting for the sheriff," she said, smoothing her long cotton blouse with large hands. Dura smelled like flour and oranges, Bo noticed. She'd been preparing breakfast when something drew her outside. But what?

"Let's sit down," Dura went on, selecting one of the benches beneath the tree. "Something terrible has happened."

Bo felt a contraction beneath her lungs, followed by a chemical taste at the back of her throat. The vitaminlike taste of the medications dissolving in her stomach.

"What?" she whispered.

"Mort Wagman has . . . has died," Dura said. "He went for a walk late last night, to Yucca Canyon. When he hadn't returned by the time we got up, Zach went looking for him. He found Mort's body at the rim of the canyon."

Bo gasped. The news was too shocking to internalize immediately, but her mind quickly created reasons, made sense of the unthinkable.

"Was it the Clozaril?" she asked.

The medication that stood between Mort Wagman and the

distorted thinking of schizophrenia could be dangerous. People using it had to have weekly blood tests and had to be scrupulous about taking every dose at the prescribed daily intervals. But Bo knew the answer even as she asked the question. Mort had been fanatically careful about his meds.

"No, I'm afraid it was—"

"A rattlesnake," Bo finished Dura's sentence, the syllables desperate. "Mort and I walked out to Yucca Canyon all the time. We kept watching for them. But Mort knew to make noise on the trail and keep his eyes open. I can't believe . . . "

A clammy hand seemed to be closing around her heart, and her breath felt stringy and shallow. Across the pale blue sky a dull curtain fell like a fine-meshed screen. Beyond the shadow cast by the fig tree a tumble of pink, daisylike fleabane turned gray against a backdrop of murderous cholla cactus. What was the point in fighting to keep going? Death was everywhere. You couldn't win.

"Mort was shot," Dura said softly. "Zach saw a wound in the middle of his chest. That's why we phoned the sheriff. Zach sent Ojo back out there with a rifle to guard Mort's body until the sheriff gets here."

"Yes," Bo answered, seeing Zach and Dura's oldest boy in her mind. The vultures that would soon come. The other predators. A difficult task for a boy of eleven, but Ojo was a man in Kumeyaay terms. He'd been through the ceremony that ended his childhood; he'd do what was expected of him. Bo wasn't sure why the image was so comforting, but it was. Nothing would vandalize Mort's body. Nothing would disturb what she'd just realized was a crime scene. Mort Wagman had been murdered!

"I heard a sound during the night," she told Dura. "It woke me up. That must have been the shot that . . . that killed Mort."

Inside her head the gray landscape was turning to flickers of pale gold and then deepening to oranges, reds. Anger. It felt like a flood of electricity blasting through the depression, the medications, the whole structure of her being. This was not a natural death like Mildred's, ordained by the cycles of life. This death was unnatural, unnecessary. And this death had stolen a friend. The anger cooled to flecks of steel Bo could feel hardening behind her eyes.

Dura noticed. "This is a terrible thing for you," she said. "I should call Dr. Broussard. Maybe a sedative . . ."

"No," Bo answered. "I'm all right. And I can help with the arrangements for Bird. The sheriff will take him, you know. Bird will have to go to the receiving home in San Diego and then to a foster home until Mort's family can be located. He can't stay here unless the mother or some other relative is notified and on the way by the time the sheriff arrives."

In Dura's puzzled silence Bo recognized the cultural gap between Indians and the dominant culture, whose rules were often cruel and always unassailable. "You'll have a file on Mort, or the psychiatrist who's monitoring his meds will," she thought aloud. "We can get phone numbers for the family from that."

Dura frowned and led Bo to the lodge office adjacent to the kitchen. As she unlocked a filing cabinet Bo admired the array of photos adorning the office walls. John Crooked Owl with an Indian man Bo thought must be Catomka. Zach as a boy, holding up a dead snake. Various men and women, hundreds of them, who had been guests of the Kumeyaay since John Crooked Owl learned that San Diego County would pay money to people willing to care for those nobody wanted— the chronically mentally ill.

"There's nothing listed in the file under 'next of kin' but a theatrical agent in Hollywood," Dura said uncomfortably. Then she grabbed a portable phone from its cradle and hurried through the kitchen and out through a back door.

"What about his doctor?" Bo asked, wondering why they'd left the relative cool of the office.

"One of our volunteer doctors has been monitoring Mort's meds and watching the bloodwork," Dura explained. "But

Mort was brought here from Los Angeles by his agent, Billy Reno."

"Nobody's named Billy Reno," Bo snorted. "But it sounds like he's the one who'll know how to reach Mort's family. Let's call him."

In seconds Bo heard the efficient voice of a woman who identified herself as "Mr. Reno's administrative assistant." After hearing the shocking news of Mort Wagman's death she was happy to contact Mr. Reno by cellular phone in his car.

Billy Reno, genuinely affected by what he heard, parked his Lexus in a yellow zone on Beverly Hills's trendy Rodeo Drive and wept. Then he told Bo he was pretty sure Mort Wagman had no family. Bird's mother was a girlfriend Mort had never married, and she'd died years ago. Billy Reno said he didn't know Bird's real name, that Mort had just called the boy by pet names on the few occasions Reno had seen them together. Bird had gone to a private school in Pasadena called the Tafel School, he told Bo. He was sorry he didn't know anything else, but he'd phone Mort's lawyer and see what could be done to help the boy. There was plenty of money, he said. Mort Wagman had just been paid close to a million dollars to go crazy over a gym shoe.

From the lodge's driveway in front Bo heard the crunch of tires on gravel, businesslike voices. Sheriff's deputies. It was too late to keep Mort's son out of the government bureaucracy she worked for. And too early to plan what a thrumming anger in her heart demanded—the capture of Mort's killer. For now she'd just do what the County of San Diego had trained her to do. Watch. Listen. Investigate.

Walking back through the lodge, she was aware of the high desert framed by window arches, the landscape where she'd found a friend in a man half her age. A brother. "There *are* sharks in the desert," she whispered to the ghost of Mort Wagman. "And I'm going to find the one that made your son an orphan."

Chapter 5

After gulping a cup of coffee in the deserted kitchen Bo forced herself to go outside and approach Bird, try to explain the inevitable sequence of events. She wished she felt affection for the little boy, but she didn't. A nervous, restless child, Bird had often been merely an annoyance. Bo was particularly unimpressed with his short attention span and habit of catapulting himself into chairs and couches when she was occupying them. But Mort had said the boy's IQ tested close to the genius range. And he was cute, Bo admitted, with his flashing blue eyes and penchant for dramatic posturing. The Indians called him Moonbird for his pale and prone-to-sunburn skin, but Bo had thought more than once that Roadrunner would be a more appropriate sobriquet.

Often he burst into spontaneous recitations of the nonsense children's poetry he and his father both loved. The favorite, which Bo had heard several times more than her fragile mental state could bear, had given him his nickname and was called "The High Barbaree." It involved a Crumpet Cat and a Muffin Bird.

"When you see a Crumpet Cat," she hummed the poem's final stanza as she headed out into the desert glare, "Let your shout be heard; For you may save the life of . . . A pretty Muffin Bird!"

Zach was directing the sheriff's deputies to an obscure little canyon where Mort Wagman's body lay as Bo approached. Bird ran back and forth between Zach and the Backcountry Sheriff's Department's green and tan four-wheel drive.

"Bird!" she called in the no-nonsense voice she'd heard Mort use. "I want to tell you what's going to happen now."

The child ran toward her, flailing his arms in a windmill pattern.

"Let's walk," she said.

Bird would never sit still for the detailed explanation of Child Protective Services he needed to hear. Bird rarely sat still for anything. Bo placed a firm hand on the boy's thin shoulder under his biker-style black T-shirt with the sleeves ripped off.

"I know you've already been told about what happened to your dad," she began. "It's terrible for you."

That's it in a nutshell, Bradley. But don't plan on getting any awards for diplomacy.

A month away from work, she thought, and already she'd forgotten how to talk with children. Bird merely grabbed a rock from the ground and threw it angrily in the direction of a small cholla cactus.

"Daddy's dead," he pronounced, kneeling to gather more rocks. "Like your dog, Mildred. Do I have to cut my hair off like you did?"

Bo winced as the boy's bare knees pressed against the rocky ground. The sharp stones would hurt, but Bird appeared to feel no discomfort. In seconds he'd filled both front pockets of his baggy tan shorts with rocks. Bo wished she were on Mars.

"I don't think you need to do that," she replied, failing to address the real issue. "Your hair's already pretty short."

Bird ran a hand over his prep-school crew cut.

"Yeah," he said, dodging to one side of the paved walkway around the lodge and throwing another rock at the cholla. The rock missed its mark by a yard.

"Until we can find your relatives and they can come get

you, you'll be cared for in San Diego," Bo pushed on. "First
you'll go to a place where there are lots of other children, and
then you'll probably go right away to a family who are called
'foster parents.' It'll be okay. Right now I need for you to tell
me the names of your relatives—grandmas, grandpas, aunts,
or uncles—and where they live. Can you do that, Bird?"

The boy's blue eyes narrowed.

"I don't have any relatives," he said, dashing ahead of Bo on
the walkway. "I know Billy Reno, though. He's a friend of my
daddy. Why don't you call Billy Reno?"

"I've already . . ." Bo began.

But Bird had doubled back and sped past her into the
group surrounding the sheriff's deputies. One of the deputies
was talking on a shortwave radio in the Jeep while the other
wrote on a form attached to a clipboard. Zach, his chocolate-
colored skin ashen in the morning light, was moving through
the group, talking to each person. Bo could see the deep fur-
row in his forehead as she ambled back, thinking.

Mort might have been shot by some random drunk roam-
ing the desert at night with a gun, Bo conjectured glumly,
but it wasn't likely. Things like that didn't happen. So who
had been out there on an Indian reservation sixty miles east of
San Diego in the middle of the night? Who could have
known how to find Yucca Canyon, accessible only on foot?
And why would anyone want to kill Mort Wagman, anyway?
It occurred to Bo that she really knew absolutely nothing
about the raven-haired young man she'd imagined was like a
brother.

"Zach, why is everybody outside?" she asked a few minutes
later. "It's getting hot."

"The Kumeyaay believe that a house where death comes
has to be destroyed," he said. "Burned. There is a fear that the
soul in the loneliness of death will try to take a companion
from among the living. We don't want to burn the lodge, so
we keep the awareness of the dead one outside. And no one
can talk about him or mention his name. It's to free his spirit,

not keep pulling his spirit back here by saying his name. It is to be kind to the spirit of the dead that we do this, and to protect ourselves. But . . ." he paused to gesture at the deputies, "we have to talk about Mort to these people. So we will stay outside to do it. Inside the lodge nobody will mention his name again."

That explained why Dura had taken the phone outside to call Billy Reno, Bo thought. She wished the Indians would occasionally just explain things instead of telling symbolic stories, but that wasn't their way. "And a Kurok," she asked, "the ceremony like you did for me or, well, for Mildred last night. Will there be a Kurok for Mort?"

Zach glared irritably at the sky as though it, and not he, should be providing explanations. She could see that the whites of his eyes were bloodshot.

"A Kurok is traditionally done one year after the death. In the old days only certain people could make the dolls, the effigies that were used. Now it's just clothes on a stick frame. We might do one next year if . . ." His voice trailed away as he stared at the distant ocotillo.

"If what?" Bo asked.

"I don't know," Zach said, distracted.

"Mildred hasn't been dead for a year and she had a Kurok."

"We sometimes stretch the rules for our guests if we think it might help," Zach admitted. "We thought that might help you."

Bo nodded. "It did."

Behind Zach she could see one of the deputies approaching. A young woman with sandy hair held off her face by a red bandanna tied Indian-style around her head. On a plastic rectangle over her left shirt pocket was the name "W. Barlow."

"Hello, W. Barlow," Bo said, noticing a stiff bulkiness under the woman's tan uniform shirt. Body armor, the cops called it now. The thick undershirt they used to call a bulletproof vest. Bo guessed the deputies had all felt like wearing them into what they probably thought was a nest of psychotic killers.

"Wick," the young woman answered, nervous. "Wick Barlow. It's really Victoria, but I couldn't pronounce Vs as a kid. Uh, Mr. Crooked Owl here said, uh, said his wife told him you heard something, a shot maybe, during the night?"

Bo couldn't help smiling at the clipboard visibly trembling in the woman's hands.

"Let's go sit in the shade and I'll tell you everything I know," she said, indicating a picnic table under a large live oak near the lodge gate. "And don't worry, I haven't massacred anybody since that group of retired nuns who—"

"Bo . . ." Zach's voice rumbled ominously.

"Right," she answered.

Once seated at the picnic table, Wick Barlow smiled as if she were interviewing a convicted murderer additionally burdened with leprosy.

"I'm sorry I'm acting weird," she began. "It's just that your hair . . ."

Bo had forgotten about that. "An Indian ceremony last night," she explained. "See, my dog died, and . . ."

The young woman's wide hazel eyes softened as she impulsively touched Bo's hand.

"Oh, no, I'm so sorry," she said. "I know what that's like. Our family's schnauzer died three years ago—his name was Max—and we still miss him every day. But I didn't know people came up here for, you know, things like that."

Wick Barlow seemed even younger than Mort Wagman. It occurred to Bo that the exponentially increasing youth of cops, doctors, and Hollywood comedians might suggest an alarming maturity in the eyes of the beholder.

"I'm here because I have manic-depressive illness and I'm just crawling out of a depressive episode," she explained. "And yes, I did hear a loud sort of cracking sound sometime during the night that could well have been a gunshot. It came from the south, from the direction of Yucca Canyon. I'd guess it was sometime between three and four A.M."

The words gave reality to what lay at the lip of a desert canyon less than a mile away. Just a still form on the ground, Bo imagined. And an Indian boy with a rifle on some nearby rock. Already two more cars had pulled into the lodge driveway. There would be photographs of the body, a chalk outline on the gritty, baked desert dirt. Then Mort Wagman's body would be gone.

"Have you called Child Protective Services about Bird, Mort's son?" she asked the young deputy.

"First thing. We called just as soon as Mr. Crooked Owl told us the little boy was here. There's a social worker on the way to get him right now."

Bo looked at the lodge with its massive walls, the people who had cared for her during the doomful exhaustion of depression. She didn't want to leave, but it was time. There were things to do. The social worker would be somebody from one of the CPS Immediate Response units. He or she would transport Bird to the receiving home, complete a preliminary file documenting the circumstances, and then transfer the case over for legal investigation. By this afternoon Bird's case would be assigned to a Court Investigation unit, one of which employed Bo. She knew all the investigators. She'd have no trouble tracking Bird through the system.

Giving Wick Barlow her office phone number, Bo walked through the Kumeyaay staff and other guests back to the lodge. Everybody was still outside except Old Ayma, who no longer lurked on the fringes of the group.

From the lodge phone Bo called her own office in the heart of San Diego. Estrella Benedict answered on the second ring.

"Es," Bo said, "can you drive up here and get me as soon as possible? And would you mind calling Maria at Hair & There in Ocean Beach? See if I can get in for a haircut this afternoon. Yeah, I'm coming down the hill. I'll be back at work tomorrow."

Chapter 6

Bob Thompson woke with the grandfather of all hangovers and a hotel bedsheet roped across his chest. Somebody had thrown the heavy quilted bedspread over his lower half, making him sweat like a racehorse. Probably Tamara, he assumed. Or was her name Tabitha? Tamika? Something that began with a T. Whatever her name was, if she didn't stop flipping TV channels with the damned remote control he was going to vomit. The kaleidoscoping screen only increased the nauseating spin of the room.

"Stop," he managed to say, lurching to his feet and pointing at the remote. She'd opened the drapes and a slice of yellow sunlight caught him in the throat like the side of a board. Bathroom. Fast.

It wasn't the first time he'd tossed his cookies in a hotel crapper, he smiled to himself five minutes later. And it wouldn't be the last. He felt better already as a hot shower washed the night's residue from his well-maintained body. No point in letting yourself go to seed just because you were fifty-something. Flab was bad business.

Whatever-her-name-was had already showered, he noticed. And left that woman-smell of lotion and makeup in the air. He loved the smells that women had, both the tantalizing promise of their perfume and the salty pungency that came later. He'd fallen in love with it at fifteen when his uncle took him to a pricey whorehouse for his birthday. He never tired of it. But it was expensive. Women were expensive.

In the magnifying mirror he shaved carefully and arched his chin to both sides. Nobody could see the hairline scars from the facelift. He couldn't even see them himself without his contacts. And the surgery had removed the neck folds and jowls that made him look like his father. He'd told Darcy, his wife, that the surgery was a necessity of his business. His investors expected an image, he said. And it was true.

"You're pathetic," Darcy had answered, "but you're not as bad as most."

He figured she was right. And they'd both settled for that, years ago. She loved the ranch he'd bought her near Santa Fe, and she'd raised three great kids there. Now that one was on his own and the other two in college, Darcy had gone back to school for some accounting classes and started a travel consulting business with a friend. They spent their time checking out resort accommodations for business meetings and seemed to be having a ball.

She knew what he did when he was out of town. She'd always known, had left him a couple of times because of it. Eventually she decided to stay with him anyway, under two conditions—that he only whore around away from home and that he never approach her side of their king-sized bed without a condom. He'd agreed to both conditions. He loved her.

Tabitha or whoever was half dressed when he came out of the bathroom.

"Bob, sweetie, listen," she smiled over a delectable shoulder, "I've got an eight o'clock class, so I'm gonna pass on breakfast, okay?"

"Take a cab," he agreed, scooping some bills from his wallet and tucking them into her purse on the dresser. "On me."

"You're a doll," she said. "And last night was terrific."

At the door she turned to give him a wink, and then was gone.

He'd put five hundred-dollar bills in her purse, three more than the expected gratuity. Guilt money. She was younger than his daughter.

From items hidden in his suitcase he selected a can of vanilla-flavored Ensure, popped the tab and poured it into an ice-filled glass. The stuff was horrible but full of vitamins and easy to keep down. Then he found the prescription pills designed to stop the cramps and diarrhea that always followed if he drank too much. After swallowing the pill with the thick, white liquid, he pulled on a jockstrap, skimpy athletic shorts, and a T-shirt.

He couldn't work out at the moment if somebody paid him a million bucks, but when you were working a conference it was smart to be seen in the hotel gym early in the morning. Usually only a few women would be there, using the exercycles. Maybe a couple of guys if there were weights or a banked running track. Nobody talked much, but the image was reinforced. Bob Thompson, a disciplined man who's up at dawn safeguarding his health. The sort of man people trust. With their money.

This Houston conference was fairly small potatoes. Pharmaceutical company managers jockeying for job offers. A few heavy-hitters, officers of the big companies, in and out as speakers but not conference participants. Thompson, as Med-Net's public information officer, had arranged the usual discreet "hospitality suite" on Friday night when everybody was fresh. Complimentary drinks, hors d'oeuvres, and conservatively dressed call girls from one of Houston's best services. Never more than two working the suite at the same time.

At every such occasion he'd stand well away from the expensively designed investment literature placed about the room. When someone inquired, as most had this time, he'd merely gesture at the embossed packets as if he'd forgotten they were there.

"There will probably be some interesting opportunities," he'd mentioned when asked about MedNet's response to its legal situation. "Say, didn't I hear your son's interested in law school? Ethan, isn't it?"

Names. People liked you if you remembered their names. Their wives' names, kids' names, dogs' and cats' names. Bob Thompson had a knack for remembering, but he worked at it, too. Before every conference, every meeting, he reviewed the list of players and brought up their files from his database. Bob Thompson knew when somebody's wife was detoxing at Betty Ford and would just happen to send the kids tickets to the Ice Capades. He knew who got fired, who got hired, and who was supporting the family of a brother in prison for mail fraud.

He judged nobody. He just remembered people and made sure they remembered him. Bob Thompson liked people, and they repaid him with their business. Investments. He was MedNet's secret weapon, and he didn't like what Alexander Morley was doing. He didn't like it because he didn't know what it was.

The old man, Thompson thought as he pushed open the glass doors of the hotel gym, was making mistakes. Hiring an unknown to negotiate this Indian deal was a mistake. Med-Net didn't contract with people Bob Thompson didn't know. MedNet had never done that in the fifteen years he'd been there.

Nodding to the controller of a solid Midwestern company whose portfolio he was about to seduce away from French cancer research, Bob Thompson sat on the carpeted floor. Then he began an elaborate series of warm-up stretches that would forestall actual exercise. A woman account exec from a Dallas company smiled from her exercycle. Her company was about to be bought by a diversifying food chain that would, Thompson knew, mismanage it to death within a year.

"Ride 'em, cowboy!" He smiled back.

But Alexander Morley was on his mind. The old man was up to something, and Bob Thompson wanted to know what it was. This Indian psychiatric deal was a stroke of genius, but why had an outsider been brought in to nail it? Henderson, Morley had said. A negotiator named Henderson.

Bob Thompson never forgot a name that was worth remembering. And he'd never heard of a negotiator named Henderson.

Chapter 7

The new haircut, Bo decided on Friday morning as she stared groggily into the bathroom mirror of her Ocean Beach apartment, was either hideous or a refreshing fashion statement. The short curls framing her face and neck seemed embarrassingly youthful, even *wholesome* in a rakish sort of way. Like the hair of a woman whose bath soap, if sliced in half, would produce cartoon bluebirds doing a medley of tunes from *The Sound of Music*. The image was unnerving, but short hair would be less of a hassle during the tail end of the depression, in which everything continued to be a hassle.

On the floor of the bedroom closet she found the laundry basket of clean but unironed clothes and grabbed a pleated white blouse. Unworn since the last time she'd ironed it over a year ago. Wrestling the ironing board from its clamps in the hall closet, Bo paused to wonder why she was bothering. It had something to do with white, she decided. "Chinese white mourning," like Emily Dickinson. With a long white duck skirt she'd bought for its row of tiny buttons down one side and then never worn, the pleated blouse would look appropriately austere. And a white ensemble would covertly honor the deaths of both Mildred and Mort Wagman while reinforcing the clean-cut image bequeathed by short hair. She wondered what Dickinson had done about accessories.

"*Madre de dios!*" Estrella exclaimed an hour later as Bo opened the door to their shared office at San Diego County's Child Protective Services. "You look like a nun."

Bo switched on her desk lamp. "They said that about Emily Dickinson, too."

Estrella's dark eyes widened in alarm. Actually in panic, Bo thought.

"Bo, it's too soon for you to come back to work," Estrella said. "I knew it yesterday when you were in such a rush to get your hair repaired. Look, I know you want to help Mort's little boy, but why don't you just let me do that while you . . . you know, stabilize for a few more days?"

"*Stabilize?*" Bo repeated dramatically, pushing her dark glasses down her nose in order to glare over them. "If I were any more 'stable' I'd have to become a right-wing religious fanatic with a petition to abolish votes for women. Surely you don't want that."

"No," Estrella agreed. Her manicured fingers drummed thoughtfully on her abdomen. "The baby can't have a right-wing godmother."

"There you have it then. So who got Bird's case?"

The little office felt at once familiar and hostile, Bo noticed. As if the walls and utilitarian furnishings had taken her absence personally and were at best ambivalent about her return. The awareness, if permitted to expand, could become paranoia. But the medications would control that, Bo reassured herself. In the meantime she rearranged items on her desk with large and proprietary movements, dramatizing for the furniture her right to be there.

"You're in luck; it's Nick Paratore," Estrella answered. "The case file's on his desk across the hall, but he isn't in yet."

Bo sank into her swivel chair with a determined smile. Things were falling into place. "Does Madge know anything about Mort, about Bird and his dad being at Ghost Flower with me?" she asked. If their supervisor, Madge Aldenhoven, knew anything of the connection there would be no chance of getting the case. It was a flat rule that investigators with any connection whatever to a child could not investigate that child's case. Not that it mattered in this situation, Bo thought. There were no allegations of child abuse, just a need to locate the family. No conflict of interest.

Estrella stood and faced the window as if modeling her layered maroon knit maternity ensemble for the eucalyptus tree outside. "Bird's file says he was picked up from Ghost Flower Lodge after the death of his father," she answered slowly. "Does Madge know that's where you were?"

Bo remembered an absence of get-well cards from her supervisor during her recuperation, a complete dearth of concerned phone calls. "Not unless you told her."

Estrella adjusted a carved wooden comb in her upswept hair and then sighed. "She didn't ask."

"Well, then," Bo grinned, rubbing her palms together, "where's Nick?"

"At a save the sharks demonstration," Estrella whispered, eyeing the door as if Madge Aldenhoven were glued to its other side. "You know how he's into diving and snorkeling and all that? Well, after the death of that woman yesterday, shark-hunters descended on San Diego in droves. And this marine life protection group Nick's in—it's called Scales of Justice if you can believe that—is sponsoring a demonstration against the big hunt that's going out this morning. Nick and the others are in the water in wetsuits waving white flags at boatloads of heavily armed shark haters. He told Madge he had to go to the dentist."

"What does Nick's group think . . ." Bo began and then stopped as the door swooped open, propelled by Madge Aldenhoven in an astonishing navy silk blouse with huge white polka dots. The blouse's floppy bow completed a look Bo associated with clowns.

"I see you're back early," Madge addressed a space two inches to the left of Bo's broad grin. "And dressed as a bride. No doubt this has something to do with your illness and so everyone is expected to ignore it. But most people don't wear white after Labor Day, Bo. Surely you'd be more comfortable if you made *some* attempt to fit in."

Bo couldn't stop envisioning Madge in a sawdust ring, juggling bowling pins. "The Labor Day rule doesn't apply in the tropics," she replied. "Everyone in Boston knew that when *I* was a kid."

Madge Aldenhoven sighed and handed a case file to Estrella. "Hand-shaped bruises on the baby and the three-year-old sister has worms as well as lice," she outlined the case. "Reporting party is a barrio priest. There won't be any problem getting the petition. And Bo . . ." she glowered levelly through contact lenses tinted to make her blue eyes violet, ". . . this isn't the tropics. You'll get the next case that comes up. Don't go anywhere."

Bo saw her chance. "I thought I'd take the free time to do a little decorating in here," she said. "Maybe redo my bulletin board, change the plants around, you know."

Madge believed in sterile work spaces, almost as zealously as she believed in the Protestant work ethic. It was rumored that even plastic plants died in her office.

"Nick is at the dentist," Madge said with sudden purpose, grabbing a pen lodged in her flyaway white hair and pointing it at Bo, "so you might as well take his new case. It's a six-year-old boy whose father was accidentally shot up in the desert near Campo. If you can find the mother or some other family before the weekend we can close it without involving juvenile court. The file's on Nick's desk. Let me know by this afternoon what you turn up. Your hair, by the way, looks much better short."

When the door had slammed shut after Madge, Bo looked at Estrella. "Accidentally?" she said. "Mort wasn't shot accidentally, he was murdered!"

"You don't know that. It might have *been* an accident, Bo." The word was pronounced "bean," a sure sign of anxiety. Estrella's Spanish accent always escalated with her stress level.

Bo experienced a warm flutter of neck muscles. Guilt. She hadn't meant to upset her best friend.

"You're right," she admitted. "And I know taking this case is pretty dumb, but I want to do it for Mort." Striding the two steps necessary to cross the tiny room, Bo hooked both thumbs in the waist of her skirt and stared into a spindly bottlebrush shrub beneath the window. "He was . . . really close to me."

Estrella feigned interest in the case file on her desk. "Andy will be back from Europe in a week," she mentioned. "I hope you and Mort didn't get, you know, too close." Estrella's vision of Andrew LaMarche escorting Bo to an altar had reached obsessive proportions.

"Our favorite pediatrician," Bo answered, "has not been supplanted in my dubious affections *or* my bed, if that's what you're asking, and it *is* what you're asking. When he heard I was in the hospital he wanted to cancel that training program on child abuse prevention on foreign U.S. military bases he's doing for the government, but there was really no point. I wanted him to stay in Frankfurt. He's sent flowers every other day. Also an enormous cuckoo clock, three pairs of kid gloves I'll never wear unless I move back to Boston, and an illustrated strudel cookbook in German. My relationship with Mort Wagman was different. We were friends."

Estrella was pensive. "Maybe in a place like that, where everybody's just trying to get on their feet, that could happen," she mused. "I still don't really understand what Ghost Flower Lodge is, to be honest. And what are you going to do with a German cookbook?"

"I thought I'd run an ad in the personals for a German cook," Bo answered. "And Ghost Flower Lodge is a subacute psychiatric facility, like a rehabilitation center, the only one of its kind. The Neji started taking in people with chronic psychiatric illnesses years ago. It's a special purpose they have, a tradition. Now famous people go up there to rehab after a hospitalization or a medication change. Movie stars, pro sports types, everybody." Bo unbuttoned the cuffs of her blouse and rolled up the sleeves, creating wrinkles. It felt better.

"But not everybody pays at Ghost Flower," she went on. "Half the guests are indigent, trying to stay alive on Social Security Disability benefits. Ghost Flower is actually licensed by the county as a board-and-care."

"Ycchh!" Estrella said. "I've seen those places, private homes where the owners get paid to keep mentally ill people. Most of them are pits. But Ghost Flower has that fabulous building with the thick walls. It must have cost a fortune to build."

"The walls are made out of dirt," Bo answered, thinking. "And there's plenty of that on the reservation. But the Neji had an architectural firm from Los Angeles do the building, so it couldn't have been cheap. You're right. Wonder where they got the money?"

"Why don't you ask them?" Estrella said, wiping lipstick from the corner of her mouth with her little finger. "I've got to go, try to make sure these kids get sent to the same foster home."

"Maybe I will," Bo answered as the door closed behind her officemate. The other bands of Kumeyaay left in San Diego County after sequential displacement by Spanish, Mexican, and then American invaders, had all lived in grueling poverty until casino interests and waste-management entrepreneurs discovered them. Only the Neji Reservation had avoided becoming either a hazardous waste dump or a gambling mecca.

The Neji history was interesting, Bo thought. But it couldn't have anything to do with the death of a stand-up comic. Or could it? Zachary Crooked Owl would know. And she was going to ask him.

Chapter 8

Hiking her long skirt with one hand, Bo climbed into the four-wheel-drive Pathfinder she'd bought at a police auction four months earlier, and sighed. The CPS parking lot looked exactly the same as it had for three years. Her office building, a rambling two-story structure of colorless brick, also looked the same. In the yard overlooked by rows of gray windows, an unchanging eucalyptus tree wore the same mantle of dust it wore every October. What was lacking, she realized as she guided the Pathfinder carefully past Madge's immaculately clean beige coupe, was autumn. Just one red leaf anywhere on the horizon would provide a focus. But there would be no red leaf. San Diego's autumns brought nothing but dust and a nearly unendurable glare.

Sunlight's good for depression, Bradley. Enjoy it and save some money so you can fly to New Zealand in the spring, where it will be fall.

The thought was energizing. She'd embark on an austerity program, Bo decided, in order to stockpile the airfare. She'd make her own clothes, plant vegetables in pots on the deck, maybe try to sell some of her paintings at craft fairs. And if she didn't start smoking again she could save fifteen dollars a week on cigarettes alone. On that concept she was ambivalent.

Mort Wagman had talked her into quitting shortly after she'd arrived at Ghost Flower. "You're depressed, you don't care about *anything*, so you won't care about going through withdrawal," he argued while pacing in a tight circle beside Bo's nest in the couch corner. "The misery will give you something concrete to think about."

At the time his weird pacing had been irritating, its pointless energy a criticism of her sluggishness. "Either stand still or go away," Bo had told him. "You're making me dizzy."

"I'm going to tell you a secret," he answered, leaning over the leather arm of the couch. "You know how dogs circle around and around before they curl up to go to sleep?"

"Leave me alone," she said, not relishing a conversation about dogs.

"They do it because their ancestors made nests in tall grass that way, and the memory got wired in."

Bo pulled a length of tan acrylic blanket over her head, but the voice continued.

"I'm not a hundred percent human," Mort Wagman whispered as though revealing a secret thousands were dying to know. "Somebody did this surgery on me, somebody in my *family* put in pieces of animal brain. See the scar? That's why I circle sometimes. It just feels right."

In spite of herself Bo had emerged from the stifling blanket to look at his scalp beneath his long, ebony hair. There was a small scar, probably from a childhood fall or some other accident. And Mort Wagman was still delusional, she thought bleakly. Crazy. Paranoid. Good thing he was in a safe place until his meds kicked in.

"Not only that, but I've kissed a frog," he went on. "Think maybe I'll marry her."

"I won't smoke around you if you won't pace around me," Bo offered. Anything to shut him up, silence his intense, meaningless stories.

And he agreed to the deal. But then he'd been constantly at her side, joking, cajoling, dragging her out for countless walks in the desert. She'd finally quit smoking without really thinking about it. But the change wasn't permanent, she was sure. She felt none of the melodramatic idiocy so evident in nonsmokers. Not a single urge to flap her hands and cough dramatically at the mere sight of a Bic lighter. Nothing. About smoking she just felt nothing. And that, she was sure, wouldn't last.

Slipping a tape of the soundtrack from *The Mission* into the Pathfinder's tape deck, Bo watched the urban landscape revert to its natural state as she climbed east on Interstate 8. The hilly terrain was pocked with boulders and where the ground was not shadowed by coast live oaks, sycamores, and elderberry trees, an occasional cholla cactus grew, baking in the sun. They looked like the fuzzy arms and legs of dismembered teddy bears, she thought. Little forests of teddy bear limbs growing from each other at odd angles, matted with barbed spines that could bury themselves an inch deep in rubber shoe soles. What they could do to flesh did not bear thinking.

In the morning glare Bo felt a growing unease. The closer she got to Ghost Flower Lodge, the more she felt as if she were driving into an old black-and-white movie. The sun had devoured color, leaving nothing but gradations of ecru relieved only occasionally by splotches of shadow. Ennio Morricone's score blaring from her tape deck only reinforced the eerie feeling, but she couldn't bring herself to turn it off. The single oboe, the boy soprano's haunting miserere, the threat audible in a rumbling timpani, brought up an edginess that had nothing to do with depression. Something was wrong in these baking hills; Bo could sense it. Something unholy happening. Something fearful in the white glare.

As she turned off the freeway onto the patched concrete road leading toward the Neji Reservation, Bo noticed a small wooden sign professionally painted in letters reading, "Hadamar Desert Reclamation Project, Site II." Beyond the sign a narrow road wound into the hills, littered with tumbleweeds. A university project of some kind, Bo thought. Geology. "Hadamar" was undoubtedly some academic's pun on an excavation for the fossilized marine life left baking after

the retreat of ancient seas. "Mar" meant "sea" in several languages, she remembered, wondering if "had a sea" was typical
geologist humor.

Curious, Bo made a mental note to explore the area later.
For now, she reminded herself sternly, the goal was to explore
the muddy financial situation of the Neji.

Zachary Crooked Owl was standing in the courtyard as Bo
pulled up, talking to a man who looked like George Washington with a crew cut. The man had slung his dark suit coat
over a shoulder and his black wingtips were covered with a
film of dust, but even in the high desert heat he seemed cool,
composed. Zach was sweating. Bo could see dark blue arcs
under the arms of the big man's blue workshirt, and the
leather cord holding the owl's claw at his neck was dark with
moisture.

"I've already told you, Henderson . . ." Zach said as Bo
opened the Pathfinder's door to a wall of dry heat.

But the man merely nodded and turned toward a rental car
parked under the cottonwood. "We'll be in touch, Crooked
Owl," he replied and then paused to perform a smiling
appraisal of the lodge's exterior. A satisfied, self-congratulatory
look. Like a man who's just purchased an expensive toy. Then
he folded himself into the little car and drove away.

Zach stared into the dust cloud trailing the man's exit for
minutes before acknowledging Bo's presence. "Good to see
you, Bo," he finally said. "But don't stand around in the sun
without a hat. Come on in."

"Can't," Bo answered. "I've come to talk about Mort, and I
know we have to do that outside. What's going on, Zach?
Something's wrong; I can feel it. Who was that man?"

"Just business," he answered, hunching massive shoulders
as if battling a chill. His eyelids were swollen and with the
graying stubble on his cheeks his long, braided hair looked
less Indian than derelict. Zach, Bo noted with alarm, was at
this moment scarcely the pillar of strength she knew and
respected. "What do you want to know about Mort?" he

asked. "I haven't heard anything from the sheriff's people since they were here yesterday."

"You mean you haven't called? And what about Bird? Doesn't anybody care what's happened to Bird?"

"Bo, we've got eleven sick people here to manage. Until yesterday you were one of them, so you understand what I'm saying. Why'd you drive all the way up here? What do you want?"

The words drove a wedge between them that Bo felt in her stomach. She wasn't a guest anymore, wasn't going to be treated with the easy patience demanded by illness. She'd left; now she was an outsider. Hard to take. And Zach's count was off. There had been fourteen guests at Ghost Flower until yesterday. Mort's death and her return to San Diego would not leave eleven.

"You mean twelve sick people," she corrected. "And what I want to know is . . ."

Zach stared into his hands, stretched palm-side up at his waist. Then he folded each into a brown fist. "Old Ayma walked off," he said quietly, not looking up. "Nobody noticed in the mess about Mort. We searched all night. Nobody found her."

Bo felt her heart beat faster as she looked past Zachary Crooked Owl into the bleached landscape bequeathed a gentle, mystical people by the United States government. To the west lay the Campo Reservation, and north of that, the La Posta, Manzanita, and Cuyapaipe Reservations. All Kumeyaay. All desert lands now called home by the last remnants of a once-large tribe so private and unassuming it had nearly perished without a trace. Also out there, Bo remembered, were lost emerald and gold mines, a mysterious Viking ship jutting from the side of a desert wash until buried by an earthquake in 1933, and a ghostly mule-drawn stagecoach complete with its driver murdered in 1860, still seen barreling through desert canyons. A shape-shifting, dangerous place. Deadly for an old woman already hallucinating. An old woman who spit out the pills that might have enabled her to survive.

"You've informed the Sheriff's Department," Bo thought aloud. "What about the search-and-rescue teams, the trained dogs?"

"They've been out there since first light. They haven't found her." Zach's barrel chest expanded with a shuddering breath and then shrank as he exhaled. "They're bringing in cadaver dogs this afternoon."

"*Cadaver* dogs?"

"Specially trained. They can find a fresh body within eight to ten miles, less for one that's been dead longer. Ayma couldn't have gone far. They'll find her."

"My God," Bo breathed. "I'm sorry, Zach. This must be hell for you and Dura, everybody."

"Been doing this all my life, Old John before me, all the way back to my uncle, Catomka. Never lost anybody. Then two at once." His wide nostrils flared with some emotion Bo couldn't define. Anger. Or maybe despair. "It feels like a curse."

On the ground beside the lodge driveway a darkling beetle emerged from beneath a rock and moved, its rump characteristically elevated, into a clump of Mormon tea. Bo watched the bug's stiff movement and wondered what had inspired it to change locations. There was no way to know.

The universe, she thought, was comprised of such inexplicable movements. Black beetles, psychotic old women, cosmic debris hurtling through space—all intent on journeys for which explanation was simply absent. No one would ever know why Old Ayma walked into the autumn desert. Or why Mort Wagman was shot in the middle of the night on a California Indian reservation. The tyranny of not knowing made Bo feel abandoned and angry.

"How did the Neji fund the construction of this place?" she blurted. The question was completely inappropriate. "I mean, it must have been expensive."

Zach seemed to welcome a question he could answer. "A private underwriter," he answered. "That and our licensed facility status with MediCal and then some of the big insurance companies. Took us nearly twenty years to get where we are, and now . . ." He stopped and jammed his fists into the pockets of dirt-encrusted Levi's.

"And now what, Zach? Can the county pull your license because of what's happened?"

"Maybe. But it's not your problem. Look, I've got things to do and—"

"It *is* my problem," Bo interrupted, tears forming and then drying behind her sunglasses in the warm air. "This place is a miracle! There's nothing like it anywhere west of Massachusetts. For that matter there's nothing like it anywhere. Let me do something to help, Zach. Tell me what's going on."

The look in his eyes was one Bo hated. The professional look. The one separating those with psychiatric disorders from everyone else on the planet. An impenetrable wall.

"Too much stress right now can land you back in a hospital," he said. "But I'll keep Dr. Broussard informed about the investigation into Mort's death and about what happens to Ghost Flower. She'll fill you in." With that he turned and walked into the lodge.

Bo felt a tear spill from her right eye and evaporate on her cheek as she stood beside her car. Zachary Crooked Owl never called Eva Broussard anything but "Blindhawk," and was never rude. Until now. For a moment she felt a crush of responsibility for Zach's behavior that made her nose ache. The depression bogey again, insisting that everything wrong in the world was ultimately the fault of Bo Bradley, rotten person. It said she was unworthy of Zach's confidence, a failure. It said everything she did was wrong, clumsy, inadequate. It sneered that even her dog had left her. At that the downward spiral of her thoughts slammed to a halt.

Not Mildred, Bradley. No way! Drown in your damn depression if you have to, but leave Mildred out of it.

The words had an edge that made her feel better. A boundary. She might not be able to control these eruptions of self-loathing that could override the antidepressant medication, but their content was controllable. Striding to the clump of

Mormon tea, Bo addressed the beetle hiding inside. "Depression sucks," she hissed the Ss, "but it's not going to keep me from finding out what's going on around here, understand?"

Taking the long, scenic way on Highway 94 back down toward San Diego, she stopped in the dusty crossroad settlement called Campo and bought a cold Gatorade. Campo's stone store, now also a museum, was rumored to entomb a dead body in its thick, cool walls. The victim of a murder committed in 1868 and never solved. San Diego's back country kept its secrets, Bo realized. But not this time. Because this time a mad Irishwoman with nothing left to lose was going to unearth its secret or die trying. At the moment it really didn't matter which.

Chapter 9

There was something the matter with the new boy, something not right. Gussie Quinn watched uneasily as he raced back and forth on the cement patio beyond her kitchen doors. The other short-term foster children, both girls, were in school and so he had no one to play with. But Aunt Gussie Quinn, as children had called her for the three years she'd been fostering, knew boredom was insufficient explanation for a morning she could only regard as disastrous.

She'd gone to pick up the boy named Bird at the receiving home right after breakfast and had forgotten to take off her apron.

"You look like Mrs. Butterworth, the syrup lady," he told her in the lime green waiting room when they were introduced by one of the social workers. "I'll call you Gussie Butter."

In her garage was a brand-new five-hundred-dollar motorized treadmill her husband Hank hadn't wanted to get. She'd spent months talking him into it. Every morning when the kids were off at school she climbed on the thing and walked until the sweat ran down the middle of her back and the little dial said she'd used up two hundred calories, then two-fifty, then three. Every day she tried to burn ten extra calories. It was hard, but already she'd dropped five pounds. At fifty-

eight, Gussie Quinn was trying *not* to look like Mrs. Butterworth. "No, you can call me Aunt Gussie like the others, or
you can call me Mrs. Quinn," she told the boy. Always best to
let them know the ground rules right away.

"*My* name's Bird," he answered, distracted by a car pulling
into the parking lot outside. "It's for a muffin bird." Then
he'd dashed across the small waiting room, grabbed a magazine from an end table and tried to wrap it around his leg.
When it wouldn't stay he let it fall to the floor and locked his
knee, dragging the leg as if it were in a cast. The social worker's request that he pick up the magazine brought no
response.

"We're not sure how he's reacting to the death of his
father," she told Gussie quietly. "It only happened yesterday.
An investigator's tracking down the family today. You probably won't have him for long."

But it already seemed long. Bird had emptied her car's
glove compartment while she was on the freeway and couldn't
stop to control him. Then when they got home he'd run into
the house and grabbed a picture of Hank in his navy uniform
off the mantel, propped it on a stool at the kitchen counter,
and dropped to his knees in apparent fascination at a plastic
placemat under the dog's water dish. Rising, he bumped the
stool and the picture fell, breaking the glass. As Gussie hurried to sweep up the shards, he jerked the sliding screen door
off its track as he barreled onto the patio and tripped over the
sleeping Labrador her son and daughter-in-law had left while
they took a three-day trip to Mexico. In the fall over the dog
he scraped an elbow on the cement, but didn't cry like most
kids. He just let her clean and bandage the scrape, squirming
restlessly under her ministrations. Already the bandage was
dangling loose from one remaining strip of adhesive tape as
he ran back and forth outside.

Gussie looked at the clock as she made a peanut butter and
jelly sandwich for his lunch. Only noon. But it felt like the
end of a long day. Startled by a ring from the yellow wall
phone, she dropped the knife on her foot. It didn't hurt, but

left a smear of grape jelly on the white canvas of her brand-new Keds sneaker. Later she'd tell Hank that was when she made the decision. Just then, when she saw that sticky purple stain. The decision that Bird Wagman was just too much to handle.

"Yes, come on by, Ms. Bradley," she told the CPS social worker on the phone. "And, um, I'm afraid I'm going to have to ask you to return Bird to the receiving home. This placement just isn't going to work out."

By two o'clock Bo could feel the sun's glare in the bones of her wrists, her jaw, even her spine. A heavy, bitter whiteness humming and aching. She'd taken Bird back to the receiving home and watched him go straight to the playground where he twisted the swing chains together as she talked with the placement worker.

"Attention deficit hyperactivity disorder?" the woman repeated thoughtfully after Bo suggested a possible reason for Bird's incessant movement and distractibility. "You can ask the court to order a medical evaluation at the detention hearing, but I thought this was just an emergency placement until you find the family, not a real court case. There probably won't be a detention hearing. We won't have him long enough to get a diagnosis, and besides, he's traumatized from his father's death and probably just acting out. We've got some foster parents who're willing to take troubled kids. I'll find a better placement, but the sooner you find the family the better it'll be for everybody."

Bo stood in the air-conditioning for a few minutes, watching Bird through a tinted window. The fine dark hair and blue eyes were Mort's, but the graceful, almost pointed ears and prim mouth must have come from the mother. Bird didn't look much like his father, Bo thought. At least not on the outside. But there might be other similarities invisibly locked in the boy's genetic makeup. Frowning, she tried to remember something she'd read about attention deficit hyperactivity disorder as a potential childhood warning for later psychiatric problems. Not in every case, but sometimes. And Mort had schizophrenia. His son's behavior might be a red flag demanding skillful handling as a hedge against what might lie ahead. Bo sighed and made a mental note to discuss schizophrenia with Eva. It would not, she admitted, be a fun chat.

Her office smelled musty when she returned, its overwarm interior striped by shadows from half-open miniblinds she'd forgotten to close before she left. On her desk blotter was a tidy stack of pink phone memos, the top one from Billy Reno.

"Per Reno there's no problem with Wagman estate, but there will be some delays. Phone Wagman atty. Reynolds Cassidy for details," the CPS message operator had written in pencil, giving a Los Angeles number.

There was no comma separating the names, but that might have been an oversight. Bo dialed the number, unsure of whether to ask for Mr. Reynolds or Mr. Cassidy. Somehow getting it right loomed as a marker of her overall competence as a human being. Getting it wrong would constitute public evidence of stupidity and general unworthiness. In seconds she remembered where that strange scenario came from. Depression, again. It was like living in a poorly written play, she thought. A truly awful play with a title like *Bleak Raspberries,* and a minimalist set involving one uncomfortable black chair and a deep hole. Grinning, she determined to paint the scene, just to get even.

"This is Bo Bradley from Child Protective Services in San Diego," she said when the phone was answered. "I have a message directing me to phone 'Reynolds, Cassidy' in regard to my client, Bird Wagman." Making it sound as if she were reading the name from a message memo removed personal responsibility. Depression was so tedious, Bo thought. And alien. She wished she were manic instead. That state was at least familiar and didn't involve a recurrent need to redeem the world from one's personal blunders through exhaustive manipulation of trivia.

"Mr. Cassidy is in court at the moment. I'm his office manager. Perhaps I can be of help."

Bo drew tiny scales of justice on the margin of her desk calendar while explaining Bird's situation to a young woman whose level of empathic engagement with the narrative suggested a failed career in acting.

"Oh dear," she interjected sweetly. "Oh my . . . what a shame . . . how awful." Then when Bo had finished she said, "Mr. Cassidy is not at liberty to discuss any aspect of the case with you until you provide documentation establishing your agency's custody of the child. In the meantime you must provide this office with the current address and all other information pertaining to that child. And please extend to him Mr. Cassidy's sympathy for the tragic accident." She sighed contentedly as if just having read a difficult speech.

"Accident?" Bo snarled as a comforting anger made her ears lie back. "Mort's lawyer thinks his death was an *accident?* Mort was murdered, lady, and now his little boy is stuck here until I can find any relatives Mort had. That's my job, and if Cassidy's withholding names of the family from me, then he's contributing to the pain and suffering of a helpless child. In California that's called child abuse, and he knows it! Now get that file and tell me if it contains anything I need to know." The speech was impressive, Bo thought, if a total fabrication. Cassidy didn't have to tell her anything, but the breathy office manager might not know that. In a minute the shuffling of paper could be heard over the phone.

"There are no relatives of Mr. Wagman listed except for his son, Bird," the woman whispered, obviously hurt by Bo's failure to appreciate her crisp professionalism. "And Bird is the sole inheritor of Mr. Wagman's estate. Mr. Cassidy began making arrangements for the boy as soon as Mr. Reno called yesterday to tell him of the death. But this is a complicated estate to probate. It'll take months."

Bo sighed.

"I really can't tell you anything else," the woman insisted.

"I'll have Mr. Cassidy phone you when he's free. Thank you for calling."

"Uh-huh," Bo mumbled into the phone as the connection was severed.

A subsequent phone call to the Tafel School in Pasadena, where Billy Reno said Bird had attended first grade, revealed nothing that Bo didn't already suspect. No, the principal said agreeably, there were no relatives listed on Bird's registration forms. Neither was any name other than Bird given for the boy. Unusual names were not uncommon among the children of entertainment industry parents, he noted. The school had educated children named Cloud, Dalmatian, and even Broccoli. What was uncommon was that Bird had failed first grade and was considered a discipline problem even by the most tolerant among the staff. A school counselor suspected Bird might be suffering from ADHD and had asked the father to authorize psychiatric testing, but the father refused permission.

"Thank you," Bo said, and hung up. So Mort had known, or suspected what lay behind his son's unproductive behavior. But he hadn't been able to face it. The man who believed relatives had put animal brains into his head wanted his son to be "normal." Wanted it desperately enough to stand in the way of its happening.

Bo sighed and took seven pieces of paper from the file drawer in her desk and began filling them out. The legal paperwork that would give San Diego County legal custody of Bird Wagman. The petition would be granted this afternoon, pro forma. There were no relatives, no other option for Bird. Monday morning there would be a detention hearing, also pro forma. There was nobody to protest the seizure of the child by a system.

Over the weekend Bo would dictate a court report by telephone, documenting the facts of the case. She would ask that Bird be excused from attendance at this and subsequent hearings due to the emotional stress inherent in the setting. She would alert the county's Revenue and Recovery Department of Bird's financial resources, and advise the court that expenses connected to Bird were likely to be reimbursed. A probate judge could order that at any time. Then she'd ask the court to recommend psychiatric testing and to authorize ongoing medical supervision and medication if necessary.

And it would probably be necessary, she thought, staring balefully at her purse, inside which were her own medications. If Bird did have ADHD he'd be given Ritalin or some other stimulant, which in the neurochemistry of childhood would have a calming effect. And he might grow out of his restless, impulsive behavior at the end of puberty, or he might not. Bo drew a scale in which one side was loaded with rocks as she phoned Eva Broussard, outlined what she needed to know, and agreed to meet the psychiatrist for dinner. Then she drove the few miles from her Levant Street office to juvenile court, filed Bird's petition, and went home.

Her apartment was palpably empty when she opened the door. Too empty. A queasy wave of grief swept threateningly from her lungs to her stomach, but she stopped it by pounding gently on her belt buckle with both fists. A snapshot of Mildred taken at Dog Beach nearly four years ago when Bo had moved to San Diego rested on an easel in the living room studio. Behind the snapshot was a blank, gessoed canvas.

Inspired, Bo threw her white outfit on the floor and pulled on jeans and a sweatshirt. She could feel the portrait in her hands. The brush strokes needed to make paint look like fur, the precise mix of black and brown for fox terrier spots. The red leather collar Mildred had always worn lay on a Formica card table with the acrylic paints. Bo would take special care to get the collar right in the painting. It had been the last gift her young husband had given her before they parted forever. Now it would be immortalized with the dog who had worn it.

Engrossed in her work, Bo lost track of time until interrupted by the phone ringing at six. Just as well, she realized. The call would give her enough time to change and meet Eva without having to rush.

"Hello," she answered with more cheer than she'd felt in over a month. "Hello?"

But there was nobody on the line. Just some sort of scratchy noise. Thinking nothing of it, Bo hung up and hurried into the bedroom to change. It might have been Andy calling from Germany, she mused. But he'd call back if he got cut off. When the phone rang again she was sure it would be Andrew LaMarche.

"Andy!" she answered the second time, "I'm doing a painting of Mildred, and . . ."

But the scratchy noise was there again, louder this time. It was a dog barking. A small dog, like a fox terrier. The barking was urgent, frightened.

"Who is this?" Bo whispered, ripples of cold cascading under the skin of her neck. "What the hell is going on?"

But there was no answer and then the connection was broken.

Chapter 10

Shakily Bo scrubbed paint from her fingernails and grabbed a jacket for the beach walk up to Qwig's restaurant where Eva had agreed to meet her for an early dinner. Trying not to think about the strange phone call, she focused instead on her surroundings.

The sidewalk running north along the beach was more than usually populated with unsavory types, some of whom watched Bo with what seemed a covert animosity. Normally she'd stride straight through the small clusters of men holding bottles in paper bags, the sneering adolescent boys, but that took a kind of energy she didn't have at the moment. A kind of energy that was all elbows and attitude, sharp-eyed and wary. The kind of energy depression simply ate.

As an alternative, Bo stiff-armed the seawall and leaped with both feet over it into the sand. She'd walk along the beach to Qwig's, avoid the hard eyes on the sidewalk. The jump had been pretty graceful, she thought. It was nice to have lost some weight. Picking up her pace to a comfortable lope, she watched the sun spill a curved orange road on the water as her shoes filled with sand. It felt good to be on the beach. Familiar. Homey.

But there was something on the sidewalk that didn't look familiar at all. A little girl in a blue-checked dress, standing against the pink siding of a beachfront motel and holding something in her arms. In the orange-gold light of the sunset the child looked like a Wyeth painting. The old-fashioned dress, the long blond hair caught up above her ears by matching blue plastic barrettes, the determined set of her head—all seemed a pose framed fifty years in the past. Loping closer to the sidewalk, Bo saw that the child was holding a dachshund puppy with bronze-colored fur that glowed softly in the metallic light.

For a moment Bo was concerned for the little girl's safety. There seemed to be no one with her, and some of the sidewalk riffraff were potentially dangerous. Still, there were plenty of tourists and Ocean Beach residents around. And the child was only a few feet from the steps leading to the motel office. She'd be okay, Bo decided. She was just outside posing with her tiny dog, proud of the doting looks the pair of them attracted from passers-by.

A neon dolphin ahead announced the location of Qwig's, and Bo sat on the seawall to knock the sand from her shoes before going inside. Through the darkened glass wall of the restaurant she could see Eva Broussard sipping a glass of wine and gazing at the sunset. It was good to have a shrink you could trust, Bo thought with a burst of respect for the white-haired half-Iroquois woman beyond the glass. Better than good. Essential.

"You look hearty and windblown," Eva greeted Bo minutes later with a smile. "Will you join me in a glass of wine?"

Bo frowned. "I'm on *two* medications at the moment. I can't drink, and I'm surprised that—"

"And I'm the psychiatrist who prescribed those medications," Eva interrupted. "If I say one glass of wine won't hurt you, then it won't. Relax, Bo. I recommend the *blanc de noir*, but everyone else seems to have ordered the chardonnay. Now, how are you doing?"

Bo noticed her own paint-stained pants-legs and realized she'd forgotten to change slacks after the eerie phone call. "I was doing a portrait of Mildred when I got home today," she began, "and that felt good. But then there was this phone call. Well, two phone calls. It was a dog barking, a dog that might have been a fox terrier, sounding scared. I know it was just a mistake, but I couldn't help thinking, well . . . things."

Eva Broussard gazed over a tanned and aquiline nose into her wine. "Mildred was *Gayei Nadehogo 'eda,'* a dog of magical power for you," she said, lapsing into Iroquois folklore out of respect for Bo's feelings. "A lucky dog. She was never scared of anything in life, so it's unlikely her spirit is phoning you to tell you she's scared now. But I have to ask this—are you absolutely sure that what you heard in these wrong-number calls was the barking of a small dog, nothing else?"

Bo ordered a glass of chablis from a waiter who actually said, "Chablis? How retro!" before hurrying away to get it.

"I wasn't delusional," she told her abruptly serious shrink. "The first call was just noise, and I thought it was probably Andy with a bad connection from Germany. When the phone rang again immediately I was sure that's who it was, but then there was just this barking and they hung up. Probably some kid. Eva, quit worrying; I'm fine."

"You'd be more fine if you'd stayed away from work another week, but I understand your reasons. Now, what is this about Mort's son and attention deficit hyperactivity disorder? I spent the afternoon after your call checking up on some of your questions."

Bo admired her wine in its glass and then took a sip. "Bird's father had schizophrenia, and I think Bird has ADHD," she said. "And all this stuff is genetic. If he does have ADHD, is that a predictor that he'll get hit with schizophrenia or one of the other major disorders later? And if it is, what's the best thing to do with him now?"

Eva stretched her long, sinewy arms under the table and looked out to sea. "If testing indicates that you're right, then I'd say in Bird's case the ADHD suggests a need for close scrutiny and a highly structured, routinized environment, like a Catholic school, in addition to medication. Adults living successfully with schizophrenia are often those whose childhoods were rigidly circumscribed by external structures. In interviews these adults sometimes describe the safety they felt in contexts where routines were the same every day, nothing was ambiguous. It would seem that they internalized some of that safety, that external reliability, and used it to maintain a sense of self against the ravages of the illness when it came."

Bo nodded. Mort Wagman had told her he went to a Catholic boys' boarding school in St. Louis. Eva's words made sense. Outside, the lights of the Ocean Beach Pier blazed on, creating a sparkling wedge over the water. Invisible beneath it were hundreds of fish, and slim young sharks preying on them. Bo decided to order the vegetarian plate and felt uncharacteristically righteous.

"I'd recommend creating that safety net for Bird," Eva went on. "Get him into the most structured, repetitive environment you can find. Someplace with good people and rules that don't change. If it isn't ultimately needed, nothing's lost. If it is needed, by the time an illness hits him ten or fifteen years from now it will be too late to go back and provide a routinized childhood. It must be done now."

"Thanks, Eva," Bo said. "You know, it was only a few miles from here where that heiress got chomped by a great white. There's a universe of teeth out there under that black surface, white teeth in a million sizes, waiting to—"

"Bo!" Eva tapped the stem of her wine glass with a spoon, shattering Bo's reverie and creating anticipatory looks on the faces of nearby diners programmed to expect a speech. "It may be time to cut back on your antidepressant."

"Why? Everybody's talking about the shark attack."

"Yes, but everybody's not talking about universes of teeth. Antidepressants are dicey in patients prone to mania, and your imagery is escalating. Let's cut the dose to half, starting tonight."

"But I still feel like I'm neck-deep in gray Jell-O, and no power on earth could compel me to do a laundry. Isn't that depression?"

"Could be garden-variety exhaustion," Eva answered thoughtfully. "A depressive episode like the one you've just been through, close to psychotic in the beginning, is tantamount to brain surgery. It's a tremendous shock to the body and takes months to get over. You need to do nothing but rest when you're not at work. Do you agree to that?"

"Sure," Bo mumbled at her plate. Rest sounded fine, but the "garden-variety" bit rankled. "There's nothing else I can do for Mort, anyway. Just try to protect Bird. That's all I want."

After ordering, Eva continued. "Have you come any closer to locating Mort's relatives?" she asked.

Bo glared at invisible sharks swarming beneath the Pacific Ocean. "Not only are there no relatives," she answered, "but I can't even find Bird's real name. It's as if Mort didn't *want* anyone to know anything about him or about Bird. Everywhere I turn there's another blank wall. Bird's mother is supposedly dead, but that's only what Mort told his agent and Bird's school. I don't like thinking Mort lied, but . . . "

"But if the mother were still alive and wanted custody of Bird, she could have taken him from Mort at any time and no court in the world would have upheld the rights of a father with schizophrenia," Eva completed Bo's train of thought. "And you would support Mort in that lie."

Bo enjoyed another sip of wine and tugged at a loose thread in the corner of her salmon pink placemat. The thread leaped at her touch, unraveling the entire top seam before she realized what was happening. "He was like a brother to me," she replied defensively. "I'm sure he had his reasons for cutting himself and Bird off from his family and from Bird's mother, if she's really still alive." A new thought was stirring from the pile of curly pink thread left on the placemat. "Hey, what if *she* killed Mort in order to get Bird away from him?"

"We've already established that she'd hardly need to go to such lengths, and if she had, then she'd appear to claim Bird. Bo, what do you know about brothers?" Eva's smile was amused.

"Like sisters, only male?"

"If I'm intruding, tell me, but don't you mean you liked feeling close to a man in a nonsexual relationship, enjoying mutual affection without the often terminal complications of intimacy?"

"Well, yeah," Bo admitted, unraveling the left-hand vertical seam of the placemat. "Like a brother."

"No, a brother would share your genetic background, your childhood, your social history, maybe even your values. Mort was kind to you when you were ill and profoundly vulnerable, Bo, and so you liked him. But did you really get to know him well enough to regard him as a brother?"

"I didn't really know him at all," Bo sighed and snapped off the wad of thread before she decimated the entire placemat. "But that doesn't mean I don't owe him something for his kindness. I do, and I'm going to repay him by watching out for Bird. Period."

"Just remember to keep it in perspective," Eva advised as the waiter brought a broiler plate of scallop kabobs for her and a steaming bowl of vegetables over brown rice for Bo.

Reaching for the tamari sauce, Bo decided that discussing her determination to find Mort's killer with her shrink was probably ill-advised. "So what's going on at Ghost Flower?" she said, changing the subject. "Zach was a mess when I saw him yesterday, and there was this guy in a suit who looked like a used-Mercedes salesman. And did you hear that Old Ayma walked off? Zach said they were sending cadaver dogs out into the desert, uh, to look for her . . . her body, I guess."

Eva managed to grimace while beaming at her scallops. "No trace of Ayma was found," she told Bo, "and I'm afraid the lodge is experiencing some rather serious financial difficulties. Quite possibly the Kumeyaay will have to sell their program. Zach has a great deal to worry about, but there's nothing we can do about it at the moment, so let's enjoy our meal, don't you agree?"

Bo didn't agree, but recognized the social convention erected by her shrink's impossibly proper phrasing. Andrew LaMarche, she thought fondly, would have said precisely the same thing. She wondered what he was doing at the moment. And what it would be like when he returned from Germany in another week. Biting into a steamed carrot, she realized that she was ravenously hungry.

The moon had risen when Bo sauntered home an hour later, and its silver-gray ripples led in a narrowing, watery band over the edge of the planet. Watching that path gleam and fade as low clouds crossed the moonlight, she almost didn't see a familiar figure silhouetted beside the pink motel. It was the little girl with the puppy, her blue-checked dress now gray in shadows.

"Hey," Bo grinned, "isn't it past your pup's bedtime? Or are you two going to stand out here until the sea gives up its dead, as they say?" A poor choice of imagery, she realized, as the child glanced anxiously into the dark beyond the beach fires where most of the homeless were gathered in clumps. The red-brown puppy, now a washed-out black in the dark, squirmed in the child's arms.

"I think she has to go potty," the little girl finally said.

Bo stared pointedly at the grass comprising the narrow motel yard, and nodded. "Why don't you set her down?"

"I'm afraid she'll run away and one of those people will catch her and cook her. My stepfather says people like that eat dogs. Cats, too. Especially baby ones."

Your stepfather should be fried in whale oil and fed to nursing wolves.

"Why don't I sit right here on this little wall and help you watch her so she can do her thing?" Bo suggested. "You know how babies are when they have to go."

The child sized Bo up with a long, overly acute look, and

then carefully placed the puppy on the grass. The little dog wasted no time in selecting the perfect spot beneath an over-hang of trellised bougainvillea. "Her name's Gretel, because dachshunds are German and Gretel's a German name," the girl said somberly, "but my stepfather calls her mutant sausage and baloney-butt and stuff like that."

Better, your stepfather should be ground into croquettes and served in a lentil sauce to the Republican National Committee.

Gretel waddled over to sniff Bo's hand and wagged a diminutive tail as Bo gently scratched the spot under her right ear that Mildred had always liked to have scratched. The little hound ears were like swatches of velvet.

"So how come you two are just standing around out here in the dark?" Bo asked. "Where's your mom?"

The little girl sat stiffly on the low wall surrounding the motel's yard and sighed. "She's in there, in the room. See, my stepfather just got back from the navy, he's been out in a boat for a long time, and my mom said, you know, they need to be alone because, you know, they need to do stuff alone."

Bo stretched out on her back on the grass and allowed Gretel to clamber across her chest. The child wasn't much older than Bird. Did she grasp what "stuff" the adults needed to do alone? An embarrassed distaste in the child's voice suggested that she at least had an idea.

"Do you have a German name, too?" Bo asked.

"Nah, it's just American. It's Linda Sandifer, but I like Lindsey. I have my friends at school call me Lindsey because it sounds like a girl pioneer who lives in a covered wagon. I'd like to live with my mom in a covered wagon on the prairie. She got me Gretel for my birthday when I was seven last week. I didn't really want a dog; I wanted hamsters so they'd have babies. Except Danny, that's my stepfather, Danny says Gretel's more like a rat than a dog. He doesn't like her."

And I don't like him.

"Lindsey, do you remember what room your mom and Danny are in?"

"Yeah, it's upstairs, it's number seventeen."

"Well, I want you to take Gretel and stand on the porch by the office while I run up and talk to them for a minute, okay?"

"But . . . they said they'd come get me after they were, you know, done being alone. You can't . . ."

"Yes I can." Bo smiled. "Now go stand by the office. I'll be right back."

The man who opened the door of number seventeen had penny-sized beige eyes, an overlarge jaw, and smelled like beer. He was wearing nothing but a pair of gym shorts and seemed to have been asleep. "Yeah?" he said.

"Your little girl, Lindsey, has been standing outside alone for over two hours," Bo began. "It's dark now and I'm afraid it's simply not safe for—"

"It's her kid," he said, gesturing with a jerk of his head toward a woman emerging from the bathroom and tucking a new T-shirt into her jeans. "Honey, handle this." With the air of a man put upon by inferiors, he scooped a beer can from a large cooler and concentrated on the flickering light from a color TV.

"Where is Linda?" the woman asked. "Is she okay? I didn't realize it had gotten dark. I really appreciate . . ."

"Some people oughtta mind their own business," the man growled at the TV. "The kid's fine, no big deal."

Bo felt something like a miniature bolt of lightning inside her skull. It felt good. Pushing the door fully open with her knee, she let her head rotate with dramatic slowness toward the man slouching on the end of the unmade bed.

"I'm afraid it *is* a big deal, sir. You're in California, where we have some really serious laws affecting people who endanger children. I live in this neighborhood, so I know that if you'd so much as glanced at what's hanging around on that sidewalk where you dumped a seven-year-old girl, you'd have noticed what I'm talking about when I say 'endangered.' "

"Lady, get a life," the man sneered. "Go get yourself a man and quit bothering normal people. Get outta here!"

"Dan, I think . . ." the woman whispered.

"I'm not leaving until that child is safe," Bo insisted. "Lindsey tells me you're in the navy. Let me tell you I work for Child Protective Services. That way we both understand that one call from me to your CO will go straight into your service record and possibly land you in a shoreside job loading garbage for six months while you sit through an Armed Services Family Counseling Program. Now, was there anything else you wanted to say?"

The man merely glared into his beer can as though it contained something repulsive, but Bo could see a flush of humiliation and rage crawling up his thick neck. He might take his anger out on the child unless safeguards were established.

"I'll go down and get Linda," the woman said.

Bo followed her down the stairs and told Lindsey she'd come by tomorrow morning and take her and Gretel to a neat place nearby where they sold great stuff for dogs. "I'll bring my ID badge so you'll know I'm who I say I am," she told the girl's mother. "You can check it out by calling the child abuse hotline. Then I'll take Lindsey and her puppy out for a while, give you and that pinnacle of manhood another chance to be 'alone.' " Between the lines was a clear message—"I'll be back."

The woman blushed under the motel's security lights. "It's just that he's been on a tour for three months. And we only got married just before that . . ."

"Spare me," Bo said, and turned to walk home. She felt better than she had in months. Too good, probably. Eva was right. Time to cut back the antidepressants before she went too far the other way and got manic. But for the moment she was enjoying the upswing, and completely forgot to think about sharks.

Chapter 11

The shark had washed ashore during the night on a rocky beach north of Ensenada, Mexico, about eighty-five miles south of San Diego. Her death had occurred several hours before the tides beached her body amid moonlit rocks and ropes of seaweed. At dawn an old man beachcombing for plastic bottles dumped into the ocean from hundreds of pleasure boats cruising the coast saw the shark, and quickly cut off her dorsal fin with the curved knife he carried hidden in his boot. Then he packed the fin in seaweed and walked eight miles into Ensenada where he sold it for twenty American dollars to a fancy restaurant. The fin, he knew, would be made into soup.

After that he walked two more miles to the Escuela Ciencias Marinas, the School of Oceanography, on Calle Primera where a man named Professor Héctor Vincente Ortíz would pay five dollars to anybody who told him when a whale or any big fish washed up on the beach. Since it was Saturday Dr. Ortíz wasn't there, but a man at a desk inside the door phoned Ortíz at his home and was instructed to establish the precise location of the shark cadaver and to give the old man his five-dollar *mordida*.

Héctor Ortíz was excited about the availability of a great white for dissection, but he had to attend his son's soccer game and then drive his aging father-in-law to a doctor's appointment for the prostate problem that was making the old man meaner than a scorpion. There was no honorable way for a man of his character and position to avoid either of these responsibilities, but by afternoon the great white shark would be hacked to pieces for food and souvenirs. Héctor Ortíz thought about this for exactly two minutes and then phoned a promising student in his graduate marine biology seminar named José Méndez.

"I'm particularly concerned with stomach contents, crustacean-load in the gill areas, and the brain," he told Méndez. "Get those and then we'll try to take samples of everything else we can before it's too late. Don't forget ice. I'll be there as soon as possible."

An hour later José Méndez and is girlfriend, Bianca Escobedo, hauled an old metal Coleman cooler across the gray sand and black rocks to a beach between Ensenada and a village called San Miguel. In the cooler were a bag of ice, a hack saw, a keyhole saw, two pairs of pliers, a tape measure, knives in four sizes, two large C-clamps, boxes of sandwich bags and half-gallon freezer bags, a waterproof marker, and tape.

Ahead on the beach people stood in clusters staring at the shark, whose double-lobed tail, eyes, and most of its teeth had already been removed by human scavengers. José and Bianca both knew that the shark's eyes and teeth, along with mummified toads, straw dolls, jimsonweed, playing cards, snakeskins, and black chickens, would be used in primitive rituals by people like the servants who had raised them both. The tail, more easily hauled away than the unwieldy body, would be ground for fertilizer in somebody's garden.

"Ycchh," Bianca said when they were twenty yards from the baking carcass. "I'm glad I majored in business instead of this. It smells."

"Wait until I cut open the stomach." José grinned at the young woman who would be his bride after he graduated and got a job. His father had wanted him to stay in medical school, but José loved the beach and its freedom. Marine biology seemed like the easiest way to avoid having to get what he thought of as a real job. "You're going to throw up," he told her gleefully.

"I will not! I can take anything you can."

Approaching a middle-aged man with a machete who was ineffectively trying to saw chunks of flesh from the cadaver, José explained who he was and asked the man to wait until he had completed his scientific duties before hacking off stew meat to take home for his wife. The man nodded and stood back three feet, establishing José's authority in the eyes of the onlookers. Removing his shirt, José flexed his shoulder muscles, showing off for Bianca and demonstrating to the crowd how manly the field of marine biology could be. Then he selected the largest knife from the cooler and assessed the task before him.

The shark, a massive female great white, had come to rest on its left side parallel to the shore and facing south. Several metal harpoons trailed black nylon cord onto the sand. The stomach would be, José calculated, just below one of the harpoons. Measuring the distance with his eyes, he plunged the knife into the shark's side with both hands and pulled the blade laterally until the cut was wide enough to accommodate the hack saw.

"I need the big saw," he told Bianca, who was standing behind him, "then the second-smallest knife, and then the big plastic bags. When I get the stomach open I'll scoop the contents into the bags and then you seal them, okay?"

"What women do for love." Bianca grinned and handed him the hack saw.

After exposing the stomach José waited for a strong breeze off the water, made a small, vertical cut through the organ's side, and then pushed against the shark's belly with his knee. The gaseous stench escaping through the cut brought bile into his throat and made his hands shake. Bianca had a white line above her upper lip and tears in her eyes, but she didn't move even though the onlookers moaned and held their noses. In minutes he'd widened the incision and plunged an open plastic gag into the stomach.

Bones. There were bones amid the expected contents of the shark's stomach, and they weren't from fish. Bigger bones, and lacking that opaque flexibility characteristic of skeletons that would swim but never walk. In the second sample was a straight bone with three sides, too long to fit in the bag. Some animal must have fallen into the sea, he thought, and been devoured by the shark. Maybe a goat or a large dog.

Curious, he explored the stomach with his right hand and found another, larger bone, cylindrical with a big round knob at one end that was fastened to the shaft at nearly a right angle by a pyramid-shaped neck. As an undergraduate in premed, José had taken an anatomy class. He was certain this bone was a femur, a thighbone. The round knob was what fit into the animal's pelvis. And the other long bone had been a tibia. Holding the bigger bone next to his own thigh, he saw that it was somewhat shorter.

"What is it?" Bianca asked.

"I don't know. An animal of some kind that the shark ate. Could you hand me the tape measure?"

The femur was sixteen and a half inches long. But what sort of animal would have this long, straight thighbone? Maybe an ape of some kind, José thought. Except there were no wild primates for thousands of miles. The shark could have eaten a monkey that fell into the ocean somewhere, but the bones would been digested or excreted long before the shark could have swum to Baja, Mexico. These bones had only been in the shark's stomach for a few days.

From his anatomy class José remembered a formula. The femur was supposed to be a fourth of total body height. So this femur, he calculated, was from an animal that had been about five feet, six inches tall. Except that formula was only for human femurs.

The thought brought a sense of horror that was like frost

spreading inside the muscles of his chest and back. What if this bone were human? José held it in both hands, turning it in the bright sunlight. Had it belonged to a man or a woman? Either one could be five feet, six inches tall. But there was something about the angle of the knob, where the bone fit into the pelvis. Women's pelvises were much wider than men's in order to accommodate babies. So the angle of that knob was almost ninety degrees in women, he remembered. Professor Guitiérrez had made dumb jokes about it in class. This femur, José Méndez predicted, would turn out to be from a female, and a human. The realization intensified his curiosity, but also intensified his discomfort. In Mexico human remains were honored, their resting places visited by their families for celebrations. To be standing on a beach holding a dead woman's thighbone was unthinkable.

José didn't know what to do. He wanted to throw the thing down in the sand and run, but that was childish. It was just a bone. Probably a cemetery in some little seaside village had been eaten away by the surf, and . . . But no, he reminded himself, the shark wouldn't have been attracted to a dead body and besides, where was the rest of it? Well, maybe an amputation in a hospital somewhere, and the hospital had been careless about disposing of the amputated leg and it had wound up in the sea? The nausea came back, this time from someplace deep inside him. Unconsciously he rubbed his thumb against the bone where he held it along the shaft about four inches beneath the big knob.

"José, you're bleeding!" Bianca cried. "Look at your thumb!"

Looking down he saw the slice of skin from which a rivulet of his blood ran over the side of the bone. He'd cut himself on something sharp that shouldn't be there. Looking closely at the femur he saw, highlighted by his own blood, a cut in the bone. Something had gouged it and glanced off the surface, chipping the bone and leaving a small, straight, razor-sharp flap.

No triangular, serrated shark's tooth could leave a slice like that, he thought. Only something thin and straight, like a knife. When he turned the femur forward he realized that the gouge would have cut directly through her femoral artery. If the injury occurred prior to her death it would have killed her in minutes, her blood pumping in torrents from the large artery at its most unprotected point low in her groin. And if this injury happened in the sea, the pumping blood would attract sharks.

José placed the femur in the ice chest and stared at the shark, which no longer interested him. He'd used his mind to figure out part of a story. That interested him. The fact that he could do that interested him a lot. He wondered who the woman was, what had happened to her. Weren't there police doctors, medical examiners, who did this for a living? It would mean going back to medical school, but he could be such a doctor. The thought was exciting.

"This shark has devoured the leg of a woman," he told the crowd with authority. "It will be necessary for someone to notify the police."

Chapter 12

By six-thirty on Saturday morning Bo had already been to an all-night supermarket and bought groceries. Free-range eggs, a tub of medium-hot salsa, freshly ground coffee in three flavors, and a pack of cigarettes. After breakfast and two cups of hazelnut-mocha she phoned Eva Broussard.

"I'm starving, I bought a pack of cigarettes, and I've realized I need new towels," she announced without preamble. "I've cleaned out my linen closet and bagged the towels so I can take them to a women's shelter someplace. When the stores open I'm going to shop for new ones, thinner ones that don't take an hour in the dryer. I didn't sleep much last night, kept thinking of ways to conserve energy. If everyone used thinner towels like they do in Europe—"

"Bo." Eva Broussard's voice was deep with concern. "Don't take any more of the antidepressants. Throw the ones you have left into the toilet and plan a quiet schedule for the rest of the weekend. You know what's happening."

"Yeah, you said it might," Bo agreed. "You said the antidepressant might alter my normal cycle and throw me into a manic episode. But I'm not really manic, and besides, it feels good after an entire month of wanting to dig a hole, get in it, and die, and hating myself for not having enough energy to pick up a shovel. This is better. I'm okay."

"It may not stay better, and you wouldn't have called me at this hour if you were okay. Keep taking the mood-stabilizing medication; with luck it will even you out in a couple of days. In the meantime, exercise, keep the sun out of your eyes, and avoid stimulants."

Bo eyed the pack of cigarettes lying on the Formica counter between her tiny kitchen and the dining area of her beach apartment. A familiar comfort. "Does that include nicotine?" she asked.

"Yes," her psychiatrist laughed, "and as usual, I refuse to discuss smoking with patients whose vision and hearing are not so impaired as to preclude access to books, magazines, television, and billboards. I'm a little worried about you, Bo. Will you call me this evening to check in?"

"Sure," Bo answered. "And thanks, Eva. You're my lifeline."

After hanging up, Bo went out onto the redwood deck over the beach and lit a cigarette. It tasted rubbery and made her dizzy, but the physical movements, the arc of her arm and the tipping of her head back to exhale, were calming, pleasant. Beneath the light haze over the ocean a string of pelicans soared with ragged grace. When one plunged into the blue-green swells she held her breath until it emerged clasping a small fish in its beak. The day was clean and breezy with possibility, she thought. A good day to be alive.

After dressing conservatively in khakis and a clean white polo shirt, she tied a blue cotton crewneck sweater over her shoulders and added tiny lapis earrings for the necessary touch of class. The outfit would do for lunch somewhere on Cape Cod, she thought. It would also intimidate the parents of Lindsey Sandifer.

The little girl was waiting, again wearing her blue-checked dress, when Bo arrived at the motel. Gretel, recognizing Bo from the night before, scampered across several crushed beer cans littering the floor and then stopped to place a warm paw on Bo's instep as she sniffed her leather sandals appraisingly.

"Don't even think of it!" Bo told the puppy as she handed her CPS identification card to Lindsey's mother. "Just hang on and we'll get you something even better to teethe on."

To the woman she said politely, "With your permission I'd like to take Lindsey and Gretel to a dogwash about three blocks from here. The owners have a lovely boutique and will be delighted to talk with Lindsey about how to care for her puppy. Then we'll probably have an ice cream before returning. We shouldn't be gone longer than two hours. I've put the phone number of the dogwash on one of my business cards for you, and the address as well in case you'd care to join us later." The tone was the one Bo's violinist mother had used when dealing with salesmen and representatives of ladies clubs who expected her to provide free "musical interludes" for creamed-chicken fashion lunches.

"Sure." The child's mother nodded, glancing at the closed bathroom door from behind which a shower could be heard. "Go ahead."

"My stepfather says you're fustered," Lindsey mentioned when they reached the sidewalk, a worried frown narrowing her large eyes.

Bo pondered the term, momentarily taken aback. "Ah, I think he meant 'frustrated,' " she said when she'd deciphered the second-grade version. "That's just a word some men use when women aren't afraid of them. It doesn't really mean anything."

"My mom's afraid of him. She's afraid he won't stay with us," the girl went on. "I can tell. It's because of me, because I'm not his kid and he has to pay for me." The child's blond head was hunched over the puppy in her arms.

Bo entertained a private fantasy of murder, but said, "He's young and doesn't know how to be a daddy, since he wasn't there when you were a baby and didn't get to learn. He's still just like a teenager, you know? But he might shape up after he learns how to be important to you and your mom." Always disgusting to toe the conciliatory social worker line, but there was no point in doing anything else.

"Oh," Lindsey said thoughtfully. "Teenagers act dumb."

"But then sometimes they grow up, right?"

"I guess. Can Gretel have ice cream, too?"

The limits of seven-year-old insight had been reached. "No, but she can have dog candy. That's what she'd like."

The dogwash was busy as Bo steered Lindsey past several raised bathtubs in which large dogs were being lathered and scrubbed. Gretel, now riding on Bo's left shoulder, registered her alarm at these activities by sinking her tiny, sharp claws into Bo's neck and diving into her collar.

"I don't think she wants a bath," Lindsey giggled.

"Aagghh!" Bo yelped. "Mindy, Jane, get out here and sell us a harness and leash so I can get this beast out of my blouse!"

One of the shop's owners, Jane Jenkins, appeared from an office in the back. "I thought your beast was still in Germany." She grinned beneath short, wavy hair so red it made Bo's seem dull by comparison. "Oh, you mean this little scamp. And you," she addressed Lindsey, "must be the proud owner. Let's go over here and pick out something really smashing for your dachsie."

"It's 'dachshund,'" Lindsey replied regally. "But at least you didn't call her 'weenie' or something. Don't you think it's dumb when people call dachshunds 'weenie dogs'?"

"I do," Jane agreed.

Bo watched as they sorted through an array of small harnesses made of nylon webbing, holding each one next to the puppy's coat.

"Red clashes with her fur," Jane noted.

"And pink does, too," Lindsey said.

It was serious business. Finally they selected a deep yellow harness with matching leash, and Jane spent twenty minutes introducing Gretel to her new wardrobe. In her harness the little dog looked like a bright autumn leaf, Bo thought approvingly. And Lindsey was ecstatic.

After additional purchases of rawhide chewsticks, a squeaking rubber porcupine in Day-Glo orange, and a box of canine cookies, Bo and Lindsey sauntered back up the beachfront walk to an ice cream bistro and made their selections.

"We're going home tomorrow," Lindsey said without enthusiasm as they sat on the seawall licking their cones. "To El Paso. I guess Danny's gonna quit being in the navy and come live with us. He says my mom has to get a different job to make more money. She's a waitress now. He says she has to pay him back for all the money he spent when I had my tonsils out in the navy's hospital."

Bo saw an amoebic black dot with purple edges swimming in her field of vision. Anger, again. "Danny has made a mistake," she said through a fake smile. "He must have forgotten that his military insurance paid for everything the navy didn't cover. I'm sure he'll remember that when he thinks about it."

"My mom's real name is Emily," the child said softly. "I think it's like a pioneer mom's name. She reads me Laura Ingalls Wilder books. They're about this little girl on the prairie, y'know?"

Bo nodded. "*Little House on the Prairie* was my favorite. Is that one your favorite, too?"

The child scowled into the horizon, ignoring Bo's question. "He just calls her M. Sometimes he calls her B.M. You know what that means? It's bad. Sometimes I just wish he'd *die.*"

Bradley, you're meddling in the life of a kid that's not even on your caseload while neglecting the kid that is. You've opened a can of worms here. Now handle it!

"It's really good that you let your angry feelings out," Bo said conversationally to the top of Lindsey's head. "It's okay to feel angry sometimes and it's super-okay to say those angry feelings out loud when you're with a grown-up who understands that kids don't really mean—"

"I *do* really mean it," Lindsey said. "I wish his dumb boat would just sink and he'd be a skeleton at the bottom of the ocean with the pirates."

"Pirates?"

"Yeah, like at Disneyland. Pirates of the Caribbean, y'know? They've got trunks full of gold and diamonds, and they sing."

"You're right. I forgot about that."

And so much for the textbook social worker crap.

When Bo returned Lindsey and Gretel to the pink motel, the adults were sitting on the balcony in silence.

"Be sure to read Laura Ingalls Wilder books to Gretel as soon as you're old enough." Bo smiled at the little girl, and then said good-bye.

Back at her apartment there was a message from Andrew LaMarche saying he was counting the hours until he could see her again. Bo examined her reactions to this news and found pockets of interest heretofore lacking. The depression with its gloomy irritability and absence of romantic inclination was definitely waning. And there were, she calculated, about a hundred and seventeen hours left to count.

Next she phoned the receiving home, got the address and phone number of Bird's new foster care placement, and called.

"He seems to be doing fine," an easygoing male voice told Bo. "Got 'im up here on my ranch in Ramona, plenty a room to run around. Got 'im in knee and elbow guards, too. Worker tole me y'all suspect ADHD. Think you're prob'ly right."

The foster father, a retired oil rig mechanic from Texas named Dutch Stedman, had gone on fostering after his wife died "for the hell of it," he told Bo. And the wild kids, he went on fondly, the ones with problems, just seemed to mellow out with a little discipline and a lot of space. Bo made an appointment to visit Bird on Monday, and hung up. It sounded as if the boy were in good hands. So now what?

The painted rattlesnake clock in the kitchen said it was only ten o'clock. On a normal Saturday she'd just be finishing her second cup of coffee, Bo thought. But today she'd been up since six and still felt energetic enough to clean out the refrigerator, wash the car, and reorganize the federal government. It was going to be difficult to "plan a quiet schedule" as Dr. Broussard had ordered. Maybe a movie would be a good idea.

Phoning her psychiatric social worker friend, Rombo Perry, and his partner, Martin St. John, Bo heard an answering machine message accounting for the couple's absence. Their dog, Watson, was graduating from obedience school in a ceremony at ten-thirty that morning. Everyone was invited to a noontime picnic celebrating the occasion and directions to the picnic site were provided.

Bo sighed and replaced the phone in its cradle. From the easel in the dining alcove a half-finished portrait of a spirited old fox terrier seemed to cock its head expectantly.

"I couldn't stand to go to Watson's party without you, Mildred," Bo told the painting. "Everybody would be there with their dogs except me and it would just be too much."

Wandering onto the deck adjoining her living room and bedroom, Bo saw that the invisible window had closed again. The window through which the grieving observe a world whose ongoing activity seems inexplicable.

Bo had noticed the window first while sitting in a black limousine with her grandmother outside the Boston mortuary from which her younger sister, Laurie, was about to be buried. Already an adult, she'd nonetheless been surprised to see that traffic lights still changed color, that strangers drove by in cars, talking and laughing. The feeling had not abated as they drove toward the cemetery until an old man in a gray topcoat emerged from a barber shop and stopped on the sidewalk. Removing his hat, he crossed himself and then stood with bowed head for a moment as the hearse and somber black limousines passed before him. An old-fashioned Catholic, he'd known the ritual that broke the window, made a connection. Bo had never forgotten him.

"I feel like going out to the desert," she told an oblivious surfer riding the swells far out beyond the end of the Ocean

Beach Pier. At that distance she couldn't discern any detail of the wetsuited body half submerged in opaque green water, but she imagined it was the old man from Boston. Imagined he would understand.

The phone rang as she locked the door of her apartment behind her, but she didn't go back in to answer it. Bounding down the steps toward the street, she could hear her own voice on the tape announcing the usual "I'm sorry we're unable to answer your call at the moment . . ." message through the open kitchen window. And after that she was sure she heard the frantic barking of a small dog.

Chapter 13

Alexander Morley lowered his eyelids and shook his head so imperceptibly that only the most acutely attentive waiter could discern his meaning. No more wine. He'd brought the entire MedNet board to Phoenix at extravagant expense for this celebratory lunch at his club, and Bob Thompson was embarrassing him by swilling eighty-dollar-a-bottle Monbazillac as if it were grape soda. The waiter nodded a sixteenth of an inch and beckoned the server to clear the wine glasses. The subtlety was not lost on Bob Thompson.

"I'm sorry," he beamed at the server, "but I'm not quite finished with my wine." A technicality, but within the boundaries of truth. There was a quarter-ounce of liquid left in his glass. Ignoring the old man, Thompson turned his animated gaze to Elliot Kines, the board member second to himself in seniority, and asked a rhetorical question regarding Kines's opinion of South Africa as a test market for health services. Everyone at the table was uncomfortably aware that Bob Thompson had just thrown down a very large, symbolic gauntlet.

"Gentlemen," Morley boomed amiably, "you already know the reason for our little party here today. But let's make it official." In the silence that followed, a rustling could be heard from the room's heavy silk drapery as the air-conditioning clicked on. "Through a fortuitous twist of fate in the shape of a great white shark," Morley continued, "the Indian program known as Ghost Flower Lodge has fallen squarely into our hands. For all practical purposes, we now own it!"

"Excellent, Alex," Thompson acknowledged and then pushed the minuscule wedge he'd just driven into Morley's authority. "I'm sure we're all relieved that MedNet's interests no longer need be arbitrated by Mr. Henderson."

"Henderson's duties scarcely meet the requirements of that term, Bob," Morley replied, "he's—"

"How much did we pay this guy to 'negotiate' a done deal?" Thompson went on. The question was jovial, directed to the board's treasurer, Neal Brockman, whose immaculate surgeon's hands fluttered over his silverware like tethered moths.

"It's in the computer, Bob," Brockman answered and then tapped the crystal of his Rolex. "Is it really eight o'clock yesterday in Japan? Damned thing still isn't working right."

"I told you to stop wearing it in the shower," Kines sighed over the dark expanse of his pin-striped vest. "Ah, here's lunch!"

The exchange reinforced what Bob Thompson already knew—that Kines and Brockman would side with the old man through a nuclear blast if necessary. They were old buddies from their med school days, grown fat off the drippings from Morley's entrepreneurial savvy. At a meeting of the full board the three of them could command sufficient votes to rubber-stamp anything Morley wanted. Bob Thompson, the only member of the exec board who was not a doctor, would never be more than their employee, he thought for the hundredth time, a loyal and gifted trick dog.

"Is there something about the Indian deal you're uncomfortable with, Bob?" Morley asked through a column of steam rising from his beef Stroganoff. "The Japanese have just doubled their original offer, you know. I'm counting on you to package the thing. Get out there and nail the model. We'll contract with an advertising outfit for the design, once you've told us what it is." Morley's ice-colored eyes reminded Bob Thompson of a doll his sister had when he was a kid. A doll whose oddly knowing gaze followed you around a room. The relaxed smile didn't match the eyes at all. The two expressions, Thompson thought, might have been patched together from different faces.

"Anxious to get on it," he said. "Sounds like a real challenge."

In the standoff Bob Thompson felt something odd in the air, something rust-scented and chilling. But for the life of him he couldn't get a handle on what, exactly, it was.

Chapter 14

Bo took the long way to the desert, east on Highway 94 through parched chaparral and woodland, boulder-strewn meadows and glaring dirt side roads that had been there for centuries. The highway ran parallel to the Mexican border from the Tecate spur to the old settlement the Spanish had simply called Campo. At its closest, an area called Buck South, the road looped to within less than a quarter-mile from foreign soil. Except it didn't look foreign, Bo noted. The pale sand glistening with flecks of fool's gold, the eerie gray granite hills cracked and split so they looked like toy-block buildings—these merely continued beyond the invisible line separating the two nations. And the dirt roads snaking south into scrub sage and smoke trees would cross that line where it was not marked, where it remained so abstract it didn't really exist.

Bo grinned at the Pathfinder's second gearshift, the one built to regulate the vehicle's four-wheel drive. It would be so easy just to engage the four-wheel, turn off on a nameless southbound track, and vanish into the Baja Peninsula. Investigating the impulse, Bo found its origin in an urge to travel, to go somewhere. Anywhere. A raven swooped to land on a cracked oval topstone that reminded Bo of Humpty-Dumpty. The bird's black feathers reflected the glare in mirrorlike flashes. The Indians had called Mort Wagman Raven, and his pale little boy Moonbird in contrast. So maybe, Bo thought, this raven was significant. Maybe if it flew south into Mexico that would mean she should follow.

Easing the Pathfinder onto the shoulder, Bo slowed and watched the bird stare attentively at its own right leg until a cloud of dust from the dirt road below alerted her to the presence of a green-striped Border Patrol truck.

"Kloo-kluck," the raven sang as it flapped skyward and then soared north above the Pacific Crest Trail. The Border Patrolman glanced at Bo with professional suspicion and then turned to head back along the rutted dirt road.

A bird has just saved you from creating an international incident, Bradley. Don't let this go any further.

"It would have been fun," Bo told the steering wheel. "But I guess I'll just go on up to Ghost Flower, maybe build a cairn of stones out at Yucca Canyon where Mort was killed." The idea held a certain appeal. Besides, hauling rocks around in the heat might diminish this sudden inclination to travel. Inspired, Bo accelerated north, crossed under I-8 near Manzanita, engaged the four-wheel and dived off the road into the dry bed of Tule Creek. From the creekbed she could skirt the eastern boundaries of the Manzanita and Campo reservations and the northern edge of the property called Hadamar. She could get to within a half mile of Yucca Canyon from the back of the Neji land, she assessed. No one would know she was there, and no desert flora would be smashed by the Pathfinder's tires. Perfect.

After twenty minutes the creekbed forked upward into the barren In-Ko-Pah Mountains and became impassable. Bo parked on the eastern side of a pale peach-colored boulder encrusted with continent-shaped patches of lichen. The rock, she thought, looked like a swollen earth, its oceans long evaporated and its landmasses reduced to brittle distortions. The future, painted by nature on a canvas no one would ever see.

Bo sighed and grabbed her canteen and hiking boots from

behind the seat. As usual, the manicky skew of her imagination wasn't delusional, wasn't wrong. It was just true. But if she came out of the desert to stand on a San Diego street corner urging passers-by to stop blasting holes in the ozone layer with chlorofluorocarbon hair spray and the decimation of the world's forests, she'd be eating orange Jell-O from a Styrofoam cup in County Psychiatric's dining room by six o'clock that night. The real challenge in having a psychiatric illness, she thought, lay in keeping your mouth shut.

"Nobody wants to confront the truth," she told the boulder, "but thanks for trying." Already the noon light had shifted slightly, layering yellow glare with white and returning the shadowless little continents to their masquerade as patches of lichen. Bo finished lacing her boots and crammed a straw hat with a wide, sloping brim on her head. Eva had warned about excessive sun. The hat and sunglasses would have to do. After filling her canteen from the five-gallon water can strapped to the back of the Pathfinder, she began to climb toward the rim of Yucca Canyon.

The chalk outline of Mort Wagman's body was still there, a small black stain inside it obvious against the white granitic rock. Bo wrapped her arms about her ribs and remembered the kindness of a young man with raven-black hair who had reached outside his own illness to help her. Then she selected the first, melon-sized stone and nudged it with her foot to cover the dark stain where Mort Wagman's heart had been. After an hour the mound of stones was sufficient, identifiable.

"A kind man died here," Bo spoke loudly into the clean wind blowing up the canyon wall. "These stones mark the end of his life and honor the memory of his kindness."

Others would add to the cairn, Bo knew. The Neji, future guests at Ghost Flower Lodge, strangers traversing the desert for reasons of their own. People instinctively knew the meaning in a cone of stones piled at a crossroads, wayside, or precipice. And instinctively reached for another rock to mark their private acknowledgment of death.

Already the western slope of the sheer little canyon was mottled in shadow as the sun began its downward slide into the sea sixty miles away. Overheated, Bo scrambled partway down into cooler grayness and wedged herself behind a split rock for a long drink of water and a few minutes of rest before hiking back to the car. From a hole near her left boot heel a whiptail lizard emerged and dashed to the cleft in the rock, where it lay breathing and staring at a daddy longlegs nearly invisible in the shadows.

Tentatively the daddy longlegs began to move away, and Bo could see the lizard's five front claws tense against the rock as it prepared to stalk the insect. The claws were so *handlike,* she thought, looking at her own freckled hands holding the canteen. The evolution of reptile to primate was so obvious. And the old reptile brain buried deep beneath more recent human frontal lobes, that was obvious, too. Obvious whenever a human killed another not out of passion but for personal gain. The cold-blooded killer, Bo nodded at her own train of thought, was aptly named. A throwback. A reptile cloaked in human form.

Arachnid and lizard remained frozen as if awaiting a thrown switch to begin their drama as Bo pondered Mort Wagman's death. He'd been wealthy, especially after the lucrative SnakeEye promotion made him a millionaire. But as far as could be ascertained, no one would benefit financially from his death except Bird. And Bird had not stood armed in the desert dark, waiting to murder his father. But someone else had. Why?

Did Mort Wagman have an enemy, someone close enough to his daily movements at the lodge to know that he prowled the edges of Yucca Canyon when he couldn't sleep? The murderer would have to be someone at Ghost Flower, Bo thought. No one else could have known that the young comedian would be a sitting duck almost any night, silhouetted by moonlight at the edge of the canyon, and alone. But who?

The other guests were remote, wrapped up in their strug-

gles to get back to their lives. They enjoyed the program set
for them by the Neji, but worked it primarily in solitude or
one-on-one with a Neji counselor. None of them had been at
all interested in Mort Wagman. Except Old Ayma, Bo
remembered. Ayma had hovered around everything that went
on at the lodge, watching from beneath layers of castaway fabric. But Ayma was really crazy, wouldn't take her meds, and
then wandered off. It was unfortunate, but it happened sometimes. Bo didn't think Old Ayma could have shot Mort Wagman. With a twinge of sadness she faced the fact that Old
Ayma couldn't have done much of anything except be a bur-
den and an embarrassment. Nobody but the Neji had really
cared when the old woman vanished into the desert, presum-
ably to die. Certainly, Bo admitted to the lizard, *she* hadn't
cared very much.

The admission brought a flush of shame to her face as the
daddy longlegs suddenly skittered into sunlight and away,
pursued by the whiptailed lizard. Bo peered through the
rock's cleft, rooting for the smaller creature. But the desert
creatures had vanished, leaving only a narrow view of the
canyon's west-facing wall and its floor three stories below.

Something was moving on the ground where a shallow
pool would form in the spring beneath a threadlike waterfall.
The pool was just a depression of baked mud now, flaking
upward in stiff, leathery curls. But something was down
there. Something large moving about and casting quick,
jerky shadows like moving stains on the colorless rocks. Bo
remained motionless and waited for whatever it was to move
into her line of vision through the split boulder. It was Zach!

Shirtless in the afternoon heat, he wore the rattling wooden
bracelets and ankle cuffs he'd worn for Mildred's Kurok, and
seemed to be doing a shuffling dance. But he also seemed to
be searching for something. At regular intervals he ceased
bobbing and shuffling to inspect the ground and nearby
canyon rock slides. Then he danced again.

Fascinated, Bo drank the rest of the water from her canteen

and settled in to watch. Zach must be inducing some sort of trance, she thought. Dancing in the sun could quickly produce an altered mental state, a dizziness born of heat exhaustion and the effect of too much light on the brain. But it was dangerous and what could be the point? And Zach had removed his shirt, increasing the likelihood of dehydration. The Kumeyaay, Bo remembered, even the men, exhibited a characteristic modesty about their bodies and were always fully clothed. Zach might be courting more than a trance state with his exposed torso, she thought. He might be demonstrating vulnerability, even shame. This was a personal ritual, not meant to be observed.

She wished she could sneak back over the western rim of the little canyon without being seen by Zach, but it was impossible. Even if she weren't wearing a white shirt he'd be sure to notice the movement, hear the long, scrabbling fall of pebbles and dirt dislodged by her feet. There was nothing to do but wait until Zach completed whatever he was doing.

The idea seemed reasonable until a bright Sleepy Orange butterfly landed to bat its rounded wings on a cholla growing from the canyon wall two feet above Bo's left shoulder. The insect, she realized with a wave of icy nausea, had attracted the attention of eyes other than hers. From one of the million ubiquitous holes in the desert sand, this hole only inches from her left knee, a pair of tiny black orbs watched the butterfly from the black-and-orange-banded head of a snake!

You've finally done it, Bradley. Black and orange—that's a coral snake, isn't it? Don't move, don't breathe, or you're dead.

As the snake stretched another inch from its hole, Bo fought the freezing nausea that brought a taste of bile to her throat, and tried to track a sense that something was wrong with her reaction. Something about coral snakes. They were orange and black all right. She'd haunted classes at San Diego's Natural History Museum when she'd first moved from New Mexico and was curious about the local landscape. But hadn't the guy there said there were no coral snakes in

California? Only Arizona, he'd said. Then this orange and black snake was some other kind of snake.

The knowledge did nothing to slow Bo's accelerated heartbeat and inclination to throw up. There was just something sickening about snakes, period. Something to do with the way they moved. In a flash of useless insight she identified a central fallacy in the Old Testament story of the Fall. No woman, she saw with absolute certainty, would under any circumstances take a bite from an apple offered by a huge, scaled worm!

As if nothing had happened, the butterfly rose from the safety of the cholla's spines and drifted upward on a thermal of cooler air rising from the canyon floor. The snake tasted the air with its tongue several times and then withdrew into the hole. Sweating, Bo jammed a rock into the hole's opening and held it there with the heel of her left boot. Her position, she realized with amusement, would test the mettle of a contortionist. Now, if Zachary Crooked Owl would just put on his shirt and leave . . .

Glancing through the cleft rock once again, she took heart. Apparently Zach had found whatever he was looking for, because he was holding something small between the fingers and thumb of his right hand, staring at it. Then he looked upward to the spot at the canyon's rim where Mort Wagman had died. Suddenly stamping and sending staccato clatters from his wooden rattles bouncing off the canyon walls, he flung back his head, released a guttural scream of rage, and tore the owl's claw from its leather thong about his neck. Bo could see a faint stripe of red where the leather had cut into his flesh.

The owl's claw dropped to the ground as Zach turned and vanished into the path leading up behind the falls overhang. He couldn't see her now, and she clambered stiffly up the ten yards of canyon wall to safety and the short hike back to the car. What she had just seen was puzzling.

Why was Zach dancing alone in the heat? What had he

found, and why would he tear off the owl's claw that was his family's fetish? He had told her the claw would be given to Juana or Ojo, Maria Jueh or even little Cunel. It would be given to the one among his children who would grow up to assume leadership of the Neji Band and of Ghost Flower Lodge.

Bo remembered Eva Broussard's words over dinner only yesterday in Ocean Beach. "Quite possibly the Kumeyaay will have to sell." That must be it, Bo thought. The little band of Indians had overextended their resources in building the lodge, and were going bankrupt. Or else Mort's death and the disappearance of Old Ayma had prompted the county to terminate their license as a board-and-care. Either way, it couldn't be allowed to happen.

Bo skirted a particularly vicious outcropping of chollas near the Pathfinder and drank from the water can's spigot. She'd drive to the little desert restaurant where Mort Wagman had eaten his last meal, she decided. She'd grab a sandwich and then go straight to Ghost Flower Lodge for a serious talk with Zachary Crooked Owl.

The Neji, like all the Kumeyaay, were too private and self-contained to elicit help from a dominant culture that had systematically ignored them. They would simply accept whatever came their way with an accommodating fatalism. The other bands of Kumeyaay, she remembered, had fallen easily into the hands of casino sharks and dumping entrepreneurs for that reason. Only the Neji had managed to build something splendid out of their ruined history. And that couldn't be sacrificed.

She'd convince Zach to try a public appeal, borrow money, lobby the state legislature in Sacramento, *something*. And then they'd walk back down into Yucca Canyon to retrieve the owl's claw bequeathed by John Crooked Owl, who'd cared for his brother Catomka and saved the Neji land by siring a son in his old age.

It was a lovely story, Bo thought as she revved the

Pathfinder along the Tule creekbed. And something was trying to kill it. Was that something related to Mort Wagman's
murder? Could Old Ayma's disappearance be more than a sad
psychiatric accident? And for that matter, could a barking
dog on her answering machine have anything to do with the
secret that was destroying Ghost Flower Lodge?

"I'm not letting go of this!" she yelled into airy desert
silence. "Whoever you are, you're *not* getting away with it!"

Chapter 15

The food at the little desert diner was even worse than Bo remembered. After a few bites of limp salad and stale tortilla, she remembered to take her Depakote with the rest of an orange soda, paid the bill and left. The same waitress who'd sneered at Mort Wagman's medication-induced twitchiness watched Bo's exit with the air of a woman who had a loaded gun behind her counter and wouldn't hesitate to use it.

Bo caught the look and yelled, "Your lettuce might have a chance if you used Tupperware!" through the torn screen door. Later, she mused, she might mail the German strudel cookbook to the diner. In a plain brown wrapper and taped to a ticking clock. She felt alive and competent. An appropriate frame of mind from which to address some serious issues with Zachary Crooked Owl.

Driving toward the lodge through the Neji Reservation land, Bo framed the discussion. First, she wanted a report on the Sheriff Department's findings. What evidence had they found? Were there any suspects? From there she'd bring up licensing. Had the county withdrawn the lodge's board-and-care license because of Mort and Old Ayma? Maybe the lodge had just been placed on probationary status pending an investigation. That was more likely, given San Diego County's epic disinterest in funding services for poor people additionally burdened with psychiatric illness. The county's board-and-care licensing staff would be too overburdened with work to investigate Ghost Flower for months unless there were a public outcry. And there would be no public outcry because nobody would care what happened to a bunch of lunatics holed up in the desert.

Next, Bo planned, she'd ask Zach about Ghost Flower's finances. Exactly who was the private funding source he'd mentioned when she asked how the new building had been financed? And why was Ghost Flower Lodge now in danger of having to sell? Why? What had happened?

Her own month-long stay at the lodge, Bo calculated, had cost about three thousand dollars. Inexpensive by any standard for psychiatric care but still a respectable source of income for the Neji, all of whom lived in or near the lodge, and all of whom lived simply. If only half the fourteen guests who'd been recuperating at Ghost Flower with her were paying, the Neji would still gross about twenty-five thousand dollars a month, including small county welfare and Social Security benefits for the other seven guests.

None of the Neji received salaries. Their work was simply a part of their communal life. And the psychiatrists who prescribed and supervised the medications for those who couldn't afford private doctors worked as volunteers, earning substantial tax write-offs in the process. So where, Bo pondered, was the money going? How could the Neji have reduced themselves to bankruptcy? It didn't seem possible.

A dust cloud moving rapidly along the road from Ghost Flower's gate captured Bo's attention. Somebody was leaving the lodge. She slowed to allow the car, a gunmetal gray limousine, to pull onto the road in front of her. In the back seat were two men, one of them a large black man with a single braid hanging over the back of his suit jacket. Zach.

"Damn," Bo muttered, pounding the steering wheel with the heel of her right hand. "And what's he doing in a suit?" The image, even from the back, was that of a bear crammed into a lawyer's costume. Zach's companion was younger and shorter, but also dressed more formally than could be expected among the desert's coyotes and equally dangerous plants.

Bo allowed the Pathfinder to fall behind the limo, and followed. The road went nowhere except to a junction with Interstate 8, where the choices of destination were limited to west toward San Diego, or east toward El Centro. The latter featureless desert way station bearing no distinction save being the birthplace of a singer named Cher, Bo was certain that Zach and his companion were being driven to San Diego. But why? Ghost Flower had its own four-wheel-drive vehicle, and many of the Neji had their own cars and trucks. A chauffeured drive down the hill was wholly out of character for Zach. What was going on?

When the ostentatious car turned west on I-8, so did Bo. It was easy to track the limo from the Pathfinder's high cab. And Zach had never seen Bo's car. Even if he happened to glance back through the smoked glass he wouldn't recognize it, wouldn't know she was following.

"I'm not really *following* him," she remarked to the dashboard. "This is just the easiest way to get home."

But when the limo finally turned south on I-5 after the long trip down into the heart of San Diego, Bo turned, too. Impossible to quit now. There was something heady about tracking another person, knowing things you weren't supposed to know. Something arrogant about it, also something mildly shifty. In her sunglasses and straw hat Bo felt deliciously sneaky, a spy on a covert mission. She wished she had a cloak. And a dagger.

The limo then edged into a lane marked "Airport," and minutes later discharged its passengers at the East Terminal curb. Quickly parking in the short-term lot, Bo dashed into the airport terminal through another set of doors.

Zach and the shorter man were browsing at a newsstand, glancing occasionally toward the nearest gate, leased to

Southwest Airlines. Either they were meeting someone or they were going somewhere, she thought.

A brilliant leap of logic, Bradley. Now what?

Burying herself amid a tour group of Midwestern retirees wearing Disneyland T-shirts, Bo studied the airline's departures monitor. The next Southwest flight, boarding in ten minutes, was going to St. Louis. Over the beefy shoulder of a sunburnt septuagenarian in a John Deere cap Bo watched as Zach paid for a bag of M&M's and then walked with his companion through the Southwest gate. So Zach was going to St. Louis. Gone, in fact.

The moment tasted erroneous, futile. Nothing made any more sense than it had before this wild-goose chase, and now she was standing pointlessly in an airport terminal amid hundreds of people whose behavior actually had direction. The contrast was dizzying.

Worse, a familiar, nasty shadow had materialized near the baggage claim area and was roiling toward her like a dry mist. It was the texture of her inadequacy, an enveloping pointlessness. Following Zach had been dumb, she realized. She'd learned nothing except that all her attempts to avenge the death of a brother like some classical goddess who lived on figs and wine were producing nothing. And she hated figs.

The encroaching shadow was the damn depression again, she knew. It was soaking up the light, sinking toward her with every breath. The bad play. *Despair of the Rutabaga*. The fine gray foam continued its breathless progress.

"If you see the gray cloak of her
Down the boreen," her grandmother's voice echoed in her head,
"Let you close the door softly
And wait there unseen.

"For if she comes in on you
Never you'll part,

Till the fire burns out
In the core of your heart."

It was an Irish poem her grandmother had recited, one of many about sadness and sorrow. A warning. Sorrow in her gray cloak was coming down the boreen, all right. But where was the door to close softly and wait there unseen? The only "door" in the full metaphoric sense that Bo could see was the one leading to an airplane bound for St. Louis. An obvious choice over the lifelong companionship of sorrow. What the hell.

Dashing to the ticket counter, Bo smiled at the Irish poetic facility with mood. It was like a wordless language, she thought, another experience entirely that Ireland's sons and daughters would forever attempt to articulate. The Southwest ticket agent nodded that there were plenty of seats on the St. Louis flight, and took her credit card as the shadow dissolved into luggage and people and ordinary airport noise.

In a nearby gift shop Bo bought a hideous scarf with "San Diego—America's Finest City" printed over a tropical beach scene, and a tube of lipstick in a wine-red color that clashed with her hair, skin, and sense of propriety. After tying the scarf over her hair and slathering on the lipstick, she replaced her sunglasses and straw hat. With luck, Zach wouldn't recognize her.

And he didn't. Once aboard the plane, she'd grabbed a magazine, blanket, and two pillows for further camouflage as she walked past the big man and his companion. The other man seemed oddly familiar, but she couldn't place him. A nondescript, shortish guy with thick, mouse-brown hair and a darker mustache, he merely sat with his hands on his knees, staring into the seat back before him.

Zach had wadded a fist beneath his chin, and was watching through the window as the ground crew loaded last-minute baggage. From their body language Bo concluded that the two men were not friends and were not taking this trip for

fun. A sense of irritation surrounded them like a weak electric
field. Other passengers straggling onto the plane universally
glanced at them in passing, and then quickly looked else-
where.

Bo found two unoccupied seats in the back of the half-
empty plane, and stretched across them beneath her blanket
to rest. Someone wearing a musky cologne had obviously used
the blanket on a previous flight. Bo pulled it over her face and
tried to doze, images of honeymooning rodents drifting across
her mind from the scent.

Much later it seemed that the rodents were on television, or
one of them was, following a shark. The shark was already
gone, and the rodent was a criminal. Bo knew she was dream-
ing, and the dream was one of those boring, aimless produc-
tions her subconscious choreographed for its own
entertainment.

The knowledge brought an awareness of cramped long legs
and itchy upholstery against her sunburnt left arm. She was
on a plane. She was going to wake up and stretch. Except
there was something about that criminal rodent, something
familiar. In the last moments before fully wakening, Bo saw
that it had thick, dull hair and a mustache that didn't match.
It was a man, and she'd seen him on a TV screen right after a
story about a shark.

"Wow," she breathed to herself as she sat up. The man with
Zach was the organized crime figure some agency was investigating for illegal involvement in Indian gambling casinos.
The story had been on the news the night before Mort died,
right after the more riveting description of a young woman's
death from a shark attack. None of them had paid much
attention to the man. Bo was sure she hadn't even heard his
name.

In the phone-booth-sized bathroom Bo freshened her gar-
ish lipstick and frowned into the mirror. Zach must be selling
out, she thought. Sacrificing the Neji to organized crime,
turning Ghost Flower into a casino! The thought made her

maroon lip curl in distaste. From the mirror a grotesque mask stared back, an Ensor painting of dissolute carnival revelers losing the battle with death. Ghost Flower had been a garden for people like her, a haven, a place of quiet understanding. The debasement of that garden debased *her!*

"No wonder you tore off the owl's claw," she whispered at Zachary Crooked Owl beyond the narrow bathroom door. "You're selling your father's legacy, throwing it down the sewer, and for what? Money?"

A darker thought crossed Bo's mind as she jammed her sunglasses over tear-filled eyes. Zach had found Mort's body at the edge of Yucca Canyon. He'd gone looking for Mort, Dura said, early that morning. But where had he been when a bullet tore through Mort's heart? Zach knew Mort would be at the canyon. And Zach owned a rifle, the same rifle with which he'd sent Ojo to guard Mort's body before the authorities arrived. Had Zach killed Mort Wagman? Why? What did Mort have to do with casinos or with the lodge's financial crisis?

Nothing made sense. But it would, Bo promised herself as the pilot announced their imminent landing. She'd follow Zach like a bloodhound, fit piece after piece of the puzzle together until the truth emerged. She could do it.

Unless he sees you, Bradley. If he killed Mort Wagman, what's going to stop him from killing you?

Chapter 16

Andrew LaMarche was aware that he'd kicked the duvet off his narrow bed again. He'd had trouble with it every night since his arrival in Germany. The feather-filled comforter was too short for his six-foot body, and the big wooden buttons securing its cover dug into his shoulders every time he turned over. His feet were cold. The hotel room still, even with daily airings, smelled like wet cardboard. And he missed Bo.

"Vass ist Zeit?" he mumbled at the old-fashioned clock nailed to his nightstand, and then shook his head. He'd just asked, "What is time?," a philosophical conversation-stopper he was sure the clock would decline to answer. It was one-thirty in the morning, and a steady drizzle muted the sounds of Frankfurt outside his barely open window. A lonely, Victorian sort of night, he thought. A perfect night for holding Bo in his arms and listening as she told him tales of Irish banshees and haunted peat bogs.

The memory of her lying next to him in bed, talking softly after their lovemaking, made his heart pound. But Bo Bradley was thousands of miles away, and he had to finish this damned military child abuse project before he could return to her.

Grabbing the duvet off the floor, he turned on the bedside light and stomped to the electric wall heater. A confounding array of knobs with metric markings, he'd spent nearly a month trying to adjust it, to no purpose. It still refused to produce heat from midnight to six A.M., the only hours in which he wanted heat.

It would still be Saturday afternoon in San Diego. Bo might be home. He wanted to tell her why he hadn't called yesterday. She'd be pleased with the reason, he knew. Half joking, she'd asked him to go to Bremen and lay a pastrami sandwich on the grave of her first psychiatrist, Dr. Lois Bittner, who'd died and been buried by friends there while at a conference. He hadn't been able to bring himself to get the sandwich, but he'd flown to Bremen with a bouquet of bronze mums that he thought perfectly matched the color of Bo's hair, and laid them on the grave. In the mums was a note saying, "From Bo, who will bring the pastrami sandwich herself. Thank you for helping her learn to survive when she was young so that I could love her now. Andrew LaMarche."

Then he'd toured the city, enjoying himself thoroughly. At a bookshop he'd bought a charmingly illustrated edition of the Grimm story "The Bremen Town Musicians," which he and Bo would give to Estrella and Henry Benedict's baby when it arrived four months in the future. The text was in German, French, and English. Bo would be sure to approve. And maybe by then she'd agree to marry him. He was doing everything he could to promote that possibility, including remaining in Germany while she faced the demons of clinical depression alone.

In the dark he remembered an earlier tour, a day trip through the Lahn River Valley from Limburg to Wetzlar, where Goethe endured his doomed love for Charlotte. The procession of turreted medieval castles was delightful, but in a little town called Hadamar he'd seen something that froze his heart. Just an old hospital, still in use. A psychiatric hospital no different from any other except for its gas chamber and crematorium where thousands deemed "mentally defective" by Hitler's Reich had been gassed, their bodies incinerated. Thousands, any one of whom might have been Bo. And there had been, he'd learned, five other hospitals identically equipped. The trip ruined, he'd driven quickly back to Frankfurt and holed up in his room, sickened. He would never tell Bo what he saw in the nondescript Lahn Valley town, he decided. Neither would he forget.

After kicking the useless heater with his bare foot, Andrew flung himself back into bed and glowered at the rainy window. Bo had asked him not to fly to her side. She'd said it wouldn't make any difference, and Dr. Broussard had confirmed Bo's view. Only professional care, time and the right medications would make a difference, the psychiatrist had said. And emotional demands on Bo, demands that she could not meet while depressed, would only make her feel more inadequate, different, useless. In the transatlantic phone call he'd mustered enough courage to ask a final question.

"What about suicide?"

"Don't worry," Eva Broussard had answered with feeling. "Bo has no history of suicide attempts, and even Mildred's death isn't likely to prompt one. She may *think* about it; that's normal. But she'll never admit it. Bo has a spark inside that won't easily be extinguished, Andy. Some would say it's her manicky skew that makes her that way. You and I know it's more than that. But she needs downtime now, and some space from which to watch life from a remove."

So he'd stayed in Frankfurt and helped the military establish protocols for dealing with child abuse when it occurred among personnel based overseas. He'd worked sixteen-hour days for over three weeks, and the program was in place. All he was expected to do in the final week was to introduce academic authorities on various aspects of the problem at a series of formal seminars and dinners. Anybody could do it. He wanted to go home.

Bo's phone, when the rattling connection was complete, merely rang four times and then the answering machine clicked on.

"I miss you," he said simply, and hung up.

Then he strode to the room's little closet and began pulling his clothes from hangers. His suitcase was under the bed, already dusty. A sign he'd been away too long.

Within an hour he'd packed, sent a telegram to the adjutant in charge of the training program saying he'd been called home on an urgent personal matter, and arranged for a flight to Paris, from which he would fly to New York. The ticketing agent was working on a flight from there to California.

"Anywhere in California," he'd said. "I just need to get home."

Chapter 17

Bo would later define her discovery in St. Louis as one of the strangest scenarios she'd encountered, including those whispered or shouted in psychiatric emergency rooms. But the strangeness would only reveal its entirety later, like a black-and-white photographic print in its pan of developer. Vague at first, just a ghostly outline. In the beginning Bo merely thought she was, at last, truly crazy.

It was surprisingly easy to follow Zach to his destination from the airport. She selected a cab from the row waiting at the terminal curb, and said, "Follow that car," as Zach's cab pulled away.

Her driver, a grizzled version of Santa Claus in an ancient orange shirt and plaid bow tie, grinned and said, "Lady, I've been waitin' thirty years for somebody to say that. I s'pose you don't want 'em to know they're bein' followed, right?"

"Right."

"Can do."

Bo alternately marveled at the man's driving facility and at the Midwestern trees in their autumn color. Zach's cab, four cars ahead, kept a steady pace going south on Lindbergh Boulevard, skirting the city. And everywhere showers of golden cottonwood and sassafras leaves fluttered on trees or blew in clouds, tossed by the wind with the blood-red of maples and sumac or the brown-mottled orange of oak and horn-beam. She'd forgotten it would be fall here. A real fall where the sight and smell of dying leaves filled the air with coura-geous, doomed splendor.

"Everything is transient," she told the driver.

"I've noticed that," he answered. "Say, who's this fella we're followin', your husband?"

"No, it's a black Indian and a gangster, or at least a sus-pected gangster. The Indian may have killed a friend of mine. It's important that they don't see us."

The cabby rubbed his bulbous, bloodshot nose with a grimy index finger. "Black Indians? Gangsters? Lady, you crazy or somethin'?"

"There's some question about that at the moment," Bo replied, still mesmerized by the leaves. "But it doesn't matter. Just don't let them see us."

"It may not matter to *you* . . ." the man rumbled, and then fell silent. Zach's cab had swerved into a well-to-do older neighborhood of winding streets and widely spaced two-story homes. At a respectable distance Bo's driver turned as well. The neighborhood was not the destination she had imagined, which involved dim riverfront alleys or at least a garlic-scented Italian restaurant with a beady-eyed bouncer named Tony who would wear a tuxedo jacket over a torn undershirt. Nothing was making sense. Why would Zach and the gambling king-pin fly from San Diego to St. Louis only to do a house-and-garden tour?

From the curved porch railing of an expansive white frame house, a boy in school blazer and cap tossed peanuts onto the leaf-strewn lawn where several gray squirrels dashed to retrieve them. A block further, a young woman who looked like Audrey Hepburn pushed a black baby carriage briskly along the sidewalk. Bo couldn't remember the last time she'd seen a baby carriage. Bobbing on its thin tires it looked like a boat, she thought, or a little hearse, or . . .

Cut the weird imagery, Bradley. You're here on business.

"Where are we?" she asked. The area bore no resemblance to anything she'd seen in the last twenty years.

"Kirkwood," the driver replied, gauging his speed carefully to that of the car barely visible ahead.

"Oh," she answered. "I lived in St. Louis for a while. Kirkwood's pretty nice, right?"

"Everything's transient," he reminded her. "Hey, your gangster Indian's stopping." Smoothly he made a sharp right and braked on a side street in a rustle of leaves. "White brick on the right five houses up on the street we just turned off. That'll be fifteen fifty."

"Wait for me," Bo said, handing him a twenty from her purse and exiting the cab. Then she untied the blue sweater from her shoulders, pulled it on, and crossed to the other side of the wide street on which they'd entered the neighborhood. In her khakis and hiking boots she didn't look entirely out of place, she thought.

Retying the scarf Indian-style across her forehead, she removed her sunglasses, jammed the straw hat down as far as possible over her hair and began a serious walker's long stride and exaggerated arm swinging. Zach was going to see her. No way to avoid that. But with luck he'd just see a local matron out for a constitutional before her husband returned from his office in the city. To complete the image Bo stooped to gather a handful of bright leaves. Centerpiece for the dinner table. A nice touch.

Ahead, Zach and the other man had followed the winding flagstone path to a white brick colonial. The red of its bricks showed through the weathered paint, projecting a homey, quaint demeanor completely at odds with the two men on the raised doorstep. Only a block away now, Bo slowed to feign admiration of a narrow formal garden set in ivy and mums.

No one was answering the door of the white colonial, but the presence of Zach and the other man had captured the attention of several small dogs in a chain-linked run along the house's western side. Their frantic barking made Bo's palms grow clammy. Any one of them might have been the dog on her answering machine!

All small dogs sound alike, Bradley. It's ridiculous to think there's any connection. But what if there is . . . ?

The manicured neighborhood felt like a set, a facade hiding secrets tangled like frayed electrical wire. Because of it Mort was dead and Bird was alone. Because of it a noble undertaking would be abolished and the last of an ancient people prostituted to the lure of easy money. But what was it? Bo couldn't still the trembling of her hands as she drew closer to the white brick house. Soon she'd be directly across from it, shielded from sight only by the idling cab waiting for Zach and his companion. But there was no way to turn around without attracting attention.

Zach was writing something on the back of an envelope he pulled from the mailbox as Bo drew closer, her heart pounding blood against her eardrums. He jammed the envelope back into the mailbox vertically so that it bent under the lid, its edge a visible tab against the matte black metal. Then he and Zach strode quickly toward the cab.

The timing couldn't have been worse, Bo realized. The two men were now facing her as she passed directly across the street from them. How could Zach not recognize her? He'd seen her jerky, loping walk a hundred times. And her hands. Freckled hands with long, knobby-jointed fingers. Bo sensed her hands announcing the identity of their owner like neon signs. "These big Irish knuckles are Bo Bradley's!" they yelled. "And the big Irish feet, too!" Bo felt as naked and shining as a fish in the pale Midwestern sunset.

But Zach didn't see her. She heard the cab doors slam and then saw it accelerate to turn at the next corner. Propelled by fear, she walked a block past the colonial just to be sure the men weren't going to return, seize her, and throw her bound and gagged into the trunk. But only one car drove by, a metallic beige station wagon full of Girl Scouts. Bo reined in her terror and crossed the street. Unless she died of a heart attack first, she was going to see what was on that envelope.

In minutes she reached the flagstone walkway and affected a casual saunter as she approached the mailbox. Cars were moving on nearby streets, but no one was watching as she pulled the white rectangle from its black box. "You'll get the boy when you call off your dogs," it said. "Back off if you want him alive." The note wasn't signed.

"Is there something I could help you with?" an icy female voice inquired from the dog run. "Dr. Keith isn't home at the moment."

Bo stuffed the envelope back into the mailbox. "I'm, uh, I had an appointment with Dr. Keith to discuss, um, a new dog food Ralston-Purina is test-marketing in St. Louis," she told a tall woman of about seventy who was standing behind the chain link fence holding one of three Jack Russell terriers. The woman wore stylishly pleated gray flannel slacks and a red sweatshirt adorned with a cartoon of a deer in cartridge belts and a deerstalker cap over a caption that read, "Arm Deer." The hand holding the terrier was bigger than Bo's and not at all frail. "I thought maybe that . . ." Bo gestured toward the envelope, "was a message, you know, canceling the appointment."

"She didn't mention any appointment," the woman said. "I live next door, just got home from my Girl Scout troop meeting. I'm taking care of the dogs, watching the place. Why don't you leave your card. She can call you when she returns."

"She," Bo thought. So Dr. Keith was a woman. But who was "the boy," and what could this St. Louis doctor have to do with Zachary Crooked Owl and Ghost Flower Lodge? Maybe "the boy" was Bird! Had the note been a threat against Bird? ". . . if you want him alive," it warned.

"I'll phone Dr. Keith at her office to set another time," Bo said, backing down the steps into fading light.

"Office? You must mean at the university. Well, suit yourself." The woman set the dog on the ground where it jumped against her legs with the other two. In the autumn dusk their leaping white bodies glowed hypnotically. There was something about those dogs . . .

"Yes, the university," Bo concluded. St. Louis boasted several institutions of higher learning, she remembered from the time she'd spent there long ago. Among them three universities—the Jesuit-run St. Louis University, Washington University, and the University of Missouri at St. Louis. Calls to their switchboards would locate this Dr. Keith, but then what?

"Um, when do you expect Dr. Keith to return?" she called over her shoulder.

The older woman narrowed her eyes suspiciously. "I have no idea," she answered.

Bo hurried the three blocks back toward the street where the cab would be waiting. A deliciously autumnal dusk was falling fast, and warm amber light glowed from the windows of several houses. The street was a chronicle of domestic solidity from which she was excluded by nature. But maybe not, she thought. She could marry Andy, have a house like one of these. At dusk she'd turn on the lights.

The silly, simple fantasy was calming as she turned the corner expectantly. Where she'd begun this puzzling adventure a mature sugar maple dropped a cascade of leaves that rustled in the empty street. The cab was gone.

"That *jerk!*" she whispered angrily at the space where a yellow car should have been. But it was just an inconvenience. She was an adult, after all. She had money and a credit card. She wasn't dependent on cab drivers with ratty beards and no sense of honor. Lindbergh Boulevard was a few blocks away. The major street was lined with gas stations, restaurants, sundry businesses. She'd hike to it, grab a sandwich somewhere, and phone for another cab to the airport.

To her delight, a Steak'n'Shake restaurant was visible from the corner when she got to Lindbergh. Its black-and-white logo actually made her salivate as she sprinted toward the promise of a real hamburger and crispy, sinful French fries. Nobody would see her, she grinned to herself as she entered the brightly lit diner. She was out of place, unconnected, a wraith no one would notice as she savored the forbidden.

After phoning Southwest Airlines and arranging for a return flight that would leave in three hours, Bo checked with Directory Assistance and learned that Dr. Ann Lee Keith's number had been removed from the directory "at the customer's request." An unlisted number. Not surprised, she selected a corner booth and ordered a burger, fries, and a vanilla shake. Then she took a pen from her purse and began to write on a napkin.

"Who is Dr. Keith?" she wrote. "What is Keith's connection to Zach Crooked Owl, and what is Zach's connection to the gangster? Why did Zach and the gangster come here? ('To threaten Keith, but she wasn't available.) What other reason do they have for being in St. Louis? (They wouldn't fly here just for that; there's something else going on. What?) Who is the boy in the threatening note? Bird? Why would this Dr. Keith want Bird? (Is Keith Bird's mother?) Why are Zach and the gangster suggesting that they have this 'boy' and will harm him if Keith doesn't 'call off her dogs'? (If Bird is the boy, Zach and the gangster don't have him; they don't even know where he is.)"

The milkshake arrived, foamy and vanilla-scented. Before scooping the whipped cream off its top with an iced-tea spoon, Bo made a last notation on the napkin. "Call off what dogs? Why does Dr. Keith have three Jack Russell terriers? Is that a Jack Russell's bark in those weird phone calls I've been getting? What in hell is going on?"

Later in the airport ladies' room she dropped the seductively dark lipstick in a trash container and splashed warm water on her face. Her reflection in the mirror looked a little bright-eyed and tense, she thought, but within reasonable boundaries. She'd been up since six, but she'd napped during the three-hour flight to St. Louis. By most standards this impulsive trip would be judged odd, but she'd chosen to do it because not doing it made her feel worthless. And she'd uncovered something. She had no idea what it was, but it was definitely something. The trip, despite its expense, had definitely been worthwhile. She felt okay.

"Eva," she said into a pay phone near her departure gate, "I'm just calling to check in like you asked. Everything's fine. Don't worry."

Over the loudspeaker a booming voice announced a commuter flight to Peoria, Illinois.

"Yeah, I'm at the airport," Bo hedged the answer to her psychiatrist's question. "Peoria? I thought he said Petrolia. It's up in Northern California. I'll call you tomorrow, okay?" There was no point in worrying her shrink, who was in constant contact, Bo knew, with Andrew.

She had given Dr. Broussard permission to discuss her progress with Andrew. It only seemed fair not to exclude him. But neither of them would readily grasp the rationale behind her presence in St. Louis. They both loved her and she returned their feelings, but neither really understood how different from theirs her balance was, and how deadly their commonsense approach to life sometimes felt. Mort Wagman had understood, and that, Bo nodded solemnly at the pay phone, was what made him a brother.

On the plane she curled next to the window and dozed, an image of small white terriers leaping behind her eyes.

Chapter 18

Bo stretched and wrinkled her nose at an airplane headache as her flight made its approach through shining fog toward San Diego's Lindbergh Field. She still wasn't tired, and the fog seemed to swirl and clutch at the plane in vaporous despair. Not a good sign.

"This is our lucky night!" the pilot announced after touching down on the runway. "I've just heard from the control tower; we're the last plane in. As of now the airport's closed due to fog."

Several passengers cheered, but Bo continued to watch the wispy streams of water vapor as they swept past her window. There were shapes lost in the whiteness, half-formed things dissolving, dimensionless. She could feel their rage and grief. "Lost souls," her grandmother said when the fog drifted over Cape Cod and Bo and her little sister, Laurie, curled in the old woman's lap. "It's them that never was, it is, and them that was but isn't more."

A thrill of bathos made Bo shiver as she waited to exit the plane. The airport was built over a marshy trail the Kumeyaay had followed from village to summer village along the water. Now the trail was lost, and with Zach's betrayal the last band of quiet Indian storytellers would become "them that was but isn't more." Already something wept in the fog, outraged. Or maybe it had been there all along.

In the drive to her Ocean Beach apartment Bo decided to take a mild sedative and go to bed. Her imagination was locked in high gear, spinning out skeins of feeling. Dr. Broussard had warned her to rest, close the doorway to mania now gaping open. But she hadn't rested. She'd flown halfway across the continent and back, placed herself in literal and neurochemical danger. And for what? Not really for Mort or Bird, she admitted, but for a sense of movement, of being fully alive. It was worth it.

When she unsnapped her purse to retrieve the apartment key, she saw the handful of colored leaves tucked beside her wallet. A receipt from Steak'n'Shake. And a napkin covered in questions the answers to which might just save a lost soul dissolved in fog. That soul, she smiled as she climbed her apartment steps, might even be hers.

After drawing a hot bath Bo threw twelve chamomile tea bags into the tub, and then soaked in the aromatic water. Chamomile was supposed to be soothing, but she hated tea. Bathing in it seemed a reasonable alternative. There had been no further barks on her answering machine. She'd taken the sedative, and it would kick in in an hour or so. Everything seemed orderly, uneventful.

Actually, she realized while toweling her hair, everything seemed stiff and strangely lifeless. Boring. Her hairbrush was old. The perfume bottles in the corner of the sink-top were dull with dust. Her terrycloth bathrobe was uninspiring, and even her toothbrush seemed withered and drab. A hunger for new things, new colors and shapes, expanded gleefully in her mind. Too late to go shopping, she knew, but there was the all-night supermarket only blocks away.

The feeling was a kind of ecstasy unweighted by any link to consequence. Buoyant. Clean as morning light. And impossible to hate despite knowing what it was, a brain-bath of chemicals that in ordinary combinations merely attached pleasure to the acquisition of necessary things. But those chemical combinations weren't ordinary now. They were a river. And riding it required skill.

Okay, Bradley, enjoy a manic spending spree. It'll be harmless if you confine it to ten dollars. Twenty, max.

Dressed in clean sweats and tennis shoes, Bo took her keys and one twenty-dollar bill from her purse. The credit cards would remain behind. Also the checks. She'd learned several times in the past how it felt to pay, literally, the price for this experience. But it couldn't be stopped. Nobody, she thought, could resist the joy of it, the heady, generous fun. But it could be controlled. Sort of.

The supermarket throbbed with fluorescent light as she approached the automatic doors and enjoyed their woosh-clicking sound. A thousand objects gleamed for her approval. But it had to be real things, not food, and that eliminated most of the brightly lit aisles. Peripherally Bo wondered why food didn't count, wasn't attractive. Why it had to be solid, physical things that would last awhile. There was no reason.

In the health care aisle she examined racks of toothbrushes, finally selecting one in clear blue plastic with bold diagonal stripes in white across the handle. It reminded her of Andrew, and the thought of him made her smile. He'd be home soon. She'd welcome him with a new toothbrush to be kept at her apartment. The toothbrush would be a symbol for the continuity of their relationship. Toothpaste, too.

In the travel-size section Bo picked out three miniature tubes of toothpaste, a tiny can of mint shaving gel, and a bag of six disposable razors with blue handles. These she combined with other toiletries, a blue plastic spatula from the housewares aisle, and a collapsible cheese grater that fit into its own little canvas pouch for storage. He liked to cook, after all. Finally she selected a large white colander to hold the gifts, and headed for the checkout lane. Nineteen dollars and sixty-three cents. Delightful.

Outside, the fog had thickened to a cottony gray presence

that muted sound and diffused light in vaporous blurs. Bo could smell the sea, its salt and iodine and tangled kelp, blowing inside the wall of mist that parted and closed around her at every step. She'd walk home on the beach, she decided. She'd run with the fog where it rose from black water to become pale and glistening confusion. It was an image of manic depression, she thought. The dark cold and its frenzied mists. She'd run along that line, be the thing entire. For once, she belonged to the real world completely.

It was easy to walk two blocks along familiar, lighted doorways, but at the seawall Bo realized that she couldn't see her feet. They were there; she could feel them. But the absence of visual affirmation made her suddenly clumsy. Reaching into mist, she pulled off her shoes and held them up like rabbits pulled from a hat. They were still warm from contact with feet already alien and untrustworthy against the invisible surface of the ground.

In the sand it was better. Something about the gritty texture shifting under her weight was familiar and reassuring. And besides, the steady thrum of visual disorientation had become pleasantly scary. Bo slipped her shoes into the plastic bag with her gifts for Andrew and then swung the white bag in a circle about her. It was like casting a spell. Like some lonely blessing and exorcism at once.

"Aye, and it's your spawn I am, Cally," she whispered in her grandmother's Irish brogue to a crone named Caillech Beara who once haunted the myths and foggy crossroads of Scotland and Ireland, "but I'll neither be dead nor mad when mornin' comes. I've a work to do here, old poet. I've a friend's murder to see to and his wee boy to watch. It's just walkin' here we are. You'll be gone in the light, you will."

The whispered speech to an ancient goddess of death and madness had come from nowhere, but provided a sort of grounding. Wrapped in fog, Bo knew she wasn't lost. It was a game, nothing more. And a way of setting boundaries. For luck she swung the bag around her head one last time before leaving the wet sand where waves hissed and retreated unseen.

Except this time the heavy bag nicked something in its arc around her head. Bo felt the touch. Just a palpable thump, inconsequential and tiny against the plastic frame of the colander. It had been behind her, on the right. The bag had hit something close behind her. Except there couldn't be something there. She was walking along the littoral at the water's edge, twenty yards from the wooden uprights supporting a volleyball net close to the sidewalk. And there was nothing else on Ocean Beach tall enough to reach her shoulders.

In the fog she could see nothing, but she knew the beach from memory. Soon she would see the white framework of the Ocean Beach Pier looming out of the gray mist. The volleyball net was nowhere near her. But something else was. Something just out of sight in the drifting blanket of microscopic water. A cold net trembled and slid over Bo's back, up her calves, across her scalp. She wanted to run, but the net quivered against her muscles, sapping their strength. The net was in her eyes. And there was something, some*body,* behind her in the fog.

Run, Bradley! It could be anybody. You could be raped, beaten, killed out here. You're not stupid. Lose yourself in the fog. Run!

Bo felt her heels digging into sand as she propelled herself away, felt the spray of fine grit from each pounding step. A sharp rock dug into her instep, then another scraped her toe. She could hear the crash of the sea at her back. She was running in the right direction, toward the seawall and the sidewalk where hundreds of tourists would stroll in tomorrow's sunlight. She was almost there; she could sense it. And then she heard something. A sound that paralyzed her lungs and dissolved something behind her knees, sending her sprawling in the sand.

A dog. A small dog barking inside the fog behind her. The same frightened bark she'd heard on the phone. Bo felt sand in her teeth, in her eyes. The dog sounded like Mildred. But Mildred was gone. And the noise was coming closer. As she scrambled on hands and knees toward a muzzy pink light ahead, Bo was certain she heard one other sound. An empty, cruel chuckle.

Then there was only the crash of surf, and a car ahead on sibilant tires. As Bo flung herself over the seawall she noticed the white plastic handles of the grocery bag wrapped like a tourniquet around her right hand.

Chapter 19

Alexander Morley could feel the Sunday morning sunlight pooling on St. Luke's wide limestone aisle as he sat beside his wife. Seventh pew, Gospel side. They'd sat there every Sunday for years. And for years he'd gifted the suburban Episcopal church with new kneelers, organ repairs, choir robes, and tuck-pointing. He'd chaired the financial committee and headed the fund drive for a new educational wing. He knew the church better than did the succession of priests who stood in its pulpits. It felt like a second office.

As one of the priests read the collect for the Feast of St. Luke, Morley nodded to himself. St. Luke had been a physician, as he was. But St. Luke could not have written a check to cover the new air-conditioning system in a church honoring his name. Alexander Morley had written the check. A deep pleasure in the fact stretched into reverie.

Things were developing on the Indian deal. He'd assigned Bob Thompson the task of packaging it, creating the prospectus that would attract buyers for the program. A formality. And a ruse. MedNet already owned this Indian loony bin, whatever it was. The Indians had tried hooking up with the mob, offered them a gambling franchise on adjacent land, but Morley had easily put a stop to that. And Henderson had already reached a tentative agreement with the Japanese.

They'd buy the franchise with an under-the-table commitment to a ten-year consulting contract with MedNet. Plus, they'd agreed to purchase all medications and lab work from MedNet holdings, which meant expansion into the Japanese market with a built-in profit margin from the start.

Morley was glad he'd met Walt Henderson at the club and immediately sensed the man's similarity to himself. It was, he thought, a repetition of the day Randolph Mead had met a smart young doctor named Morley many years ago. Henderson was young, only in his forties, and hadn't received his medical training at an impressive school. It didn't matter. He had an attitude Morley recognized at once. Unlike Morley's own children, Henderson knew the rules.

With an imperceptible sigh, Alexander Morley acknowledged that Randolph Mead had taught him that lesson as well.

"Business sense isn't inherited," Mead explained cheerfully after birdieing the seventh hole of a Palm Springs golf course long ago. "I made the mistake of marrying at sixty and siring a son who already thinks he's slightly superior to God and a daughter who lives only to rescue things that have mange. They're still little children, but I have no hope that either of them will change sufficiently to be able to manage a business. That's why I've already established trust funds for them, and why I'm turning MedNet over to you."

When Morley nodded thoughtfully, Mead had gone on.

"When the time comes," he said, selecting one of three custom-made drivers for the next fairway shot, "remember that your own children will have been raised in luxury, which produces either arrogance or idealism. What it doesn't produce is hunger, and that's what our little enterprise runs on."

His eyes narrowed as he jammed a monogrammed tee into the ground. "At your retirement, your only job is to find a man as hungry, and therefore as unscrupulous, as you are."

Morley had understood then. He understood now.

Musing pleasantly, he realized that it was also time to do

something about Bob Thompson. The man was a pathetic, drunken womanizer and a detriment to the corporation. A salesman, nothing more. Morley had detested him for years. Now he could dispense with him.

"He that soweth little shall reap little," the priest said, heading into the long ritual of Holy Communion.

Morley braced himself for the verbose Anglican precision of prayers he could recite verbatim but had never really heard. Only occasionally did a phrase from the altar actually make sense. Like sowing little and reaping less. He'd sowed mightily in MedNet, put everything he had into it after Randolph Mead had taken him into the company just as he would now take in Walt Henderson. And he'd reaped everything he wanted. Now with retirement just ahead, he'd replace himself on the board with a man who had the guts and vision to fill his shoes. Henderson was that man.

There was a swell of rustling as two hundred people slid onto kneelers. A dull hush. Morley knelt beside his wife and placed his hand over her clasped fingers on the back of the pew before them. The gesture created an appropriate image. It was the only time he touched her.

"We acknowledge and bewail our manifold sins and wickedness," he intoned, admiring the diamond bracelet on his wife's wrist. The bracelet said a great deal about Alexander Morley, he thought. And "sins and wickedness" fit Bob Thompson perfectly.

It was going to be simple. Just let Thompson exhaust himself putting together the Indian setup, and then pull the whole thing out from under him with Henderson's coup. Make it look as though Henderson saved them from Thompson's incompetence. As though Bob Thompson was just too boorish and provincial for the international market, which was the only market left.

Kines and Brockman would see through it, of course. They already knew Thompson's head was on the block, but wouldn't lift a finger to save him. Why should they? MedNet stock would provide each of them a luxurious retirement. They'd follow Alexander Morley as they always had. He'd made them rich.

"Lift up your hearts," said the priest as light spilled through colored glass onto a limestone floor that reminded Alexander Morley of his secret. The private, chant-filled monastery where he cherished his soul.

Chapter 20

Bird sat on the floor between two of the seven beds. He'd counted the beds; they were all alike. It was like the dorm at his school where kids stayed if their parents lived someplace far away. But this wasn't Tafel. The lady said this was a group home. She said it when she came that morning in her stupid, ugly car to take him away from the old man named Dutch.

Dutch was nice and didn't care when you hit things. He had some kind of bag hanging from a chain in a shed, and real boxing gloves. Dutch would let you go in there and hit the bag over and over after he tied the gloves on. That was pretty neat.

But Dutch had a grown-up kid named Gwen, and Gwen had a baby that got sick, and Dutch said he was real sorry after Gwen called him on the phone, but he couldn't keep Bird at his house because he had to go to this town far away where Gwen and the sick baby lived. Bird could tell from the way Dutch talked on the phone that he was scared the baby would die. It would be like daddy. The baby just wouldn't be there anymore. Slowly Bird began to swing his shoulders from side to side, hitting his head against the beds.

"As I was sailing down the coast," he sang to himself,
　　"Of High Barbaree,

I chanced to see a Muffin Bird
    A-sitting in a tree."

It didn't sound right without daddy saying it, too, but there were other kids coming in the door and the words were better than the way they looked at him. Three boys, bigger than him. They smiled all together in a way that made the room feel cold.

"Oh, mournfully he sang,
And sorrowful he sat," Bird went on, banging his head in time with the poem's meter.
    "Because he was a-frightened of
        The Crum-pet Cat!"

Something hit him on the chest. A pencil. One of the boys had thrown a pencil at him. Bird closed his eyes and hummed the meter of the poem through clenched teeth. It was iambic, daddy said. The sound. He said iambic was like duh-DUH, duh-DUH, like the way his head felt hitting the mattresses.

"Hey!" one of the boys said. "You crazy? You look crazy. What's your name?"

"It's time for dinner," another one said. "We always have chicken on Sunday. Don't you want some chiiick-en?"

Bird kept humming the poem. It didn't quite block out the chicken part.

"Chicken, chicken," the first voice taunted. "Crazy chicken."

Bird knew no one else was in the room without looking. He could smell what was going to happen. A smell like waking up in the dark knowing everything had been moving until you opened your eyes. A metal smell that hurt the back of your nose.

"Hey! Get up, chicken!"

The first boy hit him on the shoulder with his fist. Bird kept his eyes closed and flailed at them with his hands, kicked at them. But they kicked back, hard, yelling, "Chick-EN, chick-EN," in iambic until Bird couldn't hear them anymore.

Chapter 21

By three o'clock in the afternoon Bo had completed Mildred's portrait, cleaned the deck, and dictated a preliminary report for Bird's detention hearing on Monday. A calming, domestic day with iced decaf and Bach on the stereo. A normal day. An illusion. Reluctantly she settled on one of the whitewashed bar stools at the counter and centered the phone in front of her. No way to put this off any longer.

"Eva," she began when the psychiatrist answered, "I need to talk to you about something that's happening, *if* it's happening. Last night . . ."

Eva Broussard listened without comment as Bo described the incident in the fog, her terror and, later, her shame.

"I think I'm hallucinating this," Bo admitted. "I think I'm trying to bring Mildred back, or trying to believe she's out there somewhere needing me. Except it isn't really Mildred. It scares me. I wouldn't be afraid if it were really Mildred, but it isn't."

"No, it isn't," Eva Broussard repeated conversationally. "That's not an option. So either you're hallucinating it, you're making it up to draw attention to your feelings of loss, or it's actually happening. I'm curious about why you've decided it isn't."

Bo stretched the phone cord across the cream-colored wall

between her living room and the deck, and stared through the open deck doors at a deceptively placid sea. "I didn't exactly take it easy yesterday," she confessed. "In fact, I flew to St. Louis and back, and before that I went out to the reservation and built a cairn of stones where Mort was killed. But I did wear sunglasses, Eva, and a straw hat."

"Go on."

Bo marveled at her shrink's ability to avoid obvious, side-tracking questions like "What in God's name were you doing in St. Louis?"

"Well, when I got back last night I took a bath and a sedative, but I was still pretty wired so I went shopping. I only spent twenty dollars. I got Andy a toothbrush."

Eva Broussard couldn't help herself. "A twenty-dollar toothbrush?" she asked.

"A toothbrush and some other stuff. And I decided to walk home on the beach, in the fog. I was manicky, Eva. Not too bad, but definitely hyper. That's why I'm afraid there wasn't really anybody there, no barking dog, nothing. By the time I got home I felt like an idiot with a mouthful of sand. There couldn't have been anything behind me. It doesn't make any sense."

"What about the answering machine messages?"

"I erased them. They're not there. I could have hallucinated those, too."

Eva Broussard sighed. "It doesn't happen that way, Bo. Oh, I suppose it could. There's undoubtedly a rare case on record somewhere in which a single hallucination may have recurred in otherwise normal contexts. But generally speaking that's the stuff of fiction. In real life even people with psychiatric illnesses don't produce such narrow, specific hallucinations. The brain isn't wired that way."

"So what are you saying?" Bo asked, scowling at a sleek seagull perched on her deck railing. "That I'm making this up to get attention?" The seagull jumped to the deck floor and walked aimlessly toward a green-and-white-striped deck

chair, its webbed feet making tiny flapping sounds against
the wood.

"It's possible. But it's inconsistent with what I know of
you. I take it there were no further barking dog calls today?"

"I unplugged the phones," Bo told her shrink. "I sometimes do that when I'm painting."

"If it happens again, don't erase it," Eva Broussard said.
"Now would you mind explaining why you flew to St. Louis
and back?"

When Bo had finished the explanation of Zach's strange
behavior, the white colonial house with its absent Dr. Keith,
and the threatening note left in a mailbox, Eva Broussard was
silent. After several seconds she said, "I can't help finding this
information as suspicious as you do, Bo. Suspicious and possibly quite dangerous. I suggest that you avoid further contact
with Zachary Crooked Owl. Let the authorities handle it."

"Eva," Bo asked as the gull dashed clumsily across her deck
and then flapped skyward, "is there any reason Zach might
have killed Mort?"

"I don't know," Eva answered, "but it seems unlikely. Mort
had offered to underwrite an advertising campaign for Ghost
Flower, allowing himself to be photographed for the promo-
tional materials. He loved the lodge, and the Neji. I had the
impression that he and Zach were quite close. Don't jump to
extreme conclusions based on sketchy evidence, Bo. Just try
to stay out of the situation altogether."

Bo chose not to share with her psychiatrist how meager
that likelihood was. "Thanks, Eva," she said, and hung up.

The phone rang almost immediately. It was the weekend
duty worker at the receiving home.

"Your Wagman case is in St. Mary's Hospital for Children,"
he informed Bo. "The foster father was called to an out-of-
town family emergency and had to leave. Apparently there
wasn't another foster home available for an acting-out kid
right away, and we're full. Something's been wrong with your
phone all day, so the placement worker called your supervisor.

Aldenhoven gave the okay for a temporary group home placement, and—"

"A group home!" Bo interjected. "Bird's only six years old!
What happened? Why is he in the hospital?"

"Three kids beat the hell out of him. He's got a broken rib,
but they say he'll be okay. I'm afraid I don't know anything
else."

"Oh, shit," she yelled, and slammed the phone down.
"Group home" was a euphemism for "trainer jail." Older kids
too young for juvenile incarceration centers, seriously troubled kids already lost to normal human interaction—these
were sent to county-run group homes after they'd bombed
out of five or six foster care placements. Some of them had
already committed violent crimes. All of them seethed with
resentment and quickly formed pecking orders in which the
weakest was routinely tormented. Bird had been a lamb
thrown to hyenas.

Bo drove inland toward the hospital through carloads of
people returning from an afternoon at the beach. Couples,
families with sandy kids and wet dogs. A parade of pleasant
normalcy to which she would never belong and which, in fact,
seemed rather tedious. But that life was critical to the healthy
development of children, and her exclusion was largely her
own choice. Bird, who might one day battle demons similar
to hers, was being denied the right to join or reject the
parade.

He was being systematically traumatized, she thought, by a
system created to protect him. On the heels of his father's death
he'd been in three placements in as many days. Even a well-
adjusted, normal six-year-old wouldn't be able to handle that.
And Bird wasn't normal. Now he'd been beaten so badly he had
to be hospitalized, and nothing lay ahead for him but more of
the same.

Parking illegally in a yellow zone, Bo tore into St. Mary's
Hospital vowing to find Mort Wagman's family Monday
morning, period. Maybe this Dr. Keith was Bird's mother. Bo

couldn't imagine Mort nearly seven years ago, when his illness would have been at its worst, romancing a doctor, but stranger things had happened. That failing, she'd call Mort's lawyer, threaten him with a malpractice suit or something, force him to remove Bird from the system and get him into a good private facility.

At the hospital's information desk she noticed that her hands were shaking. Bird had *been* in a good private facility. No matter what Zach had done, the Neji would have cared for Bird until she could do her job and find his family. But the law said he couldn't stay there. The law said he had to be protected. Bo wondered how insane it would sound if she screamed, "I hate systems!" in the visitors' elevator.

Bird was woozy when she loped into the room he shared with another little boy. The other boy's parents sat beside his bed, the father reading aloud from *Winnie-the-Pooh*. The mother smiled at Bo and said, "Josh has just had an emergency tonsillectomy. What happened to your little guy?"

"Assault," Bo answered. "Probably with intent to kill."

Bird recognized her. "Bo," he whispered, his blue eyes glassy with sedation above a hospital gown printed in race cars, "some boys kicked me."

"I know," she said, hoping he wouldn't notice the tears spilling over her lashes, "but you're still the Muffin Bird, aren't you, the Moonbird, too? Nobody gets *that* Bird down."

"Except Crumpet Cats, Bo. You gotta watch out for *them*."
Crumpet people, too. And they're everywhere.

What had happened to Bird wasn't unusual, only extreme. Children instinctively formed packs and then shunned the different ones, the ones who couldn't conform. Adults were only slightly less obvious while doing the same thing. And if there were a club, Madge Aldenhoven would be its president. Bo stroked Bird's fine, raven-colored hair and enjoyed a fantasy of pouring sugar into her supervisor's gas tank.

Madge had only followed the Department of Social Services procedures manual. Bird had to go somewhere, and there was nowhere for him to go. Nobody wanted a kid with ADHD any more than anybody wanted an adult with schizophrenia. Too difficult and unpleasant. Madge had approved nothing more than standard procedure. And standard procedure had broken a little boy's rib. Bo wasn't going to let it break his heart as well.

When visiting hours were over she got a copy of Bird's medical record from the nurse and drove home. The night wasn't as foggy as it had been yesterday, but it still made her feel alone, creepy. There would be no furry presence to greet her, no little life demanding love and care. The apartment would be empty. And there might be disembodied barking that wasn't really there.

Get a grip, Bradley. If it happens again, go stay in a motel. At least then you'll know for sure whether it's real or not.

There were two messages on the answering machine, both from Jane and Mindy at the dogwash. "Your phone's been down all day," Mindy's voice told her. "Give us a call as soon as you can."

The second message was from Jane. "Hey, check in, will ya? There's something here for you. Give us a call or come on over, okay?"

What "something"? Was somebody really playing tricks here? Who would leave a package at the dogwash? Bo fell in bed exhausted but uneasy. The apartment was empty, yet it felt as though trouble were breathing in its corners. Trouble just waiting. She set the clock radio and then listened to the rebroadcast of a local talk show taped earlier in the day, just for the reassurance of voices.

An oceanographer was talking about the shark attack a few days ago. It was perhaps distasteful, he said, but the remains of Hopper Mead's right leg had been retrieved from the cadaver of a great white shark washed up on a Mexican beach near Ensenada. There was some confusion as to the cause of death, although he was convinced that Mead had died from injuries inflicted by the shark. Before accepting questions from callers, he wanted to remind female water sports enthusiasts that ocean swimming at "certain times of the month" was ill-advised.

"Oh, for crying out loud!" Bo muttered into her pillow. "You're not saying Hopper Mead got her leg torn off because she was menstruating, are you?" Another obvious win for the guys. They'd never have babies, but, by God, they wouldn't attract sharks, either. Bo turned off the radio and went to sleep with a familiar, and comfortable, sense of injustice.

An hour later the phone rang. The sound bathed Bo in chill even before she was fully awake. By the time the message tape clicked on after the fourth ring, she was sweating. It was there again, the dog barking. A little dog. A terrier. The barking sounded the same as it had on previous occasions. Exactly the same. The rapid barks escalating, and then a particularly piercing yip, as if the dog were suddenly hurt or threatened. After the sound stopped, its echo filled her apartment, reverberating in her skull. Especially that sharp yip.

The dark felt like a boat around her, rocking. Why did the dog always sound the same? With her face buried in a damp pillow, the reason dawned on her. It was a tape! Somebody was playing the same tape over and over into her answering machine. Somebody had followed her on a fogbound beach in the dark and invisibly triggered a tape player. And he'd laughed at her terror. He'd been close enough to touch her, to sense her fear. And he'd laughed.

Bo remembered a cruel chuckle floating in the fog like audible teeth, like the smile of the Cheshire Cat just hanging in wet air. He knew her. He had to. He knew about Mildred, knew what would send her over the edge. And he knew where she lived. He'd watched her last night, followed her. He might be nearby right now, waiting to see her lose control, run to her car, try to escape.

In moonlight the yellow sunflowers on her sheets turned gray as she curled her knees toward her chest and locked her arms about them. It made no sense, and senselessness was terrifying. Somebody wanted to hurt her. Somebody wanted to drive her mad. A stranger hiding in mist wanted to see her insane, screaming, lost.

As she pushed her forehead against her knees, she heard a sound. A knock, soft and tentative. The silence that followed had a pulse, she realized. A throbbing she could almost see in the outlines of doorways, furniture. Then she heard it again, slightly louder. A knock at her door. How many times in the literature of human drama, she thought, had this moment been immortalized? A thousand closed doors spun toward her, each with an intolerable truth begging at its outer side. A drowned husband, long-dead child, or worse, nothing. Where something was hungered for, nothing.

Well, whatever it was, Bo decided, would soon meet its match. Forcing herself to unfold and stand up, Bo moved silently to the kitchen and fumbled in a drawer. Her hand found a corkscrew, a garlic press, and something scratchy she couldn't identify. The corkscrew would have to do. Pulling its two flanges upward, she exposed the length of pointed, spiral steel, locked both hands tight around the flanges, and strode to the door.

"Who in hell are you?" she bellowed. "Don't think I won't kill you if you keep this up!" It occurred to her that the threat sounded real.

"Bo? It's Andy. What's wrong?"

Andy? Andy with a recording of terrier barks? Unconvinced, she lowered her arms and looked through the door's tiny viewer. A haggard, familiar face looked back.

"Oh, God, Andy!" she breathed, unlocking the door and staring, wide-eyed.

"Bo, why are you holding that corkscrew?" he asked, extending a sheaf of wilting yellow roses toward her. "And what have you done to your hair? God, how I've missed you!"

In his gray eyes Bo saw storms of devotion waiting to enfold her, join her against anything. Dropping the corkscrew, she pulled him inside and into her arms. The roses fell at her feet.

"You're still in Germany," she whispered against his unshaven cheek. "You can't be you."

"I'm here, Bo," he answered, kissing her. "Whatever's happening, I'm here."

"I'm so glad," Bo sighed with unfeigned enthusiasm.

But in the dark beyond the open door something waited, she remembered. Something her lover's presence could not dissipate. A danger so cruelly intimate that, sooner or later, she would be compelled to face it, alone.

Chapter 22

Bo awoke amid a tangle of sunflower-patterned sheets and the arms and legs of her exhausted lover, who was going to appreciate the toiletries she'd bought for him, she thought. His scruffy, three-day beard was peppered with gray and made the usually impeccable pediatrician look like an aging wino. Singing "Molly Malone" under her breath, she slipped from her bedroom into the kitchen and measured twice the usual amount of coffee into one of the new unbleached filters made from recycled pine industrial pallets. She'd bought the filters from a door-to-door counterculture salesman who said he was working off bad karma from an earlier incarnation as John Milton. Irresistible.

"As she wheeled her wheelbarrow through streets broad and narrow," Bo hummed the Irish song as she picked up the phone. "Singing cockles and mussels, alive, alive-o." The St. Louis Directory Assistance operator provided numbers for all three universities. Only two of them, she told Bo, had medical schools. Bo called St. Louis University's switchboard first and learned that no Dr. Keith was connected to that school. Then she called Washington University. Bingo. A Dr. Ann Lee Keith was on the faculty. Professor Keith taught neurophysiology, Bo learned, and would be in class today. Bo left her home and office numbers, and an urgent message to call.

By the time the coffee was ready, Andrew LaMarche had showered and was shaving over the sink in Bo's dressing alcove.

"The razors and shaving gel are deeply appreciated," he said from inside a cloud of steam. "But what am I supposed to do with the cheese grater and colander?"

"Grate cheese, drain spaghetti," Bo answered. "I really got them because they match your toothbrush."

A puzzled silence indicated his unwillingness to grapple with this.

"You know," she explained, "like in magazines. A wooden table decorated with one peacock feather, four blue wine glasses imported from a village in Czechoslovakia, a high-tech eggbeater, and a daguerreotype of Mary Todd Lincoln in an old velvet frame. It all creates a mood, an image; it's advertising art."

"I don't see a feather anywhere," he replied. "But the coffee smells artful. I'll stir it with the spatula."

"The spatula is *blue*," Bo insisted. "It was a composition."

"I love your compositions," he smiled, managing to look dapper even in her yellow terrycloth bathrobe with the satin starfish appliqué she'd always hated.

Breakfast consisted of coffee and a selection of Gerber's baby cereals Bo had bought for Mildred. Decorating the counter where they sat were eight real autumn leaves, each protected from drying out by a coat of car wax. Andrew frowned into his barley cereal as Bo explained the leaves and what had happened in St. Louis.

"Have you informed the Sheriff's Department about this?" he asked.

"What am I going to say? That Zach and somebody I saw on TV flew to St. Louis and knocked on the door of a house? Neither traveling nor knocking on doors is a crime. I am going to call the Sheriff's Department this morning, though. I want to know what they've turned up regarding Mort's death. Then I'm going down to the County Administration

Center and do some checking on Ghost Flower Lodge. If they have a business license in addition to their license as a board-and-care, there'll be some information. Who's on their board, tax status, that sort of thing."

"I'm not officially back until next week," Andrew said, "but I'll check in at the hospital and make sure I'm informed of any plans for your boy, Bird. I may be able to arrange for the necessary psychiatric evaluation today. If he actually does have attention deficit hyperactivity disorder, the diagnosis should be made as quickly as possible."

"I love you, Andy," Bo smiled. "I really do."

Andrew LaMarche beamed and then flattened a mound of barley cereal against the interior curve of his bowl with the back of his spoon. "You said Bird's father, this Mort Wagman, was pretty young, didn't you? In his twenties?"

"Uh-huh," Bo answered vaguely.

"And you were, um, just friends?"

Bo walked around the counter to scrape her cereal into the garbage disposal. "No," she answered. "I didn't say we were *just* friends. I wouldn't say that. I said we were friends." The clattering disposal punctuated her remark.

"Oh," Andrew said miserably. "Well."

Bo stared levelly at his chestnut brown mustache, drooping now at the corners. "Friends are just about sacred to me," she said. "There have been times when I wouldn't have made it without them. You're the only man I love, Andy, the only man I sleep with. But you're not my only friend. If that's what you want, then—"

"No," he interrupted, grinning sheepishly. "I just want to be your only husband."

"Aagghh!" Bo roared. "Not now, not in the morning, not when I have to go to work, not when people are running around committing murder and playing tapes of barking dogs in the fog. I can't cope, Andy. Why start the day like this?"

"I'm sorry," he said, gray eyes twinkling.

He wasn't sorry at all.

After arriving at the Child Protective Services office building, Bo stopped in the hall to glare into Madge Aldenhoven's corner office. "You should never have okayed Bird Wagman's transfer to a group home," Bo said flatly. "He's only six and he may have ADHD. He's vulnerable. Thanks to you, three other kids attacked him, broke one of his ribs, put him in the hospital. Great work, Madge."

The supervisor didn't blink. "Your emotionalism is, as usual, completely unprofessional." She sighed into the stack of case files on her desk. "Procedures were followed. If you can't work within procedural guidelines, you don't belong here. But let's not waste time arguing. Was there anything else you wanted to say?"

"Just that this child will inherit a substantial estate," Bo smiled. "The attorney administering the will has been appointed temporary guardian. If there is any further mishandling of this case, any more endangerment of this little boy, his guardian just might sue the Department of Social Services on Bird's behalf for damages."

"In that event, your name will be the first one on the subpoena list," Aldenhoven pointed out.

"But your name is the one authorizing his transfer to a group home," Bo countered, "where he was seriously injured."

"What do you want, Bo?"

"Complete discretion from this moment on over that child's movement within the system even if it means junking the procedures manual."

Aldenhoven examined a narrow gold watch at her wrist and then adjusted the matching belt of her blue silk shirtwaist. "That's impossible," she said.

"It's that or I tell the lawyer the truth when he calls, that his client's well-being, even his client's *life,* cannot be guaranteed by San Diego County's Child Protective Services."

Madge glanced at several piles of pink phone memos on her desk.

"He's already called, hasn't he?" Bo asked.

The older woman shoved a stack of memos in Bo's direction. The one on top, a phone call made at 7:15 A.M., was from Reynolds Cassidy, the attorney for Mort Wagman's estate.

"You may do what you think is best for the boy," Madge agreed as if Bo hadn't just come close to blackmailing her. "Legal trouble is the last thing the department needs."

It was a small victory, but one Bo could relish.

"You're early, and you're glowing," Estrella noted suspiciously when Bo opened their office door. "What's going on?"

"Bird Wagman's in St. Mary's with a broken rib, somebody's trying to drive me crazy by playing a tape of a barking dog that sounds like Mildred, and Andy got back from Germany last night," Bo answered. It was impossible to halt the blush staining her cheeks a hopelessly Irish pink.

"Ah," Estrella beamed. "He came back early."

"Yeah."

"Ah."

Estrella's smile, Bo thought, rivaled that of the Mona Lisa in knowing subtlety. "Don't start planning the wedding shower," Bo warned. "I'm *not*—"

"I didn't say a word," Estrella grinned. "Although I *was* thinking of little paper parasols and salad Niçoise on crystal plates . . . "

"I hate olives."

"Okay, tarragon chicken in pastry shells on crystal plates, then. Crème brûlée for dessert."

Bo was salivating. "Can't we just have the crème brûlée and forget the shower business?"

"No."

"I was afraid of that."

Bo settled into her desk chair and dialed the Backcountry Sheriff's Department. Wick Barlow, the deputy who interviewed Bo the morning after Mort's death, had just arrived for her shift. The news was frustrating.

"Basically, we've got nada," she told Bo. "The bullet that

killed him was a thirty-ought-six-caliber soft point, time of death within an hour, give or take, of four A.M. Soft points flatten and split on impact to a cupped blossom shape about the size of a dime. From the trajectory of the flattened point through his chest, it looks like the shooter stood down in the canyon and fired upward. But we've been all over that canyon floor and haven't found the shell casing, tracks, nothing. Whoever it was got in and out without leaving a trace. To say we haven't got a suspect is stretching it. We haven't even got a *clue!*"

"Did you, ah, check to see if anyone at the lodge had any guns?" Bo asked awkwardly. She didn't want to implicate Zach Crooked Owl. Not just yet.

"You mean Crooked Owl's rifle? Sure. That was the first thing we did. It's a twenty-two and it hadn't been fired recently. That gun didn't kill Wagman. And neither did any of the other thirteen guns we pulled off the Neji Reservation. Half of 'em were so old they wouldn't fire eight times out of ten, but the Indians say they keep 'em around for hunting. Guess they bag a rabbit once in a while. Anyway, none of the reservation guns did it. And it's not likely we'll ever find the one that did."

Bo experienced a wash of relief. At least Zach's gun hadn't killed Mort. Maybe Zach hadn't, either. "So what will you do next?" she asked.

"Keep the investigation open," Wick Barlow replied. "It'll stay open for years. There's no statute of limitations on murder. But unless we get something—evidence, a witness, something—we're never gonna know what happened out there. I'm sorry."

Bo hung up the phone and watched for a while as Estrella dictated a court report. Then Bo grabbed her purse and whispered, "Back in an hour," before heading out the door. The County Administration Center would be open by now. She wanted to see what Ghost Flower Lodge looked like on paper. The CAC was an old, Depression-era structure built by the

Works Projects Administration in the early 1930s and situated on prime bayfront property. Half its offices commanded a view of naval vessels and sailboats for which nearby hotels charged two hundred dollars a night. Bo parked facing an art deco lion's head adorning the side of the building, and left her CPS ID badge on the dash. County employees could park free at the CAC, one of the countless and nearly always useless perks of the job.

In a large, second-floor office marked "County Office of Records," Bo leaned on a counter that came to her chest and looked at Ghost Flower's completed application for a business license. A rotund clerk in a flowered acetate dress fluttered eagerly nearby. The business license, she saw, had been revised at the time the lodge contracted for construction of its new building, and noted the corporation's debt in the amount of four hundred thousand dollars to a private lender who had agreed to pay the taxes on the loan as well. The name of the private lender made Bo gasp.

"Hopper Mead," it said. The deceased heiress. The woman whose right leg was retrieved from the stomach of a great white shark, Bo realized, had paid for the rammed-earth desert sanctuary where Bo and Mort Wagman met!

"What did Hopper Mead have to do with Ghost Flower Lodge?" she said aloud. "This is weird."

"Hopper Mead?" the clerk answered. "Oh, I know all about that. You see, we have this investment club, just a few of us here. It helps with the boredom, if you know what I mean, and—"

"She's the one the shark ate while she was swimming by her yacht last week," Bo said. "I know that. But I don't understand her connection to this Indian psychiatric facility out in the desert." She pointed to Mead's name on the document. "See, she loaned them the money for—"

"For construction of a physical plant," the clerk interrupted gleefully. "And then she was killed."

Bo thought the woman's attitude toward death was unnecessarily chipper. "You seem delighted," she said.

"Well, no, of course not," the clerk went on, temporarily abashed. "But you see, our investment club had just bought a thousand shares of MedNet stock right after they got that huge judgment. Rock-bottom prices, and now—"

"MedNet? What's MedNet?" Bo thought the name sounded like a hairspray for surgeons. It would be scented with ether.

The clerk pursed her lips. "Don't you read the financial pages?" she asked.

"No. I don't read the sports pages, either. But my life has been full, even meaningful, without them. Why would I read the financial pages? I'm a social worker."

"And I'm a clerk. You read them to *make money,* that's why. And let me tell you, our club's going to clean up on MedNet!"

Bo was sure she'd never seen a county employee this happy. "Okay," she smiled back, "what's MedNet?"

"It's a medical management consortium based in Phoenix," the clerk answered conspiratorially, metal bracelets jangling as she smoothed orange-black hair from her face. "It buys and manages hospital chains, nursing homes, that kind of thing. Mostly, you know, places for mental illness, Alzheimer's, stuff like that. Drug companies and labs, too. The ones that, you know, deal with that." Her voice dropped to a whisper. "You'd be surprised how many crazy people there are," she went on. "Why, over twenty percent of all hospital admissions in this country are for psychiatric illness. Lots of money in that, let me tell you!"

"Wow," Bo said, biting the inside of her cheek. "No kidding? But what does Hopper Mead have to do with this MedNet?"

"She *inherited* MedNet, or the money her father made with it, at least. That's what she was an heiress *to,* you see. She and her brother, he runs some kind of consulting business so I

guess he doesn't need his trust fund, but the young Miss
Mead did good things with hers, like make a big loan to this
place called Ghost Flower Lodge. That's a pretty name, isn't
it? I wonder how those Indians came up with it."

"It's just a little yellow desert flower," Bo answered
thoughtfully, "so pale you can almost see through it. But
inside it's got maroon speckles, and it's tough. So what happens to Hopper Mead's loan, now that she's dead?"

The clerk's eyes glowed. "The loan was made from her
trust," she explained. "And the trust, including its loans,
went to MedNet upon her death. We bought our stock *just*
before the corporation got all that money, so of course shares
went way up again."

"So MedNet now owns the loan Mead made to Ghost
Flower?"

"Owns it and is calling it," the clerk chirped. "The Indians
can't pay, so MedNet now owns this program they do out
there. Apparently it's like a spa for movie stars who go crazy,
something like that. There's a rumor they'll sell foreign franchises on this Indian thing, too, which will mean another
stock increase, maybe even a split! And they've already
applied for a business license under their name here. Would
you like to see it?"

"MedNet's license to run a business in California? So they
can run Ghost Flower, right?"

"That's right. Here, let me get you the file."

Bo chewed a knuckle and waited. This must be, she
thought, the financial crisis Eva had mentioned. The crisis
that would strip the Neji of their pride, reduce them to the
status of serfs under the dominion of a gluttonous corporation. This would end the dream of the Neji.

"Here it is," the clerk said, placing a file carefully on the
scratched counter. "MedNet's license application. Everything's in there, even copies of stuff we don't require. Everything related to MedNet taking over the Ghost Flower Lodge
program."

Bo thumbed through copies of documents she didn't understand, stopping at a letter of acknowledgment from MedNet of its role in Mead's estate. It was signed by Med-Net's chairman, Alexander Morley. The copier had blurred MedNet's printed logo, a cluster of arms holding aloft a caduceus, but a list of names was still visible in a column of tiny print down the letterhead's left margin. "Board of Advisors" was printed at the top of the list.

Bo narrowed her eyes to bring the tiny names into focus. They were all doctors. At the top of the column a familiar name appeared. Dr. Ann Lee Keith.

"Whaaat?" Bo whispered, scrunching her nose. The investment-happy clerk knew everything else; maybe she knew something about this, too. "Do you know anything about this Dr. Keith?" Bo asked her, pointing to the name.

"Nah. Just somebody who's on their board of advisors. Those people don't have anything to do with the business, really. They're not important."

Wrong, Bo thought, but said, "Thank you so much for your help," instead.

Outside the county building she sat on a bench and admired bas-relief cement swordfish pursuing unlikely schools of arthropods around the base of a WPA Federal Art Projects statue. The statue was of an enormous woman with a flat nose holding an equally enormous jug on her left shoulder as she gazed toward the naval base on North Island across San Diego Bay. Behind the statue, an inscription above the County Administration Center's doors said, "The noblest motive is the public good."

"Tell it to MedNet," Bo muttered, and headed for her car.

Chapter 23

The eyes of his father followed Zachary Crooked Owl as he paced from one side of the lodge's living room to the other. The deep black eyes of the painting over the fireplace laid blame as eloquently, and as silently, as John Crooked Owl himself would have done. There was no escaping those eyes. Zach didn't even try. He knew they were right.

"The white man hurts everything he touches," John Crooked Owl told his son years in the past. "He hurts the earth. He hurts the sky. Even the rocks he smashes for his tunnels and roads. The white man enslaves the mother of his children as he wants to enslave the spirit of life. The white man will hurt us if we are not careful. He will devour the soul of the Neji and all the Kumeyaay if we are not always careful."

Zach could hear Dura and the other women serving food in the dining hall. A balanced diet as determined by the County of San Diego. Dura had gone to classes at a community college to learn what foods the Neji must serve their guests, and had come home laughing.

"They teach that grains, leaves, stems, roots, and berries are the healthy things for people to eat," she told her husband. "What do they think Indians have been eating for a thousand years? Why didn't they just ask us?"

"We don't exist in their minds," he answered. "They only see Indians at the movies. They can't see real people."

That was still true, Zach thought as he walked slowly beneath his father's painted gaze. It would always be true. But white men and other men who adopted their ways could see money, even if they couldn't see anything else. Indian money, any kind of money. Money made them happy, and they would find ways to take it for themselves. They had found a way to take it from the Neji. And that was Zachary Crooked Owl's fault.

"Zach, come and eat," Dura called from the dining hall door. "It's a brown rice casserole with cheese. Fruit salad. Brownies." Her voice was flat with worry. "You like brownies, Zach."

"I have to think, Dura," he told her. "I'm not hungry right now."

Smoothing her apron, Dura moved to stand on the hearth under John Crooked Owl's picture. She held a brown-checked dish towel in one hand like a proclamation extended toward her husband. "We'll go on living here," she pronounced slowly. "The Neji will stay at Ghost Flower Lodge, stay on the land. This is reservation land. They can't take it, they can't come here. It's ours. You know this, Zach. They can't take Neji land or anything that's on Neji land. You have to stop worrying."

"They will steal our story, which is our spirit," he said, sitting heavily on a carved chair. "Steal it and sell it. They will take the money we earn because they will own the work that we do. You don't understand, Dura. We can stay here, but we will have nothing. The Neji were the only band of Kumeyaay they couldn't buy. Now they have. And I allowed this to happen."

Dura let the dish towel fall to her side and then sat next to him, biting her lip. He could see the pale knuckles like stones beneath the skin of her hands. A woman's hands, tied to time through the births and deaths that they cradled. Different

from a man's hands, which were meant to build and to fight
for his people. Dura didn't contradict what he'd said. She
merely took his hand and held it between both of hers. The
gesture was like a ghost of his mother.

"What are you thinking about, Zach?" she said. "What is
it that you're thinking about doing?"

"I don't know," he answered. "I'm going to walk outside."

He couldn't tell her. He wasn't sure.

Standing, he jammed his hands into his pockets and strode
into the sun. In his right pocket was the spent shell, the
bright copper casing of the bullet that had killed Mort Wagman. He'd fasted and danced to find it. He'd stripped off his
shirt and let the sun sink into his dark skin until he was dizzy
and blind. And the spirit of the canyon, or of his father, or of
the raven whose namesake had died there, had showed him
the orange glint of copper filmed in pale brown dust. But
now he was afraid.

It had to be Henderson, he thought for the thousandth
time. Henderson said he was going to become the head of this
corporation, MedNet. He had plans, this Henderson. Zach
had seen these plans in his face when he looked right through
the patients, and through the Neji. When he looked at the
lodge with its walls that would last forever, and didn't see
their beauty. He saw money.

Henderson had written a letter to Mort Wagman offering
Mort even more money than the SnakeEye athletic shoe company had given him, if Mort would star in a commercial
about psychiatric treatment at Ghost Flower Lodge. The commercial would be on television. Henderson wanted to show
Mort crazy in a breechcloth, sweating in a Yurok sweathouse,
doing a Navajo sand painting, wearing Zuñi jewelry. Then he
wanted to show Zach afterward sitting in a bar with pretty
women.

Mort had handed the letter to Zach and said, "Flush it."
Then he'd written back to Henderson telling him he'd "place
his personal resources at the disposal of the Neji" if MedNet

continued its attempts to buy the Ghost Flower program. But that was before Hopper Mead died. Before the ignorance of Zachary Crooked Owl handed Ghost Flower and the Neji legacy straight into the hands of the enemy.

Zach kicked pebbles at a young banded gecko peeking out from the deep shadow of a rock, and immediately cursed himself. The supple little creature with its pinkish legs nearly transparent in the bright sunlight looked like a human fetus. "What kind of man kicks a baby?" Zach said aloud. He knew he was going to have to do something before his self-hatred made him a monster.

Old John had wanted him to go to school, he remembered again. Had said that a business course at the community college would help in running the Neji's board-and-care business. And Zach had gone for a semester. But he was young then, and shy among the white students who called him Black Tonto and the black students whose jargon and hostility he couldn't understand, and even the Latino students, who just ignored him. There were no other Indians there. He didn't fit in, and he'd stopped attending classes.

If he'd finished, Zach thought bitterly, he might have seen the flaw in Hopper Mead's offer. He might have remembered that even young people can die, and hired a lawyer to handle the loan she offered. But he hadn't done any of those things. And now the greed of white men would destroy everything they'd worked for. The sullen finality of it made his head pound. Somebody should have to pay, he thought. One of them should die as Mort Wagman had died. He should kill one of them.

The copper shell in his pocket pressed against his thigh as he walked. He could give it to the authorities, could have done that from the beginning. They could run tests, determine the type of gun it was shot from, check records. They could see who owned guns like that from records all over the country. Maybe it would be Henderson's gun.

Zach pushed himself against the hot desert air as if it were

an obstacle. Even walking felt like a battle. He'd searched for
the shell and then kept it because it was the only thing he
could use against Henderson. He hadn't really thought he'd
need to.

When he found the shell he still thought he could get
enough money from the mob to pay off Mead's loan, now held
by MedNet. He'd agreed to let a gambling syndicate build a
casino on the Neji Reservation, even agreed that some of the
Neji would run it. It had to be owned and run by Indians on
reservation land to avoid federal and state gambling laws.
Indian reservations, he'd learned, were like sovereign nations
in some ways, not always subject to the laws of the conquer-
ing culture. Zach hated the idea of a Neji casino, but it was
better than losing the dream his father had created from nothing. That dream was Ghost Flower Lodge and its program, a
legend of kindness begun when one man did not abandon his
ill brother.

But Zach hadn't understood the game. He'd gone to St.
Louis for a meeting with the syndicate, but they'd already
said MedNet would pay them even more money than the four
hundred thousand he needed if they'd forget building a Neji
casino. MedNet wanted the Neji for its own purposes and
would pay the syndicate to back off. There was only one way
to cinch the deal for the Neji, his connection had told Zach.
And that way involved a woman. She was Mort Wagman's
mother.

She was a member of MedNet's board, the man told Zach.
And she wanted to take Mort's little boy away from him. That's
why Mort had changed his name, why he had no history. He'd
been hiding. But she'd found him. And MedNet had arranged
to have him killed at her request.

But she could stop the MedNet drive to gain control of
Ghost Flower, the man went on, if she thought her grandson's
life lay in the balance. If she thought the child had been kidnapped, she could stall the move long enough for Zach to nail
the casino deal, get the money, pay off Mead's loan. But it all

had to go down over the weekend, when she wouldn't be able to contact anybody at the agency holding the boy. When she would believe he'd been kidnapped.

Zach's hands knotted into fists when he remembered his stupidity. It all happened so fast. And the man talked so fast. But it was all a lie. A lie to get Zachary Crooked Owl's handwriting on a threatening note that would divert attention from both the mob and MedNet if there were further violence as the two jockeyed for control of the Indians. It was a joke, Zach thought bitterly. For a hundred years the Kumeyaay had survived like lizards in a barren landscape nobody wanted. Unworthy of attention, much less help. Invisible. Now powerful men offered powerful amounts of money for a chance to use that land and its lizards. Powerful men were willing to kill for that chance.

But he could fight back, Zach mused. If Henderson had murdered Mort, the shell casing would give the Neji leverage. There were countless reasons for murder, and Mort Wagman had been wealthy. Zach had stopped trying to understand the connections between Mort and MedNet. There was no source from which he could learn the truth, put the pieces together. But there had to be a connection because Mort Wagman was dead. And Henderson had been in town.

He would tell Henderson he had the shell. He would insist on a renegotiation of the loan in exchange for it. And that was blackmail. Henderson might try to kill him, but he was ready. If it would save the dream, he was completely ready.

Henderson was coming to the lodge on Wednesday. The Neji didn't have to permit him on their land, but Zach had told him to come. And now he was uneasy. He'd been in the army, seen action in Vietnam. He'd shot thousands of rounds into steaming jungles where tiny people were hiding. He might have killed them, but if he did he didn't know it. This would be different. The thought of it made him sick.

Looking up, he saw the edge of Yucca Canyon. He couldn't seem to stay away. Something was going to happen here, he could feel it. Someone was going to die. Throwing his head back, he screamed into the dry air, silent except for a ticking sound that might have been insects and might have been time running out. The echo bounced off the canyon's wall and bathed him in vibrating light.

Chapter 24

At the office Bo found messages from Andrew, Mindy at the dogwash, and Ann Lee Keith, each carefully abbreviated by the message center worker.

"Dr. LaMarche has important news. Call at home," said the first. Then, "Dog Beach Dogwash, call back." The final one was cryptic. "Urgent—phone Dr. Ann Lee Keith anytime day or night." Both Keith's work and unlisted home numbers were given.

Bo dialed Keith's home number immediately, and got a busy signal. Then she phoned the dogwash. Jane and Mindy were out, and the young employee who answered knew nothing of a package for Bo.

"Maybe it's this shipment of the new anti-matting coat conditioner," she suggested. "It comes in sage, peppermint, and unscented."

Bo ran a hand through her short curls and found no mats. "I have plenty of conditioner," she said. "Just tell Jane and Mindy I called."

Andrew LaMarche answered his phone on the first ring and sounded strangely exuberant. "Bo," he began, "I had no idea how much fun it could be not going to work. That harpsichord kit I ordered finally arrived, and—"

"Andy, where are you going to put a harpsichord? Your

condo's not much bigger than my apartment, and a harpsichord's as long as a grand piano."

"Indeed," he went on as if the dimensions of a stringed keyboard first seen in the sixteenth century were deeply exciting. "And I'm going to make the plectra out of crow quill the way they did in the beginning, not out of the plastic that came in the kit. And where to put it, well, *J'ai l'idée que—*"

"My guess is that means you've got an idea," Bo interrupted, "and I'd love to hear it, in English. Also, I'm concerned about how you plan to entertain a flock of naked, angry crows until their quills grow back. But I need to call Ann Lee Keith. When can I see the harpsichord?"

"In about three months," he laughed. "But there's something else I want you to see tonight."

"What?" Bo took the bait, resisting an urge to point out that she'd already seen it. A bawdy remark at this point would only drive him further into the Cajun French he sputtered at the slightest hint of emotional stress. She'd never get off the phone.

"A surprise."

"What kind of surprise?"

"Wait and see," he teased, filling Bo's ear with a baritone vibrato that made her think of windblown cypress trees. In Greece. "And by the way," the cypress-voice continued, "I remembered seeing this Dr. Keith's name before, in medical journals. She was a rising star in experimental neurophysiology until a few years ago, *the* name in early fetal-cell implant technology. Then she just vanished from the scene, quit publishing, dropped off the face of the earth, as they say. I seem to recall there was some kind of professional scandal, but I never knew what it was. Not surprising, though. It's a controversial field."

"Scandal, huh?" Bo mused. "Maybe you'll remember what it was by tonight. I'll call you later."

Without replacing the receiver Bo dialed Ann Lee Keith's number again. This time it rang.

"This is Dr. Keith," a well-modulated, feminine voice answered. The words were almost whispered.

"This is Ms. Bradley, calling from Child Protective Services in San Diego." Bo matched the woman's polite tone. "If you have a few moments, Dr. Keith, I'd like to ask—"

"Do you have my grandson?" Ann Lee Keith broke in. "There have been threats, you see. I've been trying to find him. Surely that's the reason you've called?"

In the interrogative statement Bo heard panic, the beginning of tears. "Who is your grandson?" she asked gently.

"Charles. Adam named him Charles for Baudelaire. His name is Charles Duncan Keith. He would be six now, almost seven. I haven't seen him since he was four."

Bo could actually feel her brain filing bits of information like tumblers moving in a lock. Grandson. Charles. Adam. Baudelaire. Little conceptual thunks. Then an awareness that discretion might be called for here. If Charles were Bird, his father had not wanted this woman to know his whereabouts. And this woman would either be Mort Wagman's mother or Bird's mother's mother. An advisor to MedNet. And a once-prominent scientist with a scandal in her past.

"Dr. Keith," Bo said, casting about for a way to get information without providing too much in return, "I'm investigating a case involving a murder near a treatment facility which is about to be taken over by a corporation called Med-Net. I'm contacting you in your capacity as an advisor to that corporation." It sounded official, Bo thought, and it said absolutely nothing.

"Murder!" the woman said. "Are you telling me that my grandson is dead? What treatment facility? And why would a representative of a children's agency be investigating a murder?"

Then her voice changed. "I'm tired of this," she pronounced in low, angry tones. "I don't know who you are or what you want, but whatever it is, I don't have it. I have nothing to do with MedNet. Those vultures bought my name, nothing more. The message you left at my home means nothing to me, except that you've somehow kidnapped Charles. The St. Louis police have your note, and now the San Diego police will have this phone number. You're not going to get away with this!"

Before Bo could reply, Ann Lee Keith hung up.

In the hall outside her office door Bo heard Nick Paratore urging somebody to join his save-the-fish group, Scales of Justice.

"It's only fifteen dollars," he insisted.

"*Madre de Dios!*" another voice answered. "I already gave you five dollars. Hit up somebody else." It was Estrella.

"Am I glad to see you!" Bo said as her friend dumped case files, purse, and briefcase on the desk across from Bo's, and slumped into a desk chair. "I can't make sense out of this Wagman case no matter what I do, and it's getting worse. Ann Lee Keith may be Bird's grandmother, but at the moment she's phoning San Diego police to have me arrested. Did you have lunch?"

Estrella grinned. "No, and I'm eating for two. Let's go up to the lunchroom before they padlock the sandwich cooler. The baby wants tuna salad on sourdough, a bag of chips, and one of those chocolate chip cookies the size of a Frisbee. I'll just have skim milk."

"That's wise," Bo agreed.

The lunch crowd had already cleared as Bo and Estrella sat facing the CPS building's overgrown courtyard. Half an immense chocolate chip cookie lay on each of their paper plates.

"Mmm," Estrella said, savoring a bite of cookie as Bo finished a narrative of the morning's discoveries. "I think you'd better tell Madge about your call to Dr. Keith before a SWAT team arrives to blow you away. Keith sounds like the type who really will call the police, file complaints, the whole thing."

"Yeah," Bo agreed halfheartedly. It was nothing unusual.

Parents and relatives of children picked up by CPS often called the police demanding help, as if the police and CPS weren't two sides of the same coin. And when the parents' demands weren't met, they often filed complaints, creating another whole office just to shuffle the paper. But Ann Lee Keith wasn't just another disgruntled relative. Bo didn't know what she was.

"Keith doesn't know I really work here," she explained as Estrella continued to erode the slab of cookie. "I didn't want to tell her anything about Bird until I knew more about her, about why Mort wasn't in contact with her. So I handed her a line of bureaucratic bull and she saw straight through it. Now she thinks I'm part of whoever's threatening her, leaving messages at her house. That was Zach and the gangster, Es. They left that note in her mailbox. But I don't want to tell Madge about that."

"Don't. She'd have you in a straitjacket before you got out of her office if she knew about your little trip on Saturday."

Bo sighed. "California outlawed straitjackets in public facilities thirty years ago. People choke to death in the damn things. They're barbaric!"

"It was a figure of speech, Bo. Sorry."

"Keith will find out I'm legitimate as soon as she does some checking," Bo went on. "Then she'll call back. I need to know something about her before then. I can't keep putting her off if she really is Bird's grandmother."

"Why not?" Estrella grinned. "This system's set up to put people off."

"Because Bird needs somebody to take care of him *now*. Somebody who can understand him and love him and provide the environment he needs. A grandmother would do nicely, but is Bird really this Charles she talks about, and who's Adam?"

"Maybe Adam was Mort," Estrella offered. "He looked like an Adam, don't you think?"

"He looked like a raven," Bo mumbled through her last

bite of cookie. "The Neji called him Raven. My brother Raven and his fledgling, the Moonbird, backlit by moonlight atop a desert mesa. That's the picture in my mind."

"Um," Estrella answered, standing and brushing crumbs from a gold knit maternity top. "Don't put that in the court report."

Five minutes later Bo was on the phone with Eva Broussard.

"I need to learn something about a neurophysiologist on the faculty at Washington University in St. Louis," she told her psychiatrist. "It's Ann Lee Keith, the woman at whose house Zach and that organized crime guy left the weird note. Andy says she's famous, or was. There was some kind of scandal. How can I find out about her?"

"First, how are you doing?" Broussard asked. "Are you sleeping, eating, moody, manic? All the usual questions."

"Actually, I'm fine," Bo answered. "This case is really interesting, I'm taking my meds right on schedule, and it helps that Andy's back. It's funny, but the depression seems like something that happened a long time ago. I don't think about it."

"Less than a week ago you were still in a psych rehab facility," Eva pointed out. "Of course you don't want to remember why you were there, but you have to. Am I being too direct?"

"You're shattering my illusion of normalcy." Bo grinned, drawing a row of round, imbecilic "happy faces" on the margin of a county directive regarding possible changes in dental insurance. "But thank you."

"Always delighted to help. And as to your question—I'd recommend the medical library at the University of California, here in San Diego. Do you know Keith's area of research?"

"Something about fetal implants," Bo answered. "Andy said it was controversial."

"He's correct. It's an area fraught with ethical dilemmas, but also one of the most exciting new fields in medicine. Your research should be fascinating."

"I'll let you know," Bo concluded. "Thanks, Eva."

After explaining to Madge Aldenhoven that an irate grandmother would probably be phoning the San Diego police to complain that Bo Bradley was impersonating a child abuse investigator, Bo made her own call to the police. Specifically, to Dar Reinert, a detective in the San Diego Police Department's Child Abuse Unit. Bo had worked with the crusty detective on previous cases and knew he wouldn't flinch at a little rule bending.

"Dar," she began, "I need to see a copy of the report on that shark attack. You know, the Hopper Mead thing."

"Mead didn't have any kids," Reinert resisted. "What the hell does CPS want with a shark story?"

There was no point in trying to con Dar Reinert. "I don't really know, but there's some kind of connection to this case I've got. A money connection. When Mead died her trust went to a corporation called MedNet, and—"

"MedNet was her daddy," Reinert growled knowledgeably. "Guy that's heading the investigation is a buddy of mine, told me all about it waiting in line at the firing range Saturday night."

"What did he say?"

"Daddy was Randolph Mead, Sr. Started the first chain hospitals years ago after he married into money, wife's name was Delores Hopper. Hopper Feeds. Big poultry feed company outta Kansas. It's defunct now, but—"

"Dar," Bo interrupted, "chicken feed isn't what I'm looking for. Did the investigation turn up anything suspicious about Hopper Mead's death?"

"You and the whole town wanna think she was murdered," he laughed. "You and the whole town and some Mexican graduate student named José Méndez who dug Mead's leg out of a dead shark down near Ensenada. The kid's been up here, hanging around the investigation. But our guys have run every possible lead. Bottom line—no motive, no suspects, no crime. An old sow of a shark saw lunch and chomped it. End of story."

"A shark can't be an old sow," Bo said defensively. Impossible to explain to Reinert why the term got her Irish up. "And a copy of that police report would really help me get a picture of how MedNet figures in what's happened to the boy in my case. He's only six, Dar. And in the hospital after some kids in a group home used him for a soccer ball."

"Quit," the detective said. "You know I'm a sucker for kid stories. But you owe me one for this, Bradley. I'll bring a copy by your place tonight. Read it and shred it. This didn't happen, got it?"

"I don't even know you," Bo agreed.

By late afternoon Bo had read and copied a score of articles by Dr. Ann L. Keith at the university library. All were published at least ten years in the past. Most were incomprehensible, but Bo managed to grasp the theory underlying them.

Fetal cells, taken from embryos, would adapt to host organisms and grow into whatever they were originally programmed to grow into. And the host organism would not reject them as it would identical cells taken from an adult. Thus, Bo read, mouse embryo cells programmed to become skin could be implanted in an adult mouse, and would grow into a patch of skin. The problem of tissue incompatibility was diminished, but the ethical considerations were staggering.

Most of Ann Lee Keith's research seemed to involve Parkinson's disease and the possibility for use of dopamine cells from human fetal brains in reducing its symptoms. Bo felt her eyes glazing over words like "mesencephalic" and "putamen," but beneath the technical jargon she could see a chilling beauty in what the researcher had held out as a possibility to her peers. The repair of broken people. A way of healing never before imaginable.

But something had stopped Dr. Keith's research almost

overnight. One year her name was mentioned in eight of every twelve scholarly articles, and the next year it was mentioned nowhere. What had Keith done, Bo wondered, to merit such universal disapprobation that her work was uncited even in historical articles?

It was late afternoon by the time Bo decided she couldn't face another word like "immunosuppression." The reading had provided a glimpse into a world about which she knew nothing, and the view was unsettling. A futuristic science-fiction fantasy in which new body organs would be grown in place from the seeds of embryonic cells. The technology was available. Only time would reveal what the human race might do with it.

From the exterior, Bo thought as she left, the library looked less academic than theatrical. The building's unusual architecture suggested a Martian civic center or Andromedan hospital. A set from *Star Trek*, dropped amid eucalyptus trees in Southern California. From hidden speakers in the grove of tall, shaggy trees between the library and its parking lot, students broadcast music, poetry, dramatic readings. Bo found the experience eerie as disembodied electronic music followed her on the dusty path through the grove. Minor chords accompanied by a tinkling percussion that sounded like crystal chandeliers being hit with marshmallows.

You're tired, Bradley. And hungry. Get out of here before you start seeing gnomes. Selling hamburgers.

She was almost to the parking lot when she saw it. A narrow flag of red at eye level on one of the trees beside the path, almost lost in late afternoon shadow. A circle of red fastened over a delicate, lower limb.

"Oh, my God," Bo whispered.

It was a little red leather dog collar, hanging empty in the weak breeze. The music seemed suddenly sad, unbearable. Bo felt tears burn her eyes, the hurt all over again. And beneath that a murderous anger.

"You . . . have . . . no . . . right," she yelled into the camphor-scented air, "to . . . do . . . this!"

Nothing stirred in the grove, but Bo could feel an alien awareness bathing her, hating her, laughing at her. The feeling followed her all the way to her car.

Chapter 25

Before going home, Bo made a detour inland to St. Mary's Hospital for Children. Bird was up and dressed, watching a video of *Pocahontas* in a dayroom with several other children. But he sat apart, Bo noticed, hugging his ribs with both arms and rhythmically scuffing his heels against the tile floor.

"Hey," she said when the film was over, "I found a lady who says she's your grandmother. She's worried about you, Bird. She wants to take care of you."

"What grandmother?" he asked, his blue eyes following the pink-smocked volunteer as she took the cassette from the VCR and turned off the monitor. "I don't have any grandmother."

"Her name is Ann Lee Keith."

"She's Annabel Lee," he said immediately, turning to face Bo with a curious expression animating his small face. "The moon never beams without bringing me dreams of my beautiful Annabel Lee. That's what we say about *her*." The expression was sadness, Bo realized, mixed with comfort at hearing a familiar name. The Poe was pure Mort Wagman.

"That's what who says? You and your dad?"

"Yep. It's iambic."

Bo remembered Mort Wagman's endless collection of unusual information, quips, quotes, lines of poetry. She knew he used these in his stand-up routines, which were geared to an educated audience with quirky sensibilities. Apparently he used them to teach his son as well. And it worked.

"Come over here." Bo smiled, taking his hand and pulling him toward a padded rocker. "Sit right here in my lap. We're going to say a poem."

"Okay," Bird agreed.

"There was an old parrot with teeth," she made up, "who ate crackers above and beneath. With a mouthful of snarls, he phoned his friend Charles, whose other names were ... uh ... "

"Duncan Keith!" Bird completed the limerick, giggling. "That's pretty good, Bo. That's like daddy did. Do another one."

Bird remembered the name. Charles Duncan Keith. His own name, except he probably hadn't used it since he was four, since his father renamed him Bird. Young children, Bo knew, were so psychologically flexible that they would easily adapt to new names, new identities given them before the age of five or so. But the old names would remain familiar, like names of distant relatives or characters on TV.

"Let's see," she said, enjoying the game, "pick a word."

"Pony," he said quickly. "Blue pony with wings."

"There was a blue pony with wings," Bo began, "and he dined very often with kings. He liked chocolate ice cream, and lobsters in nice steam, but ... "

"But he'd rather go sing on the swings," Bird finished, delighted. "Do another one, Bo."

His flashing blue eyes looked exactly like Mort's now, Bo noticed. Alive with an engaged intelligence. All it had taken was someone willing to speak his language, play by his rules for a change. She wished she'd known how all along. Mort had known. But then Mort was his father, and Bo had been lost in her own depression when she first met the boy. Still, she'd almost missed seeing the real child altogether.

"It's time for your dinner, Charles Duncan," she teased

him. "Charles Duncan Keith, the guy the Indians call Moon-bird."

"Can I stay with you, Bo?" he asked as they walked back to his hospital room. "I'm not sick and I can't stay here. They'll make me go back where those mean boys are. I want to stay with you."

Bo nodded thoughtfully, honored by his trust. "That would be fun," she agreed. "But you need a real home with your real family, where you can stay and grow up. Do you remember this Annabel Lee?"

Bird sat on the side of his bed to inspect the hot dogs and baked beans an aide had just brought in on a tray. "I think she has black hair," he said. "And a big white house."

"I'm gonna check her out," Bo said. "And don't worry, you *won't* go back to that group home with the mean boys. That's a promise, okay?"

"Okay, Bo." He was already distracted by the hot dogs. A good time to duck out.

"Hang in there, Bird," Bo said at the door. "Things are going to get better."

At the nurses' station Bo copied a new report from the boy's medical chart. A "psych eval," everybody called it. This one provided a guarded diagnosis of attention deficit hyperactivity disorder for a male Caucasian child, Bird Wagman, aged six years, seven months. The evaluation had been done "stat" at the request of Dr. Andrew LaMarche, director of the hospital's child abuse program.

The psychiatrist recommended a trial of standard medication, such trial to be initiated only after the child was legally declared to be under the control of the juvenile court, or after a legal guardian other than the court provided permission. The evaluation also noted that while Bird couldn't read, his intelligence measured near the genius range in verbal subtests of the Wechsler Intelligence Scale for Children. Bo wasn't surprised.

From the nurses' station phone Bo called Andrew

LaMarche and then Eva Broussard, neither of whom was at home. After leaving messages, Bo contemplated her options. It was after five o'clock. I-8 would be clogged until six-thirty, no point in trying to go home.

Face it, Bradley. You don't want to go home because you're afraid of what you'll find there. Somebody's trying to break your heart with reminders of Mildred. Somebody's trying to make you crazy.

"Okay, I'm scared," Bo said aloud as she left the hospital. The admission was difficult, but cleared the way to deal with the problem. She didn't have to go home. She could avoid whatever might be waiting for her there until someone was with her. The lack of independence was repugnant, but justified in this case, she thought. Meanwhile, she'd have dinner. There was a new low-fat cuisine place in Hillcrest she'd been meaning to try. And the trendy neighborhood was only minutes away.

Over eggplant steaks in a succulent tomato and roasted garlic sauce ten minutes later, Bo allowed herself to wonder who was following her, stalking her, trying to use her grief to erode her sanity. And why? It had to be someone connected to this case, she decided. Someone who knew about her manic depression, about Mildred's death, about her stay at Ghost Flower Lodge. Someone who didn't want her looking too closely at Mort Wagman's history, maybe?

Zach had access to the necessary facts about her, she thought, but he couldn't spend days and nights following her around San Diego playing tapes and leaving dog collars in trees. He had to be at the lodge most of the time. But he could pay somebody else to follow her, Bo thought. The idea was ridiculous. Zach Crooked Owl was incapable of psychological torture. He might be involved with criminals, but his motivation for that was desperate and obvious. This was different. This was sick!

Bo finished her meal certain that her tormentor wasn't Zach, and equally certain that it had to be someone close either to her or to Ghost Flower Lodge. An image of Madge

Aldenhoven lurking around foggy beaches in kid-leather pumps made her smile. Impossible. Madge would be happy to see her foaming at the mouth in some nineteenth-century Bedlam, but scarcely possessed the imagination necessary to create the dog collar scene in UCSD's grove that afternoon.

The thought reminded Bo to call the dogwash again. She'd have Jane or Mindy check out this mysterious package someone had left there before she saw it. If it were something left by the stalker, they could destroy it. And they closed their shop around seven. One of them would be happy to accompany Bo the few blocks to her apartment, just to make sure no further painful symbols were in evidence.

"Mindy," Bo explained from a pay phone in front of the restaurant, "I'm on my way there now, but will you make sure this package you've got for me isn't something awful? See, somebody's stalking me, and . . . "

"Oh, it's nothing awful," Mindy assured her, "but what's this about a stalker? When will you be here?"

"Half an hour," Bo told her, feeling supremely rational. The plan to enlist help was a model of sanity, she thought. An impressive step.

Her friends were scrubbing the dog tubs when she arrived, identical grins on their faces.

"Okay, what's this unknown package?" she grinned back.

"Who said package?" Mindy asked as her partner leaned to lift something from a box behind the counter. Something coppery in the bright overhead lights, with droopy hound ears and a round, pink stomach. Its tail wagged tentatively at the sound of Bo's voice.

"It's Gretel!" Bo gasped. "It's that little girl, Lindsey's puppy. What's she doing here? Where's Lindsey?"

Jane handed the dog to Bo. "Lindsey and her mother brought Gretel in yesterday morning," she said. "There's a letter from the mother for you. Lindsey wants you to adopt the puppy."

"What? No. I don't want another dog. It's too soon. I may

never want another dog. Mildred was my only dog. I'm going to have her ashes buried with mine. This is Lindsey's dog. What happened to Lindsey?"

The little dog stopped licking Bo's face as if she understood what was being said, and struggled to be released.

"See?" Bo nodded at the dog. "She doesn't want me, either. She wants Lindsey. What happened?"

"It's probably all in the letter, but the mother told us everything yesterday," Mindy said, continuing to polish the interior of a tub. "She's leaving her husband. Apparently he hit the little girl, bloodied her nose. The mother said she's been afraid this was coming. He didn't do any serious damage this time, but she's not waiting to see what he does next."

"He's a vicious jerk," Bo agreed. "Mental age of two. Good for Lindsey's mother; she's doing the right thing. But why didn't they take the dog?"

"Mom's taking Lindsey to live in a mobile home the grandparents keep for winter vacations near Phoenix. They're willing to let Lindsey and her mom live there free until mom can get on her feet again financially, but the mobile home park has a no-pets restriction. Lindsey said you understood puppies. She wanted you to have this one."

Bo couldn't help rubbing her nose against the soft fur atop the little dog's head. "Well, I'm honored," she said, "but I just can't handle it. I really can't."

Jane had resumed work on one of the tubs, her back to Bo. "We thought you'd feel that way," she said. "But we didn't want to contact anybody else about adopting her until we heard from you."

"Can you find somebody?" Bo asked, admiring a fat little paw wedged in the crook of her left arm. "Somebody who'll really love her and take proper care of her, I mean."

"Sure," Mindy answered, her voice echoing from within a tub. "We'll start calling some of our customers tomorrow. They're all dog lovers."

"Great," Bo agreed, kissing the little muzzle and placing

the dog carefully back in her box. "She's perfect for a home where there's a child. Uh, would one of you mind walking back to my apartment with me? Somebody's been following me and playing tapes of a terrier barking, and . . . "

"What!" the two women said in unison.

Bo explained the situation in detail, including her lack of clues to the possible identity of her tormentor.

"That's seriously sick!" Mindy said. "Don't worry. We'll go with you. We'll *stay* with you until Andy gets there no matter what time . . . "

"Um," Jane said, suddenly turning back to polish a gleaming tub Bo was sure needed no further attention, "remember we have to be at that Business Association meeting by seven, and then you wanted to take your brother's Jeep up to Oceanside so we don't have to get up at four in the morning."

"Oh, yeah," Mindy replied, her blond curls also again bobbing over white ceramic, her back to Bo. "Well, one of us could go to the meeting while the other one stays with Bo. And we could wait till morning to drop off the Jeep, or just go really late and stay at my brother's house. Except I think he wants to leave before dawn, anyway, so we might as well come back."

Bo felt as though she were listening to the audio of a Keystone Kops routine. A strangely rehearsed quality.

"Look, it's nothing," she said, puzzled. "You've got a meeting and then a two-hour drive. I don't want anybody to stay with me, just check my door in case this cretin's painted my name on it in paw prints. You're going to be busy until dawn. Hey, where's the puppy going to be?"

"That's a problem," Mindy acknowledged.

"I think she'll be all right in the store all night," Jane said, "although she'll be terrified here all alone."

"Is there any chance you could keep her at your place, just for tonight?" Mindy asked. "We'd get her before we open in the morning at seven-thirty."

"Well, I guess so," Bo answered. It was the least she could do for Lindsey. "I have to be at work by eight."

"No problem!" her friends agreed with a bright-eyed enthusiasm Bo found peculiar. For the moment she was just glad they'd both stopped buffing bathtubs that were already immaculately clean when she walked in the door.

"Her toys are in this bag, and I've included a couple of cans of puppy diet and some treats," Jane said, pulling a packed tote bag from under the counter. "By the way, Bo, did I mention how terrific your hair looks short?"

When the four of them arrived at Bo's apartment a few minutes later, there was something taped to the door. Mindy ripped it off with a lean, tanned hand, and stuffed it in the pocket of her bright blue dogwash T-shirt. Bo was still below urging the puppy to attend to personal matters, but heard Jane's muttered, "Oh, shit!"

"What is it?" she called up the apartment stairs.

"Just a calendar picture of some dogs," Mindy answered. "Dalmatians." She didn't mention that the dogs' eyes and tongues had all carefully been painted black.

Chapter 26

The office was dark. Only a red indicator light on the CD system punctuated the soft gloom in which Alexander Morley stretched in his orthopedic chair, listening. The Gregorian chant's melismas, single Latin syllables sustained through ten or more musical notes, hypnotized him. In the repetitive sound his soul could breathe, even as his heart struggled to maintain the rhythm he'd felt in his chest for nearly seventy years.

That rhythm was flagging now. The best doctors money could buy had told him nothing he didn't already know. That it was time to rest, hand over the reins, retire. With a pacemaker he might live for another ten years, they told him, if he were careful. He might live if he avoided every physical and emotional stress that could, and eventually would, reduce his weakened heart to a limp bag of randomly squirming muscle fibers, and then stillness.

Morley understood his heart's condition. Everything was in place for the announcement of his retirement. All that remained was the closure of this Indian deal in California, and Henderson would manage those formalities on Wednesday, only two days in the future.

As the voices of monks rose and fell about him, Alexander Morley listened to his heart and breathed with the ancient music. He'd felt an arrhythmia earlier and carefully placed the correct medication under his tongue. Then he'd stretched out to rest in the darkening office. It was his favorite time now, the quiet hours of early evening when everyone was gone and he could feel the power MedNet commanded. It was a vibration more intellectual than visceral, a cool, deep awareness beneath the chanting, beneath everything.

There were bigger companies than MedNet, but none as perfectly tuned to the most profitable dimensions of human suffering. That was his gift, the ability to exploit hope. He'd molded MedNet from its earlier identity as a hospital management concern into a leader in the field, known for its dynamic marketing strategies and impressive profit margin.

The medical community damned him as a charlatan, but he didn't care. It didn't matter. Because the only dimension of Alexander Morley still pure and innocent enough to care about opinion was hidden safely in a fantasied monastic sanctuary only accessible through the haunting music that now bathed him. He'd cut out his soul and preserved it there, apart. Everything else was business. Everything else was money, and power.

As he relaxed in the darkness he imagined that for this moment the two parts of himself were one. Alexander Morley the successful businessman and Alexander Morley the idealistic boy in medical school were one person, the soul no longer held apart from the man. It would happen in this place, he thought. And it could happen only now, as he prepared to leave MedNet behind him. But strangely, it didn't feel good. It made him sick.

"How could you do this?" his own young voice rang in his head. "You're no doctor, you're nothing but a salesman, a con artist. You've spent your life selling empty medical packaging to people so blinded by anguish that they'd pay for illusion. As a doctor you're a joke. But as a human being you're a fraud!"

Morley felt his heart twitch beneath his sternum. His own

naive young voice had made him ill. He was ill, and there was something wrong in the room. A noise, barely audible under the soaring chants. A door opening, then closing.

There shouldn't be anybody in MedNet's offices now. He'd personally made the arrangement with the cleaning service. None of the crew who cleaned the building at night were to enter MedNet's offices until after eight-thirty, when he would be gone. The intrusion made him angry, but he deliberately calmed himself with deep breaths, used the remote control to diminish the music's volume, and slowly turned his chair toward the door.

What he saw set in motion a sequence of events that his mind tracked and defined even as they were happening. There was someone there. Morley could see the shapes of head, shoulders, arms against the teak double doors leading to Med-Net's reception area. It was someone large, taller than he. Someone covered in cloth, like a sheet. A child's Halloween nightmare.

As it began to move toward him, he felt a tightening of his skin. That was the constriction of blood vessels, he knew, caused by a hormone called epinephrine his adrenal glands released when he experienced fear. The epinephrine was also causing his heart to pound. His adrenal glands couldn't know his heart was weak; there was no way to stop their automatic response to his sense of alarm.

"What are you doing here?" he barked, lowering the chair's footrest and standing. "Get out!"

The strange figure was close now. He could see something in its right hand. A knife. It had to be one of the syndicate goons, he assumed. This sort of cheap nonsense was their style. But why? MedNet had paid them to back off the deal the Indian was trying to grab. Why would they send one of their lackeys to intimidate him?

"You've been paid," he insisted over the rapid thumping in his chest. "This is a mistake."

But the raised knife kept coming.

And then the thumping ceased. In its place was a frenzied squirming sensation that Morley's mind quickly named "ventricular fibrillation." Wildly he pulled open his desk drawer and wrenched the top from a vial of tiny white pills. But the force of his movement sent them scattering like insects across the expensive carpet at his feet.

His heart was no longer pumping blood to any vital organ in his body. Already, he knew, his oxygen-starved brain had begun to shut down, sacrificing the luxury of consciousness to conserve resources for its most primitive segments. The old, reptilian brain segments without the direction of which every organ would stop functioning. A crushing pain had already filled his chest and spilled down his left arm.

Falling to his knees, he groped for the white specks on the floor. But a huge, sandaled foot had covered the only pills within reach, and was grinding them into the carpet. The toenails, Morley noticed with frantic acuity just before darkness swallowed him, were painted.

For several seconds nothing moved in Alexander Morley's office. Then his body shuddered briefly and a strangled, guttural sound came from his throat to join the ancient music in which he'd imagined his soul could hide. Shortly after that the only living thing remaining in the room opened the teak double doors and was gone. In the dark a choir of Spanish monks sang sonorous monophonic chants, over and over.

Bob Thompson had never seen MedNet's offices at night. For that matter, he thought, he'd rarely seen them during the day either. For the last ten years there'd been no reason to go to Phoenix at all, except for the occasional command get-together, since MedNet's board communicated hourly during the business week through an elaborate electronic network. He kept an office in Santa Fe where he lived, and the other board members did the same. But the Phoenix offices were MedNet's hub, the panopticon from which Alexander Morley oversaw the corporation's every move.

Thompson wondered if the old man was up there right now, listening to his church music. Everybody knew about Morley's hobby. Brockman had even given him a cat-o'-nine-tails one year as a birthday present, and Morley had smiled genially at the joke. But he never explained why he sat listening to monks singing in his office, and nobody asked.

The night cleaning crew was in the building. Thompson decided to risk it, go on up and beard the lion in his den. Maybe this would be the right time. Maybe he could actually talk to Alexander Morley.

He'd flown into Phoenix cold with panic. He knew Henderson had already worked a deal with the Japanese for the first franchise on the Ghost Flower model. And the deal was a gold mine. A man named John Takuya had heard about it in Tokyo from a friend whose bank had been approached for a loan to fund the endeavor. And Bob Thompson had sent Takuya's teenaged kids a couple of pairs of highly prized Levi's after Takuya mentioned at a meeting in San Francisco that he hadn't had time to get out and buy them. When he called to thank Bob Thompson for the gesture, he also congratulated Thompson on the MedNet deal. That was when Bob Thompson knew what Alexander Morley was doing to him. Two hours later he caught a plane to Phoenix.

The security guard at the lobby desk checked him against a roster of MedNet personnel, and then told him to take the service elevator to the twelfth-floor suite. Morley was still up there, the guard told Thompson. Later than usual.

When the elevator door opened to admit him, one of the cleaning staff brushed past him holding a bundle of sheets. Thompson noticed her because she was almost as tall as he, even in the flat sandals that showed off her painted toenails to dramatic advantage against smooth skin the color of bittersweet chocolate. No longer in her prime, the woman still carried herself with a sardonic worldliness he recognized. She'd been a hooker when she was young, he was sure. And even pushing sixty, as he was sure she was, she had a style, an attraction.

As he hit twelve on the panel of floor indicator buttons, Bob Thompson grinned and shook his head. Morley was throwing him in the toilet, he was being replaced in the job he'd given the best years of his life, and he still couldn't stop looking at loose ladies. Even loose *cleaning* ladies who hadn't seen twenty since he'd learned to love them at fifteen. He guessed it was just the way he was.

From MedNet's reception area he could hear the old man's music howling through the doors of his office. It was creepy, Thompson thought, like something from another world. The reception area lights were left on until the cleaning crew finished, but only darkness was visible beneath Morley's doors. Thompson knocked on them, waited, and knocked again. Then he opened them.

"Alex?" he said in the gloom. "I need to talk to you."

In the wedge of light falling through the open doors nothing answered except the sound of voices chanting in a language he couldn't understand. Then he saw the old man on the floor.

"Oh, my God!" he exhaled, kneeling to touch a hand that had been clawing for something on the carpet. The hand was cool. And the wrist had no pulse.

From the receptionist's desk he called 911 and then security. But there was nothing, he knew, that anyone could do for Alexander Morley now. He hoped the old man had gone to whatever his music meant to him. And he hoped there would be enough time to decipher Morley's files and get to San Diego before it was too late. Before a man named Henderson stole his future.

Chapter 27

Bo put a bowl of fresh water on the kitchen floor and watched as the puppy's pink tongue sent splashes flying in every direction. Had Mildred been this messy as a pup? Bo found the memory missing, obscured by other long-ago events. The fights with Mark. The divorce. The crushing sense of failure that was worse than everything else. And then her sister, Laurie's, suicide. Mildred had been with Bo through it all, a stalwart presence. But her puppy days were lost in the kaleidoscoping human drama that was Bo's past.

"You're making a mess," Bo told the little dachshund, "and now your ears are all wet." The dog merely shook her head and then began a series of bounding dashes through the apartment, stopping abruptly to sniff at the leg of Bo's easel, a stack of magazines under the TV, the bedroom carpet where Mildred's basket had been.

"There was a fox terrier there," Bo explained, scooping the dog into her arms. "She was my best friend. Let me show you her picture." In her tiny dining room studio Bo pointed to the painting of Mildred still on the easel. "See?" she said. "That's what she looked like." The puppy seemed to contemplate the painting briefly and then licked Bo's cheek.

"Thank you," Bo said. "I'm glad you understand because . . . "

"Bo?"

It was Andrew waving through the front window. Bo set the dog down and opened her apartment door to a smiling pediatrician holding a sheaf of white daisies and a beribboned wine bottle. He was wearing jeans, a chamois shirt, and a new Portuguese fisherman's hat and looked, Bo thought, quite dashing.

"The wine's for after I show you what I found today," he said, kissing her. "Aagghh! Something's eating my ankle!"

"I think she's just sniffing it." Bo grinned as she took the flowers to the sink and then reached under it for a vase. "I'm just keeping her tonight. It's a favor to Jane and Mindy at the dogwash."

Andrew LaMarche was already on his stomach on the floor, making uncharacteristic noises at the puppy dancing around his head. "What's her name?" he asked.

Bo was pouring 7-Up into the vase. "Gretel. The little girl who owned her called her Gretel."

"She doesn't look like a Gretel," Andrew observed thoughtfully. "Bo, why are you putting the flowers in 7-Up?"

"It's half water, half 7-Up. I read somewhere that lemon-lime soda pop makes flowers last longer. And you're right, she really doesn't look like a Gretel."

"We should think of a more suitable name," he said, rolling onto his back with the puppy in his arms. "How about Daphne?"

"Daphne Dachshund?" Bo answered, making a face. "Sounds like Daffy Duck. And we can't give her a new name because I'm just keeping her for the night. So what's this surprise you've found?"

"Oh. Well, it's a shame. She's really cute. And the surprise," he said, standing, "is a surprise. I'm going to take you to see it."

Waves of enthusiasm seemed to cascade from him, making invisible patterns in the room. A sense of change, things going forward headlong and sparkling as if propelled by light. The sensation made Bo dizzy. "Okay," she said. "Just let me change clothes. Can I go look at this thing in sweats?"

"Sweats are fine. And we'll take Daphne."

"Her name isn't Daphne!" Bo yelled from her bedroom closet, which suddenly felt safe and familiar. A snug, shadowy haven. For a moment she considered just closing the door and staying there. But of course that would be insane. Grinning, she buried her face in the sleeves of her own blouses hanging in the dark. "I'm just tired," she told them. "And I have this sense that the world's shifting." Then she pulled on her favorite gray sweatshirt with its hood and deep pockets, found the matching pants, and emerged. Next, socks.

"In Dublin's fair city, where the girls are so pretty," she sang in her grandmother's brogue while scrounging through a dresser drawer, "I first set my eyes on sweet Molly Malone. As she wheeled her wheelbarrow through streets broad and narrow, singing cockles and mussels, alive, alive-o." There were no socks that matched.

"What's that song?" Andrew asked from the bedroom door.

"Just an Irish song about Molly Malone. She was a fishmonger. My grandmother used to sing it. And I'm not wearing socks."

"I gave up socks when I fell in love with you," he said solemnly. Then he began the song again an octave lower than Bo had sung it. Joining him, Bo noticed that their voices blended nicely before drifting out the deck doors and vanishing over the sea. After a few practice verses, he felt for the alto part, found it, and belted out the chorus with a spirit that her grandmother, Bo thought, would have applauded. From the floor near Bo's remaining tennis shoe another voice joined them in a small but heartfelt howl. The puppy, her still-stubby hound nose aimed at the ceiling, was singing. There was no denying the message.

"You're Molly Malone!" Bo cried, dropping to her knees. "That's who you are." The puppy scrambled into Bo's arms, her little tail wagging furiously. Bo felt common sense, the entire world of order, crack and slide away like pond ice in the spring. "And it's way too soon for another dog," she went on, "but since you can't be with Lindsey, you belong here, with us. I'm not letting them take you back, Molly. You're staying!"

Bo was sure she was crying, although it was hard to tell with Molly licking her face and Andrew wrapping her in chamois.

"You said 'us,' Bo," he whispered as they all sat on the floor. "You told Molly she belonged with us. That must mean there *is* an us. Oh, Bo, I'm going to get that dog her own portfolio of growth stocks and a lifetime supply of T bones!"

"She'll take the stocks," Bo sniffled. "And there's been an us all along, Andy." No way to retrieve anything resembling structure now, she thought. Amazing how it's never there when you need it. "It's just that you scare me with these constant demands for something I don't want," she went on, feeling herself on a mental ski slope. "I don't want to be married, Andy. For a lot of reasons that's an identity that just isn't me. And every time you . . . "

"I know," he said, taking her hand and leaning his head backward to rest against her bed. "I've been thinking about it, about how I'd feel if the situation were reversed." He turned to face her, his gray eyes twinkling. "And I'd hate it. I'd feel that you weren't listening to me, that you didn't even know me, that you were trying to force me to be somebody else."

Bo retrieved her shoelaces from Molly's needlelike teeth and tied her shoe. The laces were wet. "You're close," she told Andrew, "but there's one thing you can't even imagine."

"What?"

Okay, Bradley, finish it. Fling yourself into thin air and just hope you don't crash and burn.

"You can't imagine what it's like to live inside my brain," she explained. "It's different, Andy. I don't just mean the obvious manic-depressive symptoms. Even when I'm fine, I'm *different.* When I was young I wanted to be like everybody else, watched people constantly so I could learn to be like them. And every time I overreacted or did something that made them shut down and turn away, I was ashamed. It was like this black wave with a bilious, purple crest sweeping over me. But I don't feel that way anymore. I really *like* being different, being completely who I am. But it's fragile, and it's something I've come to terms with on my own, alone. Now you want to rearrange that identity, and you can't, Andy. Only I can change what I am, and I don't want to. But that doesn't mean what I am doesn't want you. I do."

"I do, too," he said softly. "Just the way you are. No more demands for towels monogrammed 'Mr. and Mrs.,' I promise. My parents had towels monogrammed 'Mr. and Mrs.' They were miserable together. Hey, is it too late for me to show you my big surprise?"

Bo felt something like ground rising beneath her fall. Molly, curled like a fur donut on her stomach, had fallen asleep. "I'm pretty tired, but I'll last for another hour or so," she answered quite calmly, she thought, under the circumstances, "but what about our pup?"

"Here." Scooping Molly gently in one hand, he tucked her in the big patch pocket on the right side of his shirt and held her there as they walked to his car. During the drive she stretched her head and front paws out to rest on his shoulder. Observing this, Bo stifled a bizarre impulse to tell him she'd changed her mind and would marry him now, tonight.

"You're beautiful," she said instead, and then settled in to wonder why everything chose to happen at the same time. He was driving up the coast on I-5 toward Del Mar, the tiny, pricey beach community where he owned a condo. Bo assumed the surprise would be there. Maybe a painting he'd bought in Germany, she thought. It would be something like that. But he passed the expected street and continued along the darkened beach road where Torrey pines bent over surf gilded silver in moonlight.

"Well, here it is," he finally said after turning off the village's main street and making several turns in the residential area leading to the beach. He had stopped in a cul-de-sac with a sagging chain link fence at its end. Beyond the fence was a bristling field of dry grass sloping to the Amtrak tracks and then the beach. In the amber streetlight Bo could see a ranch-style bungalow with blue shingles, white shutters, and white window boxes trailing pink Martha Washington geraniums into the night. The bungalow was on the left. On the right was a looming shadow in a yard overgrown with weeds.

"Here what is?" Bo said.

"The house I'm going to buy."

Bo squinted into the darkness. "Ah," she said. "For the harpsichord. Which one?"

He pointed, as she had known he would, to the right. "Wait till you see it!" he began, handing Molly to her and digging a flashlight from the Jaguar's glove box. "Come on. I've got the key."

Bo found the prospect less than appealing. "Andy." She smiled dramatically. "I've been out of a psych rehab program, near which my friend was incidentally murdered, for less than a week, and somebody's chasing me around in the fog trying to scare me back in. The only relative I can find for my friend's son is a grandmother whose career sounds like a science-fiction thriller of dubious taste, and I've just made a serious commitment I'm not ready for to a new dog, not to mention you. Now you want me to prowl around what looks like the Bates Motel in the dark with only a flashlight that's sure to go dead the second we hear the creaking door slam shut, followed by low, malevolent laughter. Let me sum it up this way: hell will freeze before I leave this car."

"Oh," he said, jaundiced by the streetlight. "Well, of course. We'll come back tomorrow and see it in daylight. I didn't realize it would look this disreputable at night. I quite agree with you, Bo. This is ill-advised." Masterfully contained disappointment throbbed in every word.

In Bo's lap Molly circled restlessly, then clambered to the floor. "I think she needs to go out," Bo sighed. "And I didn't bring her harness and leash."

Andrew quickly unbuckled his belt, pulled it from his jeans, and leaned to loop it over the dog's head. "Emergency collar," he said. "I just had the car detailed, including the carpets. Be right back." In seconds he was following the little dog onto a path through the weeds, leaning to hold the end of his belt.

"Hell just froze," Bo told the Jaguar's black floor mats, and climbed out into the dark. "Wait for me!" she called, feeling like the heroine of a bodice-ripper. The incredibly stupid heroine who, in hoop skirt and thirty crinolines, dashes after the hero into thickets of briar and poison ivy because the swash of his buckle increases her heart rate.

"Success!" Andrew called happily from beneath a large Torrey pine. Molly, flinging pine needles behind her with abandon, wagged expectantly as Bo approached.

"Good girl," Bo told her. "Good dog. Now can we get out of here before the guy with the prosthetic hook shows up?"

"Of course," Andrew said, not moving.

Away from the obscuring glare of the streetlight the house was more visible, less ominous. A two-story mock Tudor, someone had nonetheless wrapped a wide porch around the three sides from which ocean views were possible through the pines. Bo couldn't help envisioning a rope hammock slung in one corner. Lemonade set out on a wicker table. Adirondack chairs on the lawn.

"Oh, Andy," she said admiringly, "that porch reminds me of my family's summer place on Cape Cod."

"It reminded me of the Garden District in New Orleans where I grew up," he nodded. "And look at this." Strolling casually through pine needles toward a driveway on the house's north side, he pointed to a detached two-car garage, also mock Tudor. "A previous owner converted the garage loft to a small apartment for the rental income. A granny flat, they call them here. I'm going to install a skylight," he said, inhaling the salty, pine-scented air as if he'd just arrived from the Sahara and didn't live two miles down the same coast, "in case an artist friend of mine would care to rent the apartment as a studio."

The word "bribe" formed itself nastily in the back of Bo's throat and sat there, while a warring part of her brain said, "Must you translate everything he offers you into a threat? Relax."

"Of course the renovations will take months," Andrew went on, ignoring her unease, "and whether you decide you'd like to live with me here, or live in the apartment, or use the apartment as a studio from time to time, or none of the above, I hope you'll at least agree to help me with decisions about fixing the place up. I'm not very good at that sort of thing, and you are. No strings, Bo." He was all business, a veritable model of detachment.

No strings, he said. Bo looked at Molly sniffing warily at a hole in the ground, Andrew proud and nervous about a major decision, the soft lights of nearby houses in which people were linked, wrapped, woven, and tied to each other and to still other people in a huge web that could either support or strangle any individual at any time. There were strings. There was no escaping strings. The trick, Bo thought, was to pick the right ones and cut away the rest.

"I love your porch, Andy," she sighed. "And I love you. But I can't cope with this right now. Too much is happening; I'm overwhelmed. I just want to take Molly and go home."

"Of course," he said, pointing the flashlight toward the weed-lined path. "After you."

At her apartment there was nothing taped to the door, no barks on the answering machine. Molly settled into her box after dragging one of Bo's dirty sweatshirts from the closet floor and stamping around on it in a circle. Bo allowed the puppy to have the sweatshirt in the box, thinking of Mort Wagman as the dog circled again and then curled up to sleep.

Ancestral dogs had circled to flatten nests in tall grass, Mort said. Bo imagined prehistoric, saber-toothed dachshunds with woolly coats, circling in prehistoric grass.

"Bo?" Andrew inquired from the bed where he was unaccountably reading the *Sunset* guide to container gardening Bo had bought when the idea of a small farm on the deck seemed appealing. "Why are you giggling?"

"There were no ancient dachshunds," she said, falling into bed beside him.

"The name is German for badger hound, but I think they were originally bred in France from basset hounds and terriers," he nodded, "although they may have descended from the medieval spit dog, which is said to have originated in ancient Egypt. There's a long, low-slung dog on the statue of an Egyptian king. The dog's name is inscribed as Tekal, and in Germany Teckel is the affectionate name for dachshunds. So it may be that there were ancient dachshunds, you see."

"Andy," Bo sighed, snuggling against him, "why do you know *everything?*"

"I don't know," he answered happily, turning off the light and kissing her with an expertise he hadn't, she was sure, learned from a book.

Chapter 28

In the morning Andrew found a manila folder wedged into Bo's apartment door on his way to get the paper. "I'm going to kill this bastard if I ever get my hands on him!" he muttered, crumpling the entire folder in his fist. "I'll dump whatever this is in the trash downstairs. I don't want you to——"

"Andy," Bo said from the kitchen, "isn't there some rule about doctors not murdering people? And don't throw it away yet. Let me see it first."

"Why?"

"Because it's probably something I was expecting. Let me see it."

"It's from the police," he said after tearing the top from the crumpled folder.

"Andy!"

"Well, here. But why would the police . . . ?"

Bo ran both hands through her short curls and sighed. "I have a job that involves working with the police," she reminded him. "And this report may shed some light on what's happening to Ghost Flower. Could you take Molly down while I make the coffee? Here's a paper towel and a baggie."

"I'm not sure I can handle this," he groaned, fastening the yellow harness around the gamboling puppy.

"For crying out loud, Andy, you're a pediatrician. Don't you ever change diapers?"

"No," he answered without, Bo thought, any real grasp of the issue. "The nurses do that."

Reality check, Bradley. He may be wonderful, but he's still a man. They assume all women were born with a natural affinity for bodily wastes.

"Then it's time you had a lesson." She beamed. "Here's the bag."

After a quick shower Bo toweled her hair and decided she should have cut it years ago. Short, it dried by itself and saved her stretches of morning time better suited to facing a life that at the moment seemed about as orderly as a buffalo stampede.

"Bo," a feminine voice called through the door, "it's Jane. I came by just in case you hadn't changed your mind, but I saw Andy downstairs, and . . . "

Bo opened the door. "You knew I'd never make it through the night," she said accusingly. "Would you like some coffee?"

"Only a heart of anthracite could resist that puppy," Jane agreed, her green eyes betraying not a shred of guilt. "So we sort of set you up. She's perfect for you, Bo. Your hair even matches her fur. And thanks for the offer, but I've got to open the shop. See ya!"

"Aliens are controlling my life," Bo told Mildred's picture. "But she's a sweet dog, Mil. And I know you wouldn't want me to be alone." It was true, Bo thought, and then wondered if she'd ever be alone again at all. A ring from the phone seemed to suggest that she wouldn't. Nobody called at seven in the morning, ever. Except maybe the creep with the tape.

"Look, you pathetic jackal," Bo yelled into the phone, "I've about had it with your sick jokes. Who are you, anyway?"

"This is the child abuse hotline," a puzzled male voice answered. "Is this Bo Bradley?"

"Uh, yeah. I thought you were somebody else. What's wrong?"

"A Dr. Keith has been calling since six, says she can't wait for the switchboard to open at eight. She wants you to call her at her hotel immediately. Here's the number."

Bo copied the number secure in the knowledge that her reputation at work for eccentricity had just taken a quantum leap. And she wasn't even crazy. Out of courtesy she pretended not to hear the hotline worker's whispered, "Jeez!" as he hung up. Then with studied calm she carried her coffee into the bathroom, took the cap off a vial of pink pills, and swallowed one. Valproate, marketed under the name Depakote. A common acid that would curb her brain's propensity to grab random stimuli from everywhere. Unfortunately, the pills couldn't do anything to curb the morning's real-life activities.

"I must see you at once," Ann Lee Keith insisted when Bo called. "It's terribly urgent. I believe the people responsible for my son's murder may also try to hurt Charles. I flew into San Diego last night. I really must see you now."

Bo remembered an earlier case, another little boy almost assassinated in the same hospital where Bird was probably eating his breakfast while she talked to his grandmother. It could happen. It had.

"I'll make sure precautions are established to protect Bird, er . . . Charles," she said. "And I'll be happy to meet you at my office as soon as I can get there."

"This will sound rather strange," Dr. Keith went on, "but what I have to tell you will take some time, and I have dogs with me. Is there a park or other outdoor area where we could meet?"

"Dogs?"

"I told you it would sound strange."

"You were right," Bo agreed. There was something about the woman's voice she liked. And the attitude. Straightforward and self-effacing at the same time. Also openly eccentric. And she was Mort Wagman's mom.

"There's a beach for dogs here," Bo told her, giving directions. "I'll meet you there in half an hour."

Madge would not approve of professional meetings on dog beaches, Bo knew. Madge would erupt in a frenzy of decorum and recite things about the dignity of social work.

"This is Bo Bradley," Bo told a tape recorder in the CPS message center. "Please tell Madge Aldenhoven I'm meeting the grandmother in the Wagman case for an emergency conference this morning. It should take about two hours. I'll be in after that."

In a second call she told the security officer at St. Mary's Hospital her name and CPS ID number, and requested a confidential hold on Bird Wagman. In the event that someone phoned or came to the hospital asking about him, neither the switchboard nor the reception desk would give out his room number or even acknowledge that he was there. It wasn't enough, she worried, but she could scarcely request an armed guard on the basis of one sentence from a woman she hadn't yet interviewed.

Then she dressed in a pair of khaki shorts, sandals, and a baggy white T-shirt. Very professional. When Andrew returned with Molly and the paper, he said, "Aren't you going to work?"

"I'm meeting Mort's mother at Dog Beach in twenty minutes," Bo sighed. "And I have to read this police report before I go."

"I won't ask why you're meeting her there," he said, puzzled.

"I'll tell you when I know why myself. Meanwhile, Andy, I've got to read this report. And thanks for taking Molly down."

"We managed very well," he said airily, carrying his coffee and paper out to the deck.

Hopper Mead, the San Diego Police Department concluded in its report, died by "misadventure" when a shark tore off her right leg as she swam in seventy-five feet of water near her anchored yacht off San Diego's landmark peninsula, Point Loma. Because of the deceased's high profile in the community and the possibility of a wrongful death stemming from attempted financial fraud, an exhaustive investigation was conducted, and was still officially open.

"MEAD was the daughter of MR. and MRS. RANDOLPH MEAD, SR.," the report told Bo in traditional police style, "and heiress to a substantial fortune shared with her brother, RANDOLPH MEAD, JR., 28. Both parents are deceased. MEAD JR. heads a local conservative think tank, Mead Policy Institute. MEAD JR. denies any connection to his sister's death, saying that he was in his offices at the time of the shark attack. An employee of Mead Institute, ANSELM TUCKER, a clerk, confirms this. Further, a review of bank and investment records for HOPPER MEAD and RANDOLPH MEAD, JR. (permission given by MEAD JR.) reveals no financial motive for MEAD JR. to seek profit from his sister's death. Both were bequeathed substantial estates by MEAD SR., and the entirety of HOPPER MEAD's estate went at her death to the corporation founded by MEAD SR., MedNet, with corporate headquarters in Phoenix, Arizona.

"The executive board of MedNet includes the following: ALEXANDER MORLEY, Chairman; ELLIOT KINES, NEAL BROCKMAN, and ROBERT THOMPSON, members. Shortly before MEAD's death MedNet sustained a punitive judgment for medical fraud in the amount of four hundred and fifty million dollars. Nonetheless, a thorough investigation revealed no connection between anyone associated with MedNet and HOPPER MEAD at any time."

Here someone had penciled in, "And we thought we could prove these guys *hired* the shark."

"Cute," Bo said to the sheaf of paper in her hands, and read on.

The report continued, documenting every interrogation conducted in relation to Hopper Mead's untimely death. Many of these were phoned interviews with the young

woman's friends. And several of her friends mentioned that
Mead had been seeing someone, "a serious boyfriend" at the
time of her death.

"Hop was pretty secretive about him," a friend named
Miko Mulryan told San Diego police, "keeping him under
wraps, I guess. I think he's somebody in TV or the movies.
Hop was always running up the coast to L.A. on weekends to
see him."

Several of Mead's friends expressed concern and puzzlement
at the "boyfriend's" failure to appear at her funeral services.
Some suggested that Mead might have terminated the relationship, since in the month prior to her death she had been
in San Diego every weekend, attending various social func-
tions alone. Police had followed every lead, the report stated,
but so far had not located the young man with whom Mead
had been involved.

An appendix to the report was a document in Spanish typed
on Escuela Ciencias Marinas letterhead with an Ensenada, Baja
California, Mexico, address, signed by José Méndez. A hand-
printed explanation in English was provided at the bottom of
the last page.

"MENDEZ is a graduate student in marine biology who
aspires to become a medical examiner," it said. "He was sent
by a professor, DR. HECTOR ORTIZ, to dissect a shark
cadaver washed up on a beach north of Ensenada. MENDEZ
discovered human bones in the shark's stomach, these later
proving to be the femur, tibia, fibula, and os calcis, or heel
bone, of the deceased, HOPPER MEAD. MENDEZ noted a
gouge in the shaft of the femur which he believes could not
have been made by the shark. MENDEZ holds the opinion
that this gouge in the bone may indicate that MEAD sustained a deep laceration to the lower groin area prior to the
shark attack. Such a laceration, MENDEZ states, would have
severed the femoral artery. Examinations of the bone by
SDPD forensic specialists have produced conflicting results.
One specialist concurs with MENDEZ, while the second

believes the gouge could have been made by a shark tooth during the attack. These forensic reports are on file, and the femur has been retained as evidence by the SDPD, with permission of next-of-kin RANDOLPH MEAD, JR., who will see that it is interred with the remains when released."

"My God, they kept her thighbone!" Bo muttered as Andrew came in from the deck, folding the newspaper.

"Take a look at this," he said, handing her the financial pages. "Didn't you tell me MedNet was taking over the Ghost Flower program? Looks like the chair of its board just died."

Bo glanced at a professional photo of an older man in a business suit whose fierce scowl reminded her of her fifth-grade teacher, a nun named Sister Timothy whose habit always smelled like burnt toast. "MedNet Chair Alexander Morley Succumbs to Heart Attack," said the column head.

"He died of natural causes," Bo noted without conviction.

"Apparently he was about to retire. MedNet's PR man, Robert Thompson, says in the article that Morley was going to make the announcement just as soon as MedNet finalized arrangements to franchise 'an innovative new approach to psychiatric care based on Native American traditions.' Thompson then drops the fact that foreign franchises are already being negotiated. MedNet's stock will climb a few points after this; count on it."

"I know a county clerk who'll be thrilled," Bo replied. "Come on, Molly, we've got an appointment at the beach."

Bo would have recognized Ann Lee Keith even if she hadn't been ushering three Jack Russell terriers from a rental car in the Dog Beach parking lot. Her ebony hair, artfully streaked with silver, would have been identical to Mort's when she was younger. And she had the same full lips, carefully outlined in lip pencil and filled in with a slightly lighter shade of lipstick. In a crisp red linen blazer over tan slacks and a blouse, she looked like the social director on a cruise ship. But there were deep lines in her face, Bo noticed. And even dark glasses couldn't hide the purplish circles under her eyes. Ann Lee Keith, Bo acknowledged, was grieving the death of her son.

"I'm Bo Bradley, and I want you to know how sorry I am about your loss," Bo said, extending one hand as the other held Molly's straining leash as the dogs performed their investigatory sniffing ritual. "I know this is a terrible time for you."

The hand that clasped Bo's was cool and firm. "Thank you," Ann Keith answered. "The only thing that has kept me going since Adam's attorney called to tell me that my son was dead is that Charles is still alive. I still have a grandson. You can't imagine how important that is to me, and how frightened I am. Please, shall we sit down somewhere and talk?"

Bo looked at the postcard expanse of Dog Beach under a cloudless blue sky, waves breaking against the stone jetty extending toward a bobbing white buoy, a young couple watching two golden retrievers chase sandpipers, and wondered how Mort Wagman could be dead and his mother standing here holding three terriers on matching red leashes. The two realities were mutually exclusive, she thought. A clean, morning beach. A frightened, grieving woman. With dogs.

"Let's go over there." She pointed to the beach boundary where the San Diego River emptied into the sea. "We can sit in the sand and the dogs can run free."

Molly, attempting to keep up with the Jack Russells, fell squarely on her nose twice before Bo picked her up and carried her across the expanse of sand. "My dog, my fox terrier, died just over a month ago," Bo said as they struggled through the soft sand. "And somebody's been using that fact to harass me, playing tapes of a barking terrier on my answering machine among other things. Are you that person?"

Ann Keith's face paled visibly. "How clever of you to disarm me with polite offers of sympathy before leveling accusations of demented cruelty. I have no idea what you're talking about, nor any idea why you'd assume I would do such a thing. Please tell me where my grandson is and we can terminate this interview right now!"

She had stopped cold in the sand and removed her dark glasses to glare at Bo from Mort Wagman's deep blue eyes. The effect was unnerving, but Bo ignored it to search the woman's face for telltale signs of subterfuge, evasion, malice. The signs were absent.

"I apologize," Bo said. "Last week I followed Zachary Crooked Owl and another man to your home in St. Louis and saw the dogs. That's when it occurred to me that you might have something to do with these things somebody's doing to me. I'm sure they're connected in some way to Ghost Flower's problems and Mort's death, but I don't know how. There may be a connection to MedNet, and to the shark attack on Hopper Mead. But right now I don't know anything, and confronting you with that was a way to eliminate one variable, quickly."

Ann Lee Keith's head was tilted to one side in, Bo thought, a terrierlike attitude of puzzlement. "You followed someone named Crooked Owl to my home?" she repeated. "A shark attack? And who is Mort? Nothing you have said to me since we left the parking lot has made any sense whatever. And I still know nothing about my grandson."

"Let's just sit down," Bo said, throwing a piece of driftwood for the Jack Russells. "Some of what I have to say may be upsetting. But first let me tell you that Charles, whom I know as Bird, is fine. I may be able to arrange for you to see him after we talk. But first I need to know why Mort deliberately severed his ties with you."

"*Who* is Mort?" Ann Keith asked again, sitting cross-legged in the sand and shaking her head. "You keep saying that name."

Bo sat Molly between herself and the other woman and found a stick for the puppy to chew on. "I knew your son, Adam, as Mort Wagman," she began. "We were in a psych rehab facility together, Ghost Flower Lodge. Mort's lawyer may not have explained all of this to you when he called to tell you what had happened. It's run by the Neji Band of Kumeyaay Indians in the desert about an hour from here. Mort, er, Adam and I became friends, Dr. Keith. He was kind to me even while he was sick. I thought of him as a brother, sort of. I'm doing my best to look out for his son."

"Oh, God, Mort Wagman, of course." Ann Keith bit her lip and tried to control the tears spilling from beneath her sunglasses. "That's exactly what he'd call himself. I just can't believe he's gone, Bo. Mort Wagman. God, of course."

"He was kind," Bo said quietly, taking the other woman's hand. "He was smart and funny and successful, too. But what I'll never forget is that he was kind to me."

"Thank you, Bo. And please call me Ann. I want to hear everything you can tell me about my son."

"He had schizophrenia," Bo began.

"I know that. What I don't know is everything that's happened to him in the last two and a half years. I hired detectives, everything. They couldn't locate him. I was afraid he was dead and Charles lost somewhere with strangers."

Bo explained Mort's career as she watched the Jack Russells running toward a seagull. They looked like white birds in formation, their movements perfectly synchronized against the background of water. Molly scampered to join them and they slowed to play with her briefly before she turned and ran back to Bo.

"He went off his meds to do a *commercial?*" Ann Keith said in disbelief.

"Yeah, for a lot of money. And your detectives couldn't have tried very hard to find him, Ann. He did stand-up comedy in clubs; he was on TV, for crying out loud. How could they miss him?"

Sighing, Ann Keith took off her shoes and poured sand through her fingers onto her feet. "Because I told them to look in the wrong places," she said. "I told them to look in flophouses and SROs, state mental hospitals, filthy board-

and-cares, even jails. I have a description of every unidentified young white male corpse buried in every potter's field in this country in the last two years," she went on, arching her head backward, eyes tightly shut. "There are hundreds, Bo. And so many of them are just labeled 'John Doe, known to be mentally ill, no address.' With every report I'd rejoice that it wasn't Adam, and then I'd remember that it was *somebody,* and that there was another mother somewhere, or father, brother, or sister . . . "

"It must have been hell for you," Bo acknowledged. "I don't understand why Mort, why Adam put you through that."

"When he left with Charles he wrote me a long letter explaining that he had to be on his own, free of my control. He told me not to worry, that he'd be in touch again when he'd made a life for himself, when he felt like a man. I got one postcard over a year ago, from New York City. He said he and Charles were fine and he was 'almost there.' Then nothing until about three months ago."

"And?"

"It was a letter, with a Las Vegas postmark. He said he was working, that he had plenty of money. He said he was ready to come home again, for a visit. He said," she paused to inhale deeply, "that he would be bringing a young woman to meet me, that they were talking about marriage. Then I heard nothing until a stranger phoned in the middle of the night saying that Adam was dead and if I didn't withdraw my support for . . . he said 'this Indian deal' . . . I'd never see Charles again. Later Adam's attorney in Los Angeles called about . . . about the burial. I arranged to have Adam's body flown to St. Louis and buried next to his father. Then somebody left a note in my mailbox . . . "

Bo frowned. "That was Zach. I was there, Ann. I saw them leave that note."

"Then you can help put this Zach in jail."

Bo wiped sand from Molly's nose with her shirttail. "What's your connection to MedNet?" she asked.

In the silence that followed, the Jack Russells careened in an arc against the edge of the sea and then ran like small white deer to fling themselves beside Ann Lee Keith on the sand.

"It's a long story," she answered over the sound of panting, "involving a man named Alexander Morley."

"Morley died last night of a heart attack in Phoenix."

"Good." The older woman smiled bleakly. "On my next vacation I'll take a trip to dance on his grave."

"And the story?"

"May shock you," Keith said softly.

Chapter 29

Bo squinted at the sun, which seemed to be creating elongated bubbles in the stratosphere. She could see them at the edge of her field of vision, pulsing in and out of visibility. An optical illusion, of course. It meant she needed to get out of the glare.

"I'm not easily shocked," she told Ann Keith, "but I am, among other things, manic-depressive, and the sun is beginning to do weird things with the air. Usually it's still cloudy at this time of the morning. My apartment is only a few blocks from here. Would you mind if we . . . ?"

"Of course," Ann Keith said, standing immediately and clipping the terriers to their red leashes. "Light sensitivity seems to be shaping up as a cornerstone of manic-depressive illness, doesn't it? It's even been documented in children of manic-depressive parents and may actually be a causal factor in the etiology of the illness."

"You seem to know a lot about this," Bo said, carrying Molly with one hand wrapped under the round, pink stomach. The puppy made paddling motions with her paws.

"I'm a neurophysiologist . . . or was."

"Was?"

"What I am now is merely a teacher of neurophysiology. I'll

tell you the whole story. It's surprising that Adam didn't tell you himself."

"Neither of us was in great shape when we first met," Bo said. "I'm afraid he wasn't making a lot of sense and I wasn't listening, anyway."

"No wonder you got along so well," Ann Keith laughed.

It was a rich, husky laugh that sounded, Bo thought, like wooden poker chips poured onto a felt table. Her father had a box of wooden poker chips, red, white, and blue. She could almost see the colored discs drifting in the air beside an empty lifeguard tower on the beach to her right. It was definitely time to get out of the sun.

"Your home feels comfortable; I like it," Keith said after they were settled in Bo's living room. Molly had gone to her box for a nap, and the Jack Russells were positioned like Victorian statuary at the feet of their mistress.

"So tell me," Bo said, breathing mist from the iced Coke in her hand.

"Adam was always a strange child," Keith began without preamble, carefully placing her iced tea on one of the raffia coasters Bo had found at a garage sale for a nickel apiece. "He never outgrew his night terrors, had learning problems that defied diagnosis, but also occasional bursts of talent and brilliance, especially where words, word games, poetry, drama, that sort of thing were involved. Adam never knew his father, my husband, Duncan. Dunk was killed in the crash of a private plane when Adam was a year and a half old.

"When Adam was three he began to memorize cigarette commercials on television. Then it was a fascination with the names of plants, which he'd invariably recite in three syllables. 'Oak' was 'the oak tree,' 'tulip' was 'to a lip,' etc. Nothing clinical, you understand, just strange. Accompanying this was a complete inability to comprehend parts of a whole, fractions. To the moment of his death I imagine that Adam still thought one fourth plus one fourth equaled two eighths. So by his sophomore year in high school he was in remedial math classes while making A's in English and, particularly, in French. He was nearly obsessed with French, listened to French popular music, subscribed to *Paris Match*."

Here she stopped to watch for some reaction from Bo. When there was none, she said, "Do you know what *mort* means in French?"

"Um, dead," Bo answered. "But that doesn't necessarily mean he named himself 'dead.' He may have chosen 'Mort' because of Mort Sahl, the famous stand-up comic. Maybe Sahl was his inspiration."

"Please let me finish, Bo," Ann Keith said, stroking one of the terriers with a trembling hand. "Adam's schizophrenia hit during the summer after his sophomore year. It hit suddenly, it hit hard, and it never let up. He was only sixteen. By the time he was eighteen he'd been hospitalized over thirty times, nearly starved to death in the streets once before the police found him, had to have two toes amputated after they froze. Every medication available at the time was tried, nothing worked. On his eighteenth birthday Adam told me he didn't want to live if there was no hope he'd ever get well. He was barely shaving, just a skinny, terrified boy. A month later he tried to kill himself."

Bo was silent, felt her apartment walls detach from the ordinary world and become nothing but a space in which she and Ann Lee Keith already knew a reality too painful to define for those on the outside. Her sister, Laurie, Bo remembered with love, had been a slender youngster of twenty when her acute depression left her no option but death.

"There were subsequent attempts," Keith continued, her head bowed, "each more serious than the last. Adam was missing for weeks at a time, living in the streets. Late in that year he brought a girl to the house. He said the girl was pregnant, and that it was his child."

"Bird's mother," Bo interjected. "Who is she? Where is she now?"

"She called herself Frito," Ann Keith sighed. "I arranged

for her to enter a church-sponsored residential program for pregnant teenagers. She told the staff there that her name was Cyndi Lauper, but of course that's just the name of a singer they all admired. That's the name on Charles's birth certificate, on the line where it says, 'Mother.' Cyndi Lauper. She was, obviously, a deeply troubled young woman. She used drugs, left the program several times only to return when she was sick and hungry. The day after Charles was born, she left and didn't come back. A month later her body was found in an abandoned building frequented by drug users. I like to think that she fought to stay alive long enough to give birth to her baby. Her body is buried in our family plot. Anyway, after she left they called me to come and get the baby, or else convince Adam to release him for adoption.

"Adam was lost in his own torment, not competent to make that, or any, decision. I had taken the legal steps necessary to sign the release form myself, but something made me find Adam and force him to accompany me to the facility where they were keeping the baby. He was psychotic that day, but fighting hard to keep it under control. When he saw the baby, he . . . "

Bo studied the melting ice in her Coke as the other woman took a deep breath and then said, "These memories are so difficult now. You don't happen to have a cigarette, do you?"

Bo grinned. "As a matter of fact, yes. It was your son, by the way, who badgered me into quitting. But I got a little manic the other night and bought a pack. Only smoked one. They're out on the deck."

"It figures," Ann Keith nodded minutes later, pacing the redwood boards still shaded by the building and taking shallow drags on one of Bo's cigarettes. "He was always trying to get me to quit. I finally did, but he never knew. Amazing how one never stops craving them, isn't it?"

Bo had pulled a deck chair into the shade for herself. "What happened when he saw his son?" she prompted.

"He began to cry, to sob. The baby looked so much like

him, you see. I don't know what was going through Adam's mind, but he finally said three things. He said the baby would be named Charles, because Baudelaire wrote *Fleurs du Mal*, and Duncan, for his father. He begged me not to send the baby away. And then . . . and then he begged me either to find a way to help him, or to let him die. It was an ultimatum. He was absolutely desperate and absolutely serious. I knew that the next suicide attempt would be the last."

"But there was no suicide," Bo said. "Adam got better."

Ann Keith lit another cigarette and watched a pelican glide by, far at sea. "I've never told anyone what I'm about to tell you," she said. "It can't be proven; Adam's body has been cremated. And if you repeat this, I'll deny ever having said it."

Bo measured the woman, the manicured hands and red linen blazer, the intelligent blue eyes that both were and weren't Mort Wagman's eyes. Ann Lee Keith had once been a woman of great feeling, even drama, Bo recognized. That earlier personality lay in patches now beneath the mature one, hammered by experience to a steady, muted glow. Ann Keith was a survivor, Bo sensed, and a decent person.

"Why would you tell me whatever this is?" she asked.

"You have the power to give my grandson to me, or to keep him from me. If I were in your position I would want to know everything I could before making that decision. You have asked why Adam severed contact with me for over two years. I could lie to you, blame his behavior on the illness. But you'd know I was lying, wouldn't you? Meanwhile, I believe my grandson is in danger. Surely you can see that nothing but the whole truth will do now."

Intuition throbbed around Bo. It felt like a warm cloak on the skin rather than a process of the mind. It was what her grandmother had called "the sight," even though, Bo thought, it involved feeling more than vision.

"I've already seen the whole truth," Bo said, standing to face her friend's mother. "I saw it in your son's kindness and see it now in your courage. Don't tell me your secret. It isn't necessary in any event. The court will release Charles to you; you're his grandmother, you want him, and you can provide for him. Meanwhile, I'll release him to you immediately. All it will take is a phone call."

The Jack Russells were circling, curious, aware that something had changed. Bo scratched one behind his ear as she watched Ann Keith stub out her cigarette thoughtfully. The activity of the dogs and the scent of cigarette smoke reminded Bo of Mort at the lodge, pacing in a circle beside her, urging her to quit smoking, telling her he'd stop pacing if . . . But there was something else. Mort had said something else, Bo remembered. He'd said dogs circle around because their ancestors circled to nest in high grass. He paced in a circle, he said, because somebody, "somebody in my *family*," he said, put animal brains in his head.

Bo felt her eyes move upward from the dog to those of Ann Keith in dawning realization. Dr. Ann Lee Keith, a neurophysiologist renowned for her research on fetal cell implants! The deck, the dogs, the sea—everything seemed to diminish and fade in contrast to the awareness unfolding in Bo's mind.

"Oh, my God," she said softly. "Was it one of these dogs?"

"Adam did tell you, didn't he?" Keith nodded. Her voice was soft, almost amused.

"I thought he was still psychotic. He also told me he was going to marry a frog. I thought it was all just nonsense."

"Not all. Would you like to hear it now?"

"Only if you want to tell it," Bo answered. "Off the record."

"Thank you, Bo Bradley," Ann Keith smiled, "for being who you are. I do want to tell it. How about another iced tea, and then I'd like to get my grandson. Will that do?"

"I'll call the hospital right now," Bo agreed.

"Hospital? Why is Charles in a hospital?"

"I'll explain," Bo said, following Ann Keith and three terriers into her own living room, which did, she thought, feel comfortable. And the dachshund puppy carefully leaving a puddle on Andrew's newspaper on the floor beside the couch was an especially homey touch.

Leaning on the counter as Bo stirred another glass of tea, Ann Keith explained that Alexander Morley had made escalating monetary offers for the use of her name as one of MedNet's board of advisors. "I was the cutting-edge name," she told Bo. "I was published everywhere, got grants just by asking. My name on an advisory board meant the endeavor was not only competent but ethical, neither of which term has ever been applicable to MedNet. They're charlatans, the worst sort of avaricious medical fakes. I rejected Morley's offers for years. Any connection to that nest of sharks is instant death in the medical community. They're universally despised by serious medical practitioners and researchers. But at the end I needed money for Adam's surgery. A lot of money. To get it, I sold out. That's why my name is on their letterhead. They bought me. And overnight I was persona non grata everywhere. The university keeps me on as a professor only because I had tenure before this happened. Frankly, I wouldn't blame them if they threw me out."

"And this surgery," Bo prodded gingerly. "Did you really . . . ?"

Ann Keith jabbed at an ice cube in her glass. "Do you understand that my son was going to die?" she asked. "There was no question in my mind then, nor is there any now, that I did the right thing. I didn't perform the surgery myself. That was done by a Scandinavian neurosurgeon in a private European clinic. It's really quite simple and not at all dangerous, as invasive brain surgery goes.

"I had promised Adam I'd help him, Bo. There was nothing else I knew to do, and even that was entirely experimental. So I took MedNet's money and, well, I won't go into the details, but I was able to get the necessary fetal brain cells through a medical lab. They were from a canine embryo of three weeks' gestation. The embryo had been removed as part of another experiment, although its siblings were not. I extracted, prepared, and packed the cells, flew with Adam to Europe, and the surgery was performed. I assume you understand the principle."

"Fetal cells will grow into whatever they were supposed to grow into," Bo recited, "even when transplanted to a different organism, and the host organism is less likely to reject them than it is the same cells from an older donor."

"Sometimes. There have been exciting results using this technique with Parkinson's disease, but of course the fetal brain cells used were not animal, but human, donated by women undergoing abortion. The ethical considerations are so overwhelming that research in this area is difficult. As an alternative, another focus now is on development of 'engineered' cells grown in labs rather than taken from embryos. It's far too early to predict whether or not these cells will perform."

"But did it work?" Bo asked. "Did the fetal cells replace some segment of Mort's brain?"

Ann Keith sighed. "Possibly, but probably not. There was no way to tell without further surgery, and the mechanisms of schizophrenia are not as well researched as those of Parkinson's. Until recently there was virtually no research at all. Now we know the limbic system is involved. CAT scans had shown typical abnormalities in Adam's hippocampus and hypothalamus. Those were the sites I chose for cell transplants. This was a desperate act, Bo, not a rational one. On a par with appeals to magic. It was simply the last thing I could do to save my son. The likelihood that these fetal cells would grow and partially supplant malfunctioning cells in Adam's brain was educated speculation at best, pathetic and arguably criminal delusion at worst."

"But Adam got better. He was successful, Ann. He made a great deal of money, functioned, took care of Bird, everything. Maybe the experiment did work. He thought so. He said he paced in a circle when he was off his meds because dogs do that."

Ann Keith shook her head, smiling. "Adam loved the idea that he was part dog after the surgery. Look at the name he gave himself."

"Wagman," Bo pronounced, her eyes wide. "Mort Wagman . . . *Dead Dog!*"

"He was very aware of the embryo from which the cells were taken," Keith said. "He created a sort of mythos around it, felt that he was living its life for it in some sense."

The three Jack Russell terriers watched Bo hopefully from the kitchen floor, aware that treats were likely to be provided from kitchens. "You said the other embryos in the litter were not removed by this medical lab," she said slowly.

"The other embryos were born and are at the moment shedding on your kitchen floor," Keith nodded. "I know it's bizarre, but I had to have them. Call me crazy. They're like family."

"You're crazy," Bo agreed. "Totally nuts. And believe me, I don't say that very often. But I still don't understand why Mort got better, if the surgery wasn't responsible."

"Clozapine," Ann Keith answered. "It was finally legalized for use in this country by the Food and Drug Administration several months after our return from Europe. I believe that medication, plus Adam's maturing out of his adolescent hormonal surges, was responsible for his improvement. But the truth is, without the hope the surgery gave him, Adam wouldn't have been alive by the time clozapine was available."

"Your grandson has been diagnosed with attention deficit hyperactivity disorder," Bo told the woman sitting at her counter. "How do you feel about that?"

"I don't know quite how to respond. It's not a surprise to me. Remember, Charles and Adam lived with me until Charles was four. I suspected it. Is he receiving the appropriate medication?"

"Not yet," Bo answered. "But are you going to be able to cope with the problems?"

"Charles will attend the same private school his father did. It's very old-fashioned, traditional. All the teachers are men, so he'll have male role models. And I already know an excellent child psychiatrist. But Bo, all this depends on my getting him out of here safely. May I get him now?"

"You'll have to stay in San Diego until the court releases Charles," Bo explained, "but I can file that paperwork this afternoon. What I still don't know is why you think Charles is in danger. Who do you think wants to hurt him?"

"I believe that MedNet is responsible for the death of my son," she said angrily. "Adam's attorney, Reynolds Cassidy, told me that Adam phoned him late the night before he was killed, very upset. Adam directed Cassidy to make arrangements for a substantial loan, make the money available. Now I realize that Adam was going to rescue this Indian psychiatric program from MedNet. I believe that MedNet, probably in the person of Alexander Morley, knew what Adam planned, and ordered his death. I also believe that someone else in MedNet, someone not well placed enough to know that I have no influence there, has reason to oppose the takeover, and is using threats against Charles to compel me to vote against it, even though in reality I have no vote and no influence. Whoever it is is stupid, which makes him doubly dangerous."

What Ann Keith believed about her son's death made sense, Bo thought, if the rest of it did not. Some sense, but not quite enough. There were missing pieces in Keith's view of what happened the night a shot burst the desert sky, too many near-impossible variables falling together at once. It would mean that Zach knew of the MedNet takeover within hours of Hopper Mead's death, told Mort Wagman about it the night of Mildred's Kurok, and that Mort was so alarmed that he phoned his attorney to transfer funds in the middle of the night.

Mort might have done that, Bo conceded, since a call to his

attorney's home would skirt the runaround involved in phoning his office the next morning, when Mort and Bird would be en route back to Los Angeles, anyway. Still, Ann Keith was conjecturing from fear, not hard data. Unwise to grant too much credibility to her view of the situation. And there was no point in explaining that Zach and the mob, not MedNet, had threatened her. She wouldn't believe it, so great was her animosity toward the corporation to which she had sold her professional reputation.

"Here are directions to the hospital," Bo said, handing the other woman a map scribbled on the back of an envelope, "and my home phone number. You can pick Bird up now, but you must stay in San Diego until the petition I filed for Bird in juvenile court has been dismissed. You'll be required to provide identification to security at St. Mary's. And I need your address and phone number."

"I have a small suite at a hotel on the bay where pets are welcome," Ann Keith replied, writing the required information on a business card. "And thank you, Bo. I'll phone you this evening to let you know how Charles is doing."

"Ann, why was your son hiding from you?"

"Because there was no other way for him to grow up, find out who he was," the older woman answered from the apartment's open door. "Isn't that the point of being alive?"

Bo watched as Ann Keith and the three Jack Russells left her apartment. Then she phoned Eva Broussard.

"I'm over my head with this case," she told her shrink. "I may just have made a serious mistake, and Andy is buying a house. The story I've just heard rivals *Invasion of the Body Snatchers* in content, except without the space aliens. Also, I think it's probably true. A little girl has given me a dachshund puppy I wasn't going to keep until she sang 'Molly Malone,' and I knew I had to. She's so cute, Eva, but I'd forgotten about puppies, the housebreaking, everything. Andy wants me to live with him, although he's not being pushy, and I'm afraid this case is going to close without anybody finding who killed Mort. I'm not sure Adirondack chairs are really right for Andy's yard, either."

"I'm afraid you lost me at 'space aliens,' " Eva replied. "The term always catches my attention. I'm giving a luncheon talk on it today, in fact, to a conference of journalists at a hotel in Mission Valley near your office. Why don't we meet for coffee afterward?"

"The espresso bar at Hazard Center," Bo decided quickly. "Two o'clock?"

"Fine."

Bo wadded the soggy newspaper into a trash bag, changed clothes, and scooped Molly from beneath the television where she was shredding an advertising mailer for a Cantonese restaurant.

"Too much MSG," she told the puppy, picking bits of damp card stock out of the carpet. "And you're going to have to go to work with me until I can do something about day care."

The little dog indicated her acceptance of the plan by licking Bo in the eye.

Chapter 30

Eva Broussard was already seated at an umbrellaed table outside the espresso bar when Bo arrived with Molly. In an olive silk jacket over a pencil-thin knit dress the color of new pewter she looked, Bo thought, less like a half-Iroquois psychiatrist than a Parisian businesswoman involved in the fashion industry.

"Ah, the new baby!" Eva exclaimed as Molly sniffed her gray kid pumps with unabashed interest, tail quivering. "She's quite spirited, Bo, like her mistress. But how did you come to get another dog?"

After ordering an iced hazelnut latte, Bo explained her meeting with Lindsey Sandifer and the situation that led Lindsey to select Bo as the puppy's new owner.

"Lindsey said she wanted to live with her mom in a covered wagon on the prairie," she told Eva. "I guess a mobile home outside Phoenix is pretty close."

"The decision required great courage on the part of her mother," Eva mused over her espresso. "I can't help wondering at times exactly what combination of variables it is that we call love."

The word hung uneasily above them as Bo straightened the hem of her knit skirt, then spent the better part of a minute coaxing Molly to drink some water from a paper cup brought by the waiter. "I've been wondering about that, too," she said. "Not sex, but love. It's dangerous, Eva. It's like a sort of unending mania that takes people out of reality and into another dimension."

"Yes," Eva Broussard said. The word fell somewhere between statement and question.

"I met Ann Lee Keith this morning," Bo began, and then told her psychiatrist the story of why a young man named Adam Keith chose to call himself "Dead Dog."

"*Mon dieu,*" Eva whispered. "As a child I heard many strange stories, the old Iroquois legends full of peculiar images—a flayed skin that sang in a tree, a flying head, a beautiful, seductive man who was in reality a snake—but this story is true, yes?"

"I think it is."

"Then your work has brought you a gift."

Bo enjoyed a sip of cold latte. "Gift?"

"A story. One you won't forget as the details of the present are lost. Whenever you remember Mildred's death, your terrible sadness, Mort's friendship, the arrival of Molly in your life, Andrew's house—all the events of this difficult time— you'll remember a story of great and frightening love. What Dr. Keith did won't seem strange at all ten years from now; they're already using brain cell transplants from fetal pigs for Parkinson's disease, with astonishing results. But because Keith acted ahead of history and at great sacrifice, the story is unforgettable, a framework for your experience now, and a priceless gift."

"What Ann did for her son ultimately drove him away," Bo sighed, rattling the ice in her glass. "Her caring for him left no room for *him*. He had to flee, to hide, in order to . . . to be himself."

"Every child must do that, separate from its parents, soon-er or later. Adam's illness made the process more dramatic and difficult. But every love involves that struggle, don't you think? And sometimes it goes badly, becomes diseased and obsessive on one or both sides. Fortunately, it sounds as though Ann Keith stopped far short of the obsession Adam might have become for her after she sacrificed her career. She's a remarkable woman."

"I hope I'm right about her," Bo said, frowning. "I released Bird to her this morning, technically under my supervision until the petition's dismissed. Madge was thrilled, of course. We can close the case now. It's all ending, but there's something that's bothering me, something I can't quite see. Mort was murdered, and then somebody began trying to upset me with those tapes on the phone, following me in the fog, the red collar on the tree. There has to be a connection somewhere, but there isn't. If MedNet orchestrated Mort's death to keep him from bailing out the Neji, why would they try to drive *me* crazy? I can't help the Indians. It doesn't make any sense."

"It actually happened, therefore it does make sense," Eva said emphatically, leaning to pick up the puppy asleep on her foot. "It's just that the sense isn't apparent at the moment. It may never be apparent. Did you know that about thirty percent of homicides are never solved? In those cases the sense of a sequence of behaviors is simply not discerned by outsiders, but that doesn't mean it's not there."

"I can't live with that," Bo said. The idea was completely unacceptable. "Mort had already suffered the onset of schizophrenia before there were any decent drugs for it, starved, froze in the streets, attempted suicide. But he survived, eventually made a life, cared for his son, even became wealthy. That was so important to him he was willing to go off his meds to make that commercial for SnakeEye. I won't accept that somebody can just kill him in the middle of the night and walk away. That's not right!"

Eva smiled at Molly, curled in her lap. "Americans are culturally intolerant of moral ambiguity," she told the snoozing dog. "It's a national trait, the legacy of Puritanism I'm afraid."

"You're going to get dog hair on your dress," Bo noted peevishly.

Ignoring the remark, Eva knit her brow, thinking. "Why was money so important to him, do you think?"

"I don't know. Maybe he wanted to make sure Bird was well cared for. But I had a sense there was more to it, something about pride, something personal."

"The answers may lie in looking at questions like that, questions that seem very peripheral to the central event of his death. Seemingly inconsequential issues sometimes open doors to whole sets of motivations previously overlooked."

"A psychiatrist would say that," Bo smiled. "And you're the best. Thanks, Eva."

As they stood to leave, Eva Broussard halted, remembering something. "I'm not going to bring up your relationship with Andrew, but I've thought about the Adirondack chairs," she said, her dark eyes warm with amusement, "and after living in the Adirondacks I'm prepared to state that they're impossible to get out of gracefully. As I recall, the experience is like being a turtle trapped on its back. Perhaps that information will help you in making your decision about Andrew's lawn."

"Scratch the Adirondack chairs," Bo nodded. "I was afraid of that."

On the way back to her office Bo thought about Eva's remarks. What inconsequential issue might open the door leading to Mort Wagman's killer? The name, even in thought, seemed a caricature now. And Bo hadn't known a young man named Adam Keith at all.

"So who was my brother," she asked Molly, "Mort or Adam?"

This way lies madness, Bradley. Wouldn't it be easier to concentrate on the sound of one hand clapping?

The Indians, she remembered, frequently called each other by different names. A significant event in the life of an individual would give rise to a new name celebrating the event, although the person's previous names remained in use as well.

Zach's oldest son, Ojo, had been named, as had all of Zach and Dura's children, for Kumeyaay listed in the 1880 San Diego census. Zach explained that the Indians had not been allowed to claim identifying surnames because the white census takers thought names such as Lost Water and Eats Eyes were a joke. And so, Zach said, he'd found the names of the dead in the San Diego Public Library. Kumeyaay listed simply as Maria Jueh, Ojo, Juana, Tiron, Cunel. In naming his children with their names, he told Bo, he'd given the old ones his own surname.

But the other children often called Ojo Rabbit in honor of his hunting skill, Bo recalled. And Dura often called the boy Stone Burro for reasons known only to mother and son. Yet all the names were still Ojo, as all the names by which Adam Keith might have been known would to Bo always be Mort.

"I figured it out," she answered her own question as Molly stretched against the door in an attempt to look out the Pathfinder's window. "Nobody's just one thing, one identity. Mort was as real as Adam: it was Mort that I knew. And don't worry, tonight I'll tie a stack of towels to the seat so you can see out."

Bo parked in the shade and walked Molly around the CPS parking lot before settling the little dog with a bowl of water in her box on the back seat. The windows were down. The puppy would be all right until Bo returned, she thought, which would probably be in a few minutes. She was next up on the rotation for new cases. It would be a miracle if Madge hadn't already assigned it.

The miracle was not forthcoming. On her desk when she entered was a clean, new case file so thin Bo knew there could be nothing in it but a face sheet.

"Sounds like a weird one," Estrella said as Bo assessed the condition of her tousled curls in the mirror affixed to the back of their office door. "General Hospital emergency room staff called it in to the hotline. Seems a biker mom brought her seven-year-old daughter in with what turned out to be bronchial pneumonia, and the hospital slapped a hold on the kid. They think mom's on drugs or something. She's still at the hospital demanding to take her daughter home. You'd better get up there."

"They'll call the police if mom gets too obstreperous," Bo said, sinking into her chair. She wasn't ready for another case, not that it mattered. They kept coming.

The door opened and Madge Aldenhoven leaned in. "The court liaison just phoned," she told Bo briskly. "Your Wagman petition's been dismissed. You can close the case. Let's get it out of here this afternoon." Good old Madge, visions of "cases handled and closed" statistics dancing before her eyes. Everybody in the system knew that Aldenhoven's unit petitioned more cases than any other. Closing one only made room for more.

"Do you really think I should take the time for the paperwork?" Bo asked, feigning deep concern. "This new case sounds pretty messy. I thought I'd run up to General right away."

"I suppose you're right," Madge answered, knitting an otherwise seamless forehead. Bo had marveled for years at her supervisor's flawless complexion. Fifteen years Bo's senior, Madge nonetheless had a face betraying no more lines than Ingrid Bergman's in *Casablanca*. Probably the result of clean living, Bo thought. Living within the tidy, if incessantly changing, boundaries set by the Department of Social Services procedures manual. "If you leave now you may get back in time to complete the Wagman paperwork."

"I'll try," Bo lied. She wanted to keep Bird's case open just in case. But just in case what? As the CPS investigator she'd have access to any information she needed to determine the best plan for the child. But she'd already made that determination. The information she wanted now was something quite different.

"The Sheriff's Department is never going to find Mort's killer," she told Estrella after Madge closed their door. "And MedNet is going to take over the Ghost Flower program. They'll turn it into a marketing zoo, probably sell 'Indian headdresses' with 'Crazy House' spelled out in plastic beads on the headband. Then when they've destroyed the program and the Neji, they'll sell it and go on to ruin something else. I don't know what to do."

Estrella spun her desk chair to face Bo. "You've done what you said you wanted to," she said softly. "You found Bird's grandmother. You made sure Bird was safe. That's what you wanted to do for Mort. Now it's done. The rest isn't your responsibility, Bo. It's time to let it go."

"I still don't know who was playing those tapes, who followed me and tried to drive me crazy. I can't just let that go, Es. And there's something in all this, some piece of information, that would tie it all together, show the connection between the creep with the tape and Mort's death, but I can't see it."

"There may not be any connection, Bo. Maybe it's just somebody in your neighborhood who doesn't like you or didn't like Mildred's barking, some nasty neighbor who wants to make a point. These things happen. And you do live in a sort of odd neighborhood."

"*I'm* odd," Bo replied. "And I might buy the nasty neighbor theory if it weren't for what happened out at UCSD—the red dog collar thing. Everything else happened at or near my apartment, but somebody had to be following me to set that up, Es. Somebody following me with a red dog collar in his pocket, just waiting for the right situation. It wasn't a dog-hating neighbor following me. I don't know who it was."

"Henry's almost finished with the baby's room," Estrella said, deliberately changing the subject. "Why don't you and Andy come over for dinner tonight to see it? We decided on a vinyl tile floor because it's so much easier to keep clean than carpet, and he's built a whole wall of shelves with a built-in space for a desk later. You need to relax, Bo, get away from this case."

"Oh, Es, thanks. You're right, of course. But I'm tired, I've got Molly to train before I can take her anywhere, and tonight I think I'll just crash, read a mystery and eat corn chips or something. But how about tomorrow? We'll bring a couple of pizzas, okay?"

Estrella nodded, her dark eyes unconvinced. "You plan to have Molly trained by tomorrow?"

Bo sketched a large corn chip on her desk blotter. "I just want to think tonight, Es. Be alone."

"Ees no good, thees theenking," Estrella replied in a mock accent, snapping imaginary castanets over her head. "Especially alone."

"It's the only way to do it." Bo grinned. "And I've got to run up to General Hospital to see a lady biker. Don't worry, Es. I'm okay."

But as she closed the office door behind her a wave of concern seeped beneath it and followed her outside.

"Be careful," it said. "Something's not right. Be careful."

Chapter 31

It was almost six when Bo completed the case at General Hospital. It had been, she thought as she parked the Pathfinder and carried Molly up the apartment steps, a tribute to everything that can go wrong when one set of people judges another. Especially when those sitting in judgment have as backup a legally sanctioned bureaucracy empowered to impound children. In this situation the bureaucracy had been called for the simple reason that a woman had a tattoo.

Of course it wasn't an ordinary tattoo. Bo grinned as she spooned puppy diet into Molly's dish on the kitchen floor. It was an outrageous tattoo. A tarantula, in fact, exquisitely inked in the skin of a twenty-eight-year-old woman named Donna Sprauer, whose seven-year-old daughter, Michelle, was ill. The tattoo had been drawn on Sprauer's neck a decade earlier, and was now somewhat faded and fuzzy. But insufficiently faded and fuzzy to diminish the horror felt by the emergency room paramedical staff, some of whom maintained that the tattoo was evidence of Sprauer's devotion to Satan.

"I was *eighteen!*" Donna Sprauer told Bo in the hospital's ER waiting room. "I was an idiot! But I don't see why a stupid tattoo I had done ten years ago when I was too dumb to know my ass from a hole in the ground should mean these people can keep my kid. They can't do that."

Bo explained that they could do that, and had. "They think a woman with a tarantula tattoo on her neck must be depraved, unfit," she explained. "They put a 'hospital hold' on Michelle and called Child Protective Services. Now I have to do a complete investigation before I can release the hold."

"I should have worn a turtleneck," the young woman sighed. "I always wear one when I go out. If I could afford it, I'd have the damn thing removed, but it costs a fortune. And I was too panicky to change clothes. She was running a real high fever. Her eyes looked funny. I called her pediatrician, but the nurse said he was at the hospital. She said I should bring Michelle to an emergency room, so I did."

"Another claim is that you endangered the child by bringing her here on a motorcycle," Bo went on.

"My old man, Denny, he took the truck to work. The bike was all I had. What was I supposed to do, walk seven miles carrying a sick kid in this heat? She had a helmet on, and I had her tied to me with duct tape in case she passed out or something. I've got a license; the bike's got a license. What did I do wrong?"

"So far, nothing," Bo told her. "It sounds as if you've done exactly what you should to care for your daughter. Would you mind if I took a look at the house where Michelle lives?"

"Why?"

"It's just part of the investigation."

"This is insane," Donna Sprauer insisted, tucking a black tank top into her black Levi's, "but come on. I just want to get Michelle out of here, get her home where I can take care of her. They said she was better now. They got the fever down."

"I'll drive," Bo answered.

Sprauer's home, shared with Dennis Overholt, a general contractor, was a two-bedroom bungalow on a well-kept street in El Cajon. Except for debris from a playhouse Overholt was building for Michelle in the backyard, the house and yard were clean. No dirty dishes in the sink, no garbage in the carpet. No pornographic pictures or videotapes in sight. A waterbed in the adults' bedroom was neatly made. In the girl's room a calico cat lay among rumpled *Beauty and the Beast* sheets, clearly waiting for the return of her mistress.

"That's Angel," Donna Sprauer said, "Michelle's cat. Put that in your report."

"I will," Bo agreed. "Now let's go bring Michelle home."

The release had taken another hour, and Bo felt compelled to wait and drive the child home rather than risk more flak over the motorcycle. The little girl had been thrilled to share the ride with Molly.

"Now you know how I make a living," Bo sighed as the little dog waddled after the rubber porcupine Bo threw for her. "Sometimes it's meaningful work, sometimes it's like this afternoon. But at least it's never boring."

Molly took the porcupine onto the deck and tried to bury it in a box planter full of mummified geraniums Bo had forgotten to have someone water while she was at the lodge.

"Go for it," she told the dog. "Guess I should get you a sandbox, huh?"

It would be fun to get a sandbox, she thought. And Molly would enjoy having somewhere to dig. Dachshunds liked to dig. But if they moved in with Andy, Molly would have a whole yard to dig in. The issue seemed to permeate everything.

"I'm getting the sandbox," she told Molly. "Maybe later we'll decide to live with him, and maybe we won't. But for now I'm going to stop thinking about it."

After a call to Andrew in which she insisted on a night alone and he countered with insistence on breakfast, Bo relaxed in a steaming tub and sifted through what she knew of Mort Wagman, bit by bit. He'd been a successful stand-up comic in spite of his schizophrenia. Well, that wasn't exactly astonishing, Bo thought. It was a closely guarded secret in the psychiatric community that more than one popular comic had a mild case of the illness, one even touring with an attendant to make sure the medications were taken. Sometimes the illness provided an edge appropriate on stage, a quicksilver ability at impersonations, mimicry.

And Mort was wealthy, a status most comics working the clubs only dreamed of claiming. Was there something about his business relationship with SnakeEye, the athletic shoe company that paid him a fortune to go off his meds and become psychotic for a commercial, that could result in his death? What would SnakeEye gain from the loss of its "psycho" star? Nothing, Bo thought. Forget SnakeEye.

MedNet then. Was Ann Keith's view correct? A powerful corporation willing to kill in order to achieve a relatively insignificant takeover?

"I don't know much about megabusinesses," Bo told a floating island of lemon-scented bubbles, "but it seems to me they lean more toward twisted legalities, the purchase of elected officials, and under-the-table monopolies than they do on murder. It's so old-fashioned. The really sophisticated criminals regard it as passé, I think."

What about the brain surgery? Mort Wagman had been walking around with brain cells in his skull from a Jack Russell terrier. There were plenty of people who would lose it completely over that, run around screaming about "God's law" and signing petitions to stop fetal cell implants. But nobody knew about Mort's surgery except Ann Lee Keith and the foreign surgeon who'd performed the operation.

But Mort had told her about it, Bo thought, running additional hot water into the tub. He'd mentioned it in his characteristically odd way, explaining himself to her. And he'd said something else. He'd said he kissed a frog, that maybe he'd marry her. Bo held a bar of soap under the water and then released it. As it burst through the water's surface a train of thought regarding frogs came to its conclusion.

"Of course!" she yelled, climbing out of the tub and wrapping her terrycloth robe about her. What did frogs do? They croaked, they ate flies, and they hopped. Mort Wagman had kissed a hopper. And her last name was Mead.

It made sense. Hopper Mead's friends had told the police that she was seeing somebody in Los Angeles, somebody working in "the industry," involved in show business. A stand-up comic fit the description. And Mead had stayed in San Diego during the month Mort Wagman was rehabbing at Ghost Flower Lodge. No more weekend trips to the City of Angels. But, Bo remembered, Hopper Mead had not come to the lodge to visit Mort. No one had visited him. So what did that mean?

Bo paced the length of her apartment accompanied by Molly, who seemed to regard pacing as a reasonable, even entertaining, pastime.

"Why wouldn't she come to visit him?" Bo asked rhetorically.

She already knew the answer. Most young men in love would go to some lengths to avoid being seen in a psychotic episode by the beloved. Psychiatric illness could be a real damper on romance. Mort had probably asked the young woman to stay away until he was stable, and she'd respected his wishes. Bo felt a surge of respect for Hopper Mead, followed by a dragging wave of sadness. Mort had planned to introduce his lady to his mother, a significant event connecting tumultuous past to triumphant present. Now Mort Wagman and Hopper Mead were both dead, and within hours of each other.

"It's too coincidental to be coincidence," Bo told Molly, pulling a length of yellow cotton thread from the puppy's mouth. "And stop attacking the hem of my robe."

Ann Keith's assumption that MedNet was responsible for her son's death might be accurate, Bo mused. But what about Hopper Mead? It was, after all, her death that had transferred a four-hundred-thousand-dollar loan into the hands of MedNet, threatening the Indians' ruin, and so outraging Mort Wagman that he'd phoned his lawyer in the middle of the night to initiate fund transfers as a first step in bailing out the Neji. But Hopper Mead's death had been an accident, an ill-fated rendezvous with a shark cruising San Diego's coastal waters. The bones of her severed leg had been found in the shark's stomach. No ambiguity there. A shark killed Hopper Mead, and despite the elegance of the theory, sharks could not be hired. Still, the confluence of events suggested a pattern, a scaffold of connections with Ghost Flower Lodge at its center. But why?

Bo wandered back into her bedroom and threw on random items of clothing for a potty-run with Molly. Only ten minutes later on Dog Beach did she realize that her T-shirt was on backward and the madras plaid shorts she'd grabbed from a drawer were tight in the hips because they weren't hers, but Andy's. Fortunately, no one on Dog Beach would care.

"There's something missing in this picture," she told Molly, drawing a shark in the sand with the splintered end of an abandoned yardstick. "Even if that Mexican graduate student's suspicions are true, and somebody knifed Mead *before* the arrival of the shark, everything still points to MedNet. Nobody else stands to gain from the deaths of Hopper Mead and Mort Wagman. But the police already checked that out and found nada. Back to square one."

Molly chased the stick with which Bo was drawing a square in the sand, her paws flinging arcs of grit into Bo's shoes.

"So maybe these two deaths really are a coincidence," she went on. "Maybe somebody from MedNet arranged to have Mead knifed and thrown to the sharks within the same twenty-four hours that somebody else entirely tracked Mort to the rim of a desert canyon in the middle of the night and shot him. But if MedNet wasn't behind Mort's murder, then who was? There's something I'm just not getting, Molly, a blank space."

Over sluggish, low-tide surf a horizontal band of water vapor called the marine layer turned the sky into a gray envelope. Shut. Sealed. Occasionally a gull fell from it to strut on the beach before being driven aloft again by puppy barks, but nothing else seemed forthcoming. The ocean sky was as

impenetrable as whatever had snuffed out the life of Mort
Wagman. Bo threw the broken yardstick into the sky, half
expecting it to be swallowed, but it merely fell into the sea
and floated limply on the swells.

Back at her apartment Bo cleaned sand from Molly's ears,
reconsidered the sandbox idea. The little dog was really too
close to the ground for the endlessly blowing sand of a beach
community, Bo thought. Ocean Beach had been Mildred's
home, but Mildred was gone. Maybe it was time to leave,
move on, try something new. As if on cue, the phone rang.

"Hi, Andy," Bo answered.

"How did you know?" queried the familiar baritone.

"I was thinking about Molly's ears, about Mildred, sand,
moving, all that."

"Of course," he replied with heroic indifference to implica-
tions, "all those things are important. But I called because I
just learned that I'll need to be at the hospital early tomorrow
morning to document a particularly important surgery for a
criminal investigation, so I can't meet you for breakfast. I
thought maybe lunch . . . "

"Not tomorrow," Bo replied thoughtfully. "I'll probably
get another case since I closed the one I got this afternoon,
and I want to run by Ghost Flower and talk to Zach. Andy,
I've figured out something, a connection, in this case but still
nothing fits. I think Mort and Hopper Mead had a thing, as
they say. Mort was trying to tell me that when he said he'd
kissed a frog. But even that doesn't explain his murder
because MedNet couldn't possibly have known about Mort
loaning the Neji enough money to pay off Hopper's loan the
same night he made the call to his lawyer. It's just not possible unless MedNet had the lodge phones tapped or something, and even *then* . . . "

"You've lost me," Andrew LaMarche said as if this were
nothing new. "But why would a young woman of Hopper
Mead's background get involved with—"

"Watch it, Andy," Bo said in tones usually reserved for

street predators. "Don't say what I think you're going to say. Just don't."

"I was going to say," he went on imperturbably, " . . . get involved with someone in the entertainment industry. She was wealthy, probably privately educated, well-traveled, even pampered. The social register set. They hire entertainers, Bo, but they don't marry them."

Bo drew an ascot tie decorated in dollar signs on a dog food label. "You sound just like your parents," she said brightly, aware as the words left her mouth that her relationship with Andrew LaMarche had in the moment donned a terrible cloak of intimacy, the verbal trappings of people who know each other's secrets. The awareness had a loamy scent, like plowed fields or a dense forest floor.

"Mon dieu," he sighed. "I do."

In the silence that followed, Bo felt the swooping weight of ten thousand moments like this one, moments between friends, lovers, parents, and children. Moments on which whole dramas hinged, when a flawed human reality would meet acceptance, denial, or attack.

"It comes with *having* parents." She laughed softly. "They live in your head and blurt things out at inappropriate moments." Acceptance. She couldn't imagine where the inclination had come from, but it felt good.

"My parents were pompous and pathetic," he groaned. "I can't believe I—"

"You're definitely not pathetic," Bo replied. "But since you now owe me a little struggle to even things out, help me with Mort's murder. I can't figure out who, or why . . . "

"If your guess about their relationship is on target, then a connection between the two deaths seems likely. So what's the common link?"

"Ghost Flower Lodge. Hopper Mead invested in it and then Mort was a patient there. Also MedNet, sort of. But I want to focus on the lodge."

"Well . . . " Andrew drew out the word thoughtfully, "What's there?"

"What do you mean?"

"In the military it's called reconnoitering. It means getting the lay of the land, what's nearby, who's around, when, why. It's like a map with buildings and people. So what's out there? Remember, I was never there."

Bo thought about the desert wasteland "given" the Kumeyaay when invaders seized all the desirable properties. "Nothing," she said. "Just two or three Kumeyaay reservations, some Bureau of Land Management lands, a few parcels of private property, a state road. Lots of chollas, baked dirt, the occasional ghostly mule train with a headless driver."

Andrew LaMarche was all business. "What about the Neji property? Is there anyplace that allows easy access other than the road?"

" 'Easy' isn't a term I'd use anywhere out there," Bo answered, "and there's really nothing. Well, there is a dirt road into a geological dig, or at least I think it's a geological dig. There's a sign. It's called Had-a-something with a Roman numeral two. Had-a-sea, I thought, no . . . Had-a-mar. I think it's a university dig called Hadamar II."

- "Hadamar!" Andrew's voice boomed through twenty miles of fiber-optic filaments and Pacific Bell relays. "Is that what you said?"

"Well, yeah. It's just some cutesy geologist pun on the old seabed, Andy. It doesn't have anything to do with Ghost Flower Lodge."

"A psychiatric care facility." His voice was an octave deeper than usual and tremulous with anger.

"Ghost Flower Lodge is a psychiatric care facility," Bo confirmed. "So what?"

"Hadamar is a small town in Germany, Bo. I happened to visit it one day when I was touring. I intended never to tell you what I saw there."

Bo sighed. "Andy, every time you try to protect me from

something there's trouble. What on earth are you talking about?"

"Sit down, Bo," he said. "This may be nothing more than a coincidence, but then again it may not be."

"There are too many coincidences already, Andy. Tell me what this is all about."

"All right," he said, and began a tale that fell through Bo's mind like an intolerable light, explaining everything, illuminating a face Bo realized she had never seen. Illuminating the face of a killer hiding in fog.

When Andrew was finished with the gruesome story, she merely said, "Let me think about this, Andy. I have to think about this alone."

Then she checked a name in the San Diego police report on Hopper Mead's death, found the address in a San Diego phone directory, and grabbed her keys. If she were right, she'd just identified Mort Wagman's killer and her own tormentor. A man so obsessed with his own superiority that he'd buried a knife in his sister's groin, effectively preventing any "unworthy" new life from growing there.

They'd all been suspicious of MedNet, Bo realized, for the same reasons that the hospital staff had mistrusted a mother with a tarantula tattooed on her neck. Corporations and tattooed people were known for their nasty agendas. But not this time. Bo flung herself into the darkness beyond her door, determined to uncover the truth. Afterward, she'd notify the police. But first she had to be sure.

Chapter 32

San Diego's night streets seemed innocuous as Bo drove to the suburban University City address she'd found in the phone book. Yellow porch lights highlighted junipers, bottlebrush trees, poisonous oleander with blossoms of white, pink, or a rich buttery color precisely the hue, Bo observed, of homemade shortbread. Ordinary Southern California landscaping, ordinary residential streets. But then probably nothing in its shrubbery had advertised the town of Hadamar's hideous secret, either.

At the corner of Genesee and Governor Bo turned at a clump of decorative sycamores into the condo complex where he lived. Somebody named Anselm Tucker. Clerk to Randolph Mead, Jr., whom Bo had never met and yet knew, now, intimately. Hopper Mead's older brother, whose voice was nothing more than a distilled version of the hate spewing in rivers from a thousand gun clubs, talk shows, and diseased affinity groups masquerading in the word "Christian." Their message, Bo thought, was elegant in its simplicity. "Be like us or perish." Randolph Mead had become their very personal soldier.

After finding Tucker's address in the maze of beige stucco, Bo parked in the alley-sized street behind his numbered garage door and contemplated the lighted steps leading to a

walkway fronting the building. There were four attached con-
dos, each a two-story town house resting heavily on its
ground-floor garage. Over the walkway, jutting corners of
adjacent buildings came within three feet of touching. Bo
climbed the steps into a sense of imprisonment created by
architectural closeness. And Anselm Tucker wasn't home.

"Damn!" she whispered, standing at the gate of a front
patio so small it seemed crushed between thick stucco walls.
A window overlooking the patio's bare Mexican pavers was
dark, as was an upstairs window sliced with wide vertical
blinds. Bo rang the bell again, and looked around.

People kept to themselves in places like this, she knew. The
suffocating proximity of a badly planned condo complex
forced inhabitants to ignore each other, maintain an illusion
of privacy. Anselm Tucker's immediate neighbors probably
didn't even know his name, but Bo tried the bell outside the
next patio anyway.

"Yes?" a delicate Asian woman answered, moving toward
Bo through an attractive arrangement of potted shrubs.

"My uncle, next door," Bo improvised smoothly, "asked me
to come by and pick up some things, but he's not home. Do
you have any idea when he'll be back?"

"Uncle?" the woman said softly.

Bo realized that she had no idea how old Anselm Tucker
was. The name "Anselm" had just sounded, even to her
maturing ears, old. "It's a family joke," she grinned. "He isn't
really my uncle." That, at least, was the truth.

"He is gone," the woman went on. "My husband saw him
load things in his car four days ago and then leave. We don't
really know him. I'm sorry."

"Thanks." Bo nodded, pondering this new information.
Had Randolph Mead's only alibi for the time in which his sister met her death just blown town? If he had, it was a smart
move.

Bo hurried back to her car, got in, and then noticed that
Tucker's garage door padlock, while locked, actually secured

nothing. Through haste or carelessness, Tucker had neglected to flip the sliding bolt over the hardware's slot before snapping the padlock shut. And the presence of the padlock meant there was no automatic door-opener. Like many basementless Californians, Tucker probably used his garage for storage and parked his car on the street. In case anyone was watching, Bo waved enthusiastically to an empty window in the Asian woman's condo and called, "It's okay! He left the garage door open for me." Then she pulled up the door, slid under, and let it fall softly behind her.

In the gloom she saw the white outlines of a washer and dryer, some boxes, clothes in laundry baskets. An interior door stood open, revealing a short set of stairs that would, she was sure, lead to a kitchen. The garage felt abandoned.

The kitchen proved to be more of the same. Fiestaware dishes in a white plastic drainer, clean. Microwave under a cabinet. Toaster oven. A faint smell of bleach. The odor wafted from a larger refrigerator next to the sink. Bo stared at the appliance for a full minute before tugging skittishly at its handle, half expecting to find something unspeakable inside. But the refrigerator was glaringly empty. Disinfected. Ready to sell with the condo. The immaculate refrigerator confirmed Bo's suspicion. Whoever Anselm Tucker was, he wouldn't be coming back.

In the living room Bo could see furniture in the amber glow of the sodium lights outside. A dark leather couch with a plaid blanket folded at one end, two chairs, a glass-topped coffee table, TV. Something about the blanket felt familiar, and Bo carried it to the window.

"Ah," she breathed as a thousand short, white dog hairs became visible, caught in the weave. This would be the dog on the tape. Anselm Tucker's dog, borrowed from his factotum by Randolph Mead for the purposes of terrorism. Bo wondered what Mead had done to elicit that last, frightened yip that had enabled her to identify the sound as a recording.

At the top of a carpeted stairway were two small bedrooms

and a bath. One of the bedrooms was empty. From the other the red operating light of a fax/answering machine pierced the dark atop a low dresser. Beside the machine was a framed snapshot that explained the neighbor's reaction to Bo's "uncle." The photo was of a sixtyish black man in a pink polo shirt, holding a bright-eyed Dandie Dinmont terrier in his arms. Bo wondered when Tucker had realized that his employer was a murderer as she pulled her sleeve over her hand and pushed the machine's playback button.

"It's Tuesday at about ten and I have your quitclaim of the condo to Randolph Mead, Jr.," an efficient female voice said, "and I'll list the property, including furnishings, with an asking price of two hundred and five thousand as we agreed. It's been a pleasure working with you, Mr. Tucker, and good luck with your new job in Alaska!"

The second and final message was less polite. "You're dead, Tucker," a deep voice snarled. "Nobody steals from me, *nobody!* I'm coming after you, Tucker. I've got one more thing to do here, and then I'll find you. You're too stupid to live, Tucker. You're defective. Remember that when I come for you." Before the tape clicked off Bo heard one last sound that made her bare her teeth in the darkened room. A familiar, cruel chuckle. The second message, she knew, was from Randolph Mead.

The empty condo seemed suddenly musty, tomblike. Bo felt a film of sweat coating her forehead as she raced down two sets of stairs and across the shadowy garage. What if he'd come, locked the garage door? What if he'd set a trap for her and . . . But the garage door opened as easily as before, and in seconds she was safe in the Pathfinder.

Chill, Bradley. This was stupid, but you were lucky. Now go home and call the police.

Tucker wasn't going to Alaska, she was sure. He'd apparently embezzled money from Mead, and was bailing out. Maybe the condo was his idea of a fair exchange. It made sense to Bo.

At home she left a message for the detective investigating Hopper Mead's murder. "It's her brother," she recited for a tape nobody would hear until tomorrow. "He must have bribed his employee, Anselm Tucker, to say he was at his office when she died, but he wasn't. I'm sure that if you search Tucker's residence you'll find enough evidence to pick up Randolph Mead. And alert the Backcountry Sheriff's Department to check out a dirt road near the Neji Reservation with a sign saying Hadamar II. I think it's Mead's camp. I think he stalked and killed Mort Wagman from there."

What she didn't say was, "and he may kill again." Too dramatic for the police, and in actuality there was nothing they could do without evidence. After moving furniture over the front door and deck doors, Bo found the corkscrew and fastened its flanges up with duct tape. Placing it under her pillow, she scooped Molly from her box and curled around the little dog in sheets that still smelled like Andy's shaving cream.

She wouldn't think about Randolph Mead, Jr., she decided. Although she was sure he was thinking about her.

Chapter 33

At some point between four and five A.M., the last of several pillows fell on the floor and Bo gave up on sleep. It had been a lost cause after Andrew's story in any event. An anger still throbbing in the large muscles of her legs and arms made her movements feel jerky as she stood and walked into the kitchen to make coffee.

"So we were the first," she whispered into the damp cold released by the refrigerator door. "They practiced on us, killed more than seventy thousand of us perfecting the method. Then they built the death camps. And no one knows. No one cares."

The soft thud as the door closed on its rubber insulator brought tears to her eyes, but she curbed the impulse to cry. There would be time for that later. Plenty of time after she'd explained what she knew to Zach and then waited for Randolph Mead to make his next move, as she was certain he would. The certainty ran through every vein and artery, fed every cell, every molecule. The certainty felt cool and clean and oddly businesslike.

Hadamar. Bo couldn't stop the three-syllable drumbeat in her head. One of six German mental asylums used as extermination centers for the mentally ill, the "defective," many of whom were only small children at the time of their extermination. "Life unworthy of life" these had been named, and then their lives had been snuffed out.

The psychiatric hospital at Hadamar, Andy said, had been fitted in cellars below the right wing with a realistic "shower room" complete with benches beneath which ran perforated pipes fitted to cans of carbon monoxide outside the sealed room. A simple turn of a valve killed seventy people at a time. An hour later ventilators were turned on, and then the bodies were loaded into carts on a miniature railway leading to two crematoria. A hundred people worked directly with the extermination of the mentally ill, Andy said, and everyone in town saw trains and buses with their windows painted over disgorging thousands to a building that could only house hundreds. And then they saw the black, greasy smoke and inhaled the scent of burning flesh, and did nothing. The dead were only crazy people, after all. Defective people unworthy of life.

Bo watched coffee dripping through the filter and breathed its aroma. The sensation reminded her that she was alive, she could drink coffee, walk on the beach, mourn a beloved dog, and allow another to waddle into her heart. She could love a man and welcome him to her body, laugh with a friend, work, be tired, be bored, but be *alive*. The fact seemed suddenly fragile.

"This is the way it really is, Mil," she whispered to Mildred's portrait on its easel. "I can't tell the puppy; she's too young. But I know you can cope. It's not just Germany under the Reich, Mil, it's everywhere. When times are hard, the mentally ill are always the first scapegoats. It's happening here. There's no more money for services, desperately ill people are thrown out of hospitals because they're poor and can't get insurance. They're dying out there, Mil, and now somebody's named the property next to the Neji Reservation for a Nazi psychiatric extermination center. Two people are dead and their killer is trying to drive me crazy. Things are weirder than usual, Mil."

The bright old terrier eyes in the painting shined an

encouragement Bo knew was already a part of her soul. Mildred would live as long as she did, Bo realized. And now it was time to clean up the world a little bit for a dachshund puppy who didn't yet have a clue about how tough you had to be just to make it. Bo squared her shoulders and knocked back a Depakote with a swig of good coffee. Then she pulled on jeans and a sweatshirt, tucked the sleeping puppy's hindquarters into her bra and headed out into the predawn chill. It was quiet all the way up Interstate 8 to the Campo cutoff that would loop under the highway and become a two-lane desert road. In the hollow created by her collarbone a wet, black nose breathed softly.

Once off the freeway, Bo thought about Andrew LaMarche. He'd done well with this, she nodded to herself. He'd told her what she needed to know and then left her alone to process the information in her own way. It was a gift the value of which he wouldn't understand for years, if ever. The gift of space in which to think thoughts qualitatively different from the thoughts of other people. Even children, she mused, were not subject to the mental scrutiny and attempts at control people with psychiatric illness had to face daily.

In younger, wilder days she'd tried to make people listen, make them consider the value in a skewed perception. Depressed, Abraham Lincoln had walked the White House grounds night after sleepless night alone with the ghost of his mother, whom he said was always with him. But like all depressives, Lincoln saw reality without the scrim of comforting lies and delusion enjoyed by "normal" folk. And so he could see uncompromisingly the evil that was slavery.

"For every Lincoln, every Charlotte Perkins Gilman, there are thousands more of us with valuable viewpoints. We're *important!*" the young Bo had insisted. "We're irritating, weird, even scary sometimes, but we have a purpose. So listen."

But nobody had listened. Nobody ever listened. And Bo had learned to protect her reality in a loop of solitude like a carbon-steel ribbon. It was unassailable. And Andrew LaMarche had mustered the grace to respect it.

"He's one in a million," she told the sleeping puppy nestled in her sweatshirt. "When this is over we'll weave him a crown of laurel, maybe even cook dinner, huh?"

By the time she reached the Hadamar II sign, the sun had topped the high desert mountains and begun to pour glare like hazy yellow tea on the parched remains of an ancient seabed. Bo put on her sunglasses, turned onto the dirt track, and engaged the four-wheel drive. Then she wheeled the Pathfinder sharply to the left in second gear, and rammed the sign. Its cedar upright splintered on impact, throwing the bolted sign onto her hood. Smiling, Bo reversed onto the track, stopped, got out and gave some water to Molly, and then grabbed a hammer and screwdriver from the small tool kit behind the front seat. In minutes she'd gouged the name from the wood, if not off the face of the earth.

This would be how Jews felt about names like Dachau, Bergen-Belsen, Treblinka, she thought. This icy, absolute loathing. But trashing a sign wasn't enough, wasn't anything. Just a personal catharsis. Tying Molly's leash to the fastened seatbelt on the passenger's side, Bo revved the Pathfinder up the dirt track past clumps of bristling chollas and spindly ocotillo as the sun lay purple morning shadows across the quiet.

There was nobody there. Bo sensed the absence of human life even before she carefully circled the precise little encampment. Just two lightweight tents in desert camouflage, carefully lashed and pegged with the long, barbed tent pegs necessary in sand. One of the pegs on the windward side of the smaller tent had pulled loose and all the ropes sagged. He hadn't been there in a while. Several days, she thought. Maybe a week.

Carefully Bo propelled the Pathfinder into the corner of the smaller tent, which collapsed soundlessly as the forward movement of the vehicle tore out its supports. One of the ropes caught on the bumper, and Bo simply dragged the tan and cream mottled shell away as if unveiling a sculpture. Then she sat and stared at six five-gallon jugs of water, a propane stove leveled with packed mud atop a large rock, and a clear plastic storage chest through the sides of which she could see a box of instant oatmeal, cans of salt-free soup, a jar of Folger's instant coffee. The small tent had been a kitchen and storage area. And whoever camped here had been desert-smart. Salt-free soup would provide both fluid and nutrition without tissue-leeching sodium.

The larger tent presented a problem. Bo hadn't intended to get out of the car, just to demolish whatever was there and then leave. She didn't want her feet on the ground. Not this ground with its bitter, soul-eating name. But there might be something in there, some clue that would prove the identity of the man who had camped in a hollow just outside the Neji Reservation, less than a mile from Yucca Canyon, and then lay in wait for Mort Wagman. Reluctantly Bo switched off the ignition and jumped softly to the ground. There was nothing useful in the big tent. A camp table and folding stool, clean and bare. An empty army surplus trunk, also painted in desert camouflage. And a folding cot with some fabric tossed at one end. In the buzzing desert silence Bo frowned at the cot. The fabric wasn't a rumpled sheet or blanket, it was too small. And it was flowered, or part of it was. Forcing herself to go closer, Bo realized it was a pile of scarves, tablecloths, an old nylon blouse in lavender with sparkling, star-shaped buttons. Incongruous in the spartan setting. And familiar. Bo had seen those scarves and tablecloths before, obscuring the face and body of an old black woman lost in schizophrenia.

"Old Ayma!" Bo said aloud, suddenly shivering in the mottled light. "What happened?"

Outside the tent a tumbleweed rolled past the open flap like some brittle, sentient being pursued by demons. Bo left the tent with equal alacrity and stood watching as the tumbleweed hurried downhill, snagged on a clump of cholla, and

then broke free only to be swept into a small blind canyon at
the bottom of a wash.

Had Ayma wandered here the night she vanished? Bo wondered. And what would happen to a psychotic old black
woman in a place named Hadamar II? Had Ayma been exter-
minated? Had Mort? Maybe Ann Lee Keith was wrong and
MedNet had nothing to do with Mort's death at all. Maybe
some neo-Nazi fanatic was just camping out here and picking
off lunatics for fun!

Determinedly, Bo skirted the perimeter of the campsite,
watching the ground. If whoever was here had killed Old
Ayma, he would have to stash the body, get it away somewhere so the coyotes and vultures, then the insects, could do
their work downwind and out of sight. But Old Ayma had
been a big woman, nearly six feet tall. There was only one cot
in the tent, only one person. And nobody could haul Ayma's
body very far.

The tumbleweed was shivering in the wind, jammed into
the blind canyon. Bo scrambled downhill on instinct, watching. Maybe the tumbleweed was speaking, or maybe the wind
was. But something was pulling her toward an inconsequential little slot canyon she wouldn't have noticed if the tumbleweed hadn't found it first.

"Aagghh!" she howled within feet of the canyon. A sharp
pain shot messages from her left foot to her brain. In the
downhill rush she'd come too close to a cholla, and one of its
fat, spiny burrs was imbedded in the nylon of her sneaker. Sitting, she scraped the burr away with a rock and then removed
her shoe and sock. Only one spine had made it through to the
tender flesh of her arch, but she couldn't get it out. The spines
were barbed like fishhooks, and once embedded had to be sur-
gically removed.

"Damn," she said, limping to pull the tumbleweed from
the canyon mouth. "This is the last thing I need."

The canyon was like a thousand others carved in granite
and sedimentary stone by centuries of powerful and quickly

vanished runoff from spring rains. Wider at its sandy base than at its top, it meandered crookedly between pale pocked walls for twenty yards and stopped blind at a wall of speckled, pinkish granite. Bo limped quickly to the end and turned back. There was nothing there. Just the usual burnt-looking stems of creosote bushes, a tattered yucca, bees. Nothing had been dug, disturbed. Or had it?

Halfway out of the canyon under a rocky overhang at knee-level, she noticed an excessive accumulation of charcoal-colored creosote twigs. The strange little tubes dried and hollowed in the sun, leaving nothing but their diamond-shaped webbing like spindles of latticework. Bo had seen them everywhere in the desert, but never in clumps. Nudging the cluster apart with her good foot, she noticed something black in the sand beneath them. Something rubbery. Another sweep of her foot scattered the gray spindles and enough sand to suggest that the black shape might be a knee. It looked like a knee, bent and still.

"Oh, no," she whispered. "It wouldn't look like this. No."

Overhead a raven swooped to peer into the canyon, but said nothing. Bo watched the bird rather than her foot, which was scraping more sand off the knee. In the raven's thin shadow she imagined Mort Wagman, grinning. She had to do this, had to find what the backcountry deputies, the search parties, the cadaver dogs had not found. She had to do it for Mort.

The thing was, in fact, a knee. Bo stared at it for close to a minute before touching it. It was a black knee, but not any part of Old Ayma. It was a rubber knee attached to a rubber leg, flattened under two feet of sand, which fell away with a hiss as Bo pulled the thing from its burial. The leg was connected to a body, arms. It was a wetsuit, Bo realized, with a ten-inch, double-edged diver's knife still belted about its waist.

Sweating, she draped the heavy garment over her shoulder and hobbled out of the canyon. So he'd camped here and buried a wetsuit and a diver's knife in a blind canyon, and Bo knew why. This was the wetsuit he'd worn for the long swim away from his sister's blood, staining the water, rousing things with teeth.

"Hang in there, Mort," she yelled at the raven, still swooping in zigzags overhead. "I'm gonna find him, I promise."

Only minutes later as she gunned the Pathfinder back toward the state road did she recognize the flaw in her choice of pronouns.

"Him?" she bellowed, causing Molly's ears to lay back in alarm. "What if it was Old Ayma and not Mead at all? What if she wasn't sick but pretending to be so she could kill Mort? No wonder she was cheeking her meds—she didn't need them! And her shawls and tablecloths were in that tent. But who was she and what did she have to do with Mort, or Hopper Mead, or *Bo?* Was she the one making those phone calls, playing the taped terrier in the fog? Why?"

Molly scratched her ear with a hind paw but offered no answers.

Ten minutes later Bo roared to a stop in the driveway of Ghost Flower Lodge only to be met by Dura in the Indian version of hysteria, her eyes wild inside ashen flesh.

"Zach is going to kill a man," she said softly, and then collapsed on the ground beside Bo's car.

Chapter 34

"Where is Zach?" Bo asked after several of the Neji carried Dura into the lodge and elevated her feet. "Tell me where Zach is."

"I don't know," Dura barely whispered. "He's going to kill that man, Henderson."

Henderson. Bo struggled to retrieve information attached to the name and found nothing. But she'd heard the name before, she was sure. A rental car parked in her field of vision brought it back. She'd seen Henderson there a week ago, talking to Zach. He'd looked like George Washington. But his eyes as he surveyed the lodge had been those of a shark.

"MedNet!" Bo whispered to herself. Henderson must be a representative of MedNet. And if Zach were about to murder him, then Zach must share Ann Keith's conviction that MedNet was responsible for Mort Wagman's murder as well as the ruin of the Neji's dream. But Ann Lee Keith had been wrong. The killer's agenda, Bo knew, was measurably more diabolical than the worst a mere corporation could envision. More diabolical because it derived from twisted human feeling that had grown to obsession. Bo was sure she knew who the killer was in spite of her suspicions about Old Ayma, knew who had stalked and tormented her. Zach in his bitterness and self-loathing was about to kill the wrong man!

And there was no way to stop him. Bo shuddered as she identified something in the air. A sort of resigned shock. The aura of the hospital waiting room after disaster has claimed lives as yet unidentified. Barely seven o'clock in the morning, she thought, and time for the Neji had run out. Zachary Crooked Owl, raised as an Indian with no comprehension of the barbaric culture around him, was about to join it. And with that the dream of the Neji would vanish as if it had never been.

Finding Zach and Dura's oldest daughter, Maria Jueh, Bo handed the girl Molly's leash and said, "Your job is to care for this puppy until I get back." Then she found Ojo, tremulous as a young deer, hiding in the kitchen.

"Do you know where your father's gun is, the twenty-two?" she asked the boy.

"Dad took it the other night."

"Took it where?"

"Took it out somewhere, I don't know, didn't bring it back."

His clear, dark eyes were swimming with tears. Bo feigned interest in a cabinet door, turning her back to spare his pride. He was only eleven, but he was an adult in Indian terms, a man. He couldn't cry even though his father was about to blow his world apart.

"You know your father very well," she said to the cabinet. "Where do you think he stashed the gun? Where do you think he will try to kill this man?"

"Henderson is stealing everything the Neji worked for for so long," Ojo recited, trying for macho. "He deserves to die."

"Oh, crap," Bo exploded, turning to knot the boy's T-shirt in her fist. "Henderson's a business deal. He's nothing. But the *killer's* been living in a tent right next to the reservation. Now where's Zach?"

"I saw the man with the army tent," Ojo said, wide-eyed.

"And I think Dad'll go to Yucca Canyon. That's where he always goes."

Bo took off at a dead run, ignoring the cholla barb in her foot. If she could just get to Zach in time, she could stop whatever was going on. She could save Ghost Flower Lodge.

"Call the Sheriff's Department *now*," she yelled over her shoulder to Ojo as another car pulled into the lodge driveway.

"I'm Bob Thompson, from MedNet," she heard the well-dressed driver tell one of the Neji. In the bright morning sun, Bo could see that the man had had a facelift. Somehow the fact made her run faster.

Ten minutes later she was there, gasping painfully in the growing glare. Mort's cairn was visible, several stones larger than she had left it. The creosote shrubs, smoke trees, cholla, ocotillo, and yucca were there, as well as the million hidden lives scritching between boulders or between grains of sand. The lip of the canyon teemed with unseen things, but not with Zachary Crooked Owl, a rifle, and a man named Henderson.

"Zach!" Bo yelled into clean air that suddenly felt thick, ragged in the throat. "Zach, don't do anything until you hear what I found. It's important, Zach. You need to know this!"

But the wind merely juggled her words like birdsong and then dispersed them over the desert rubble like bits of chaff. It was pointless to yell. Zach wasn't there, unless he was *in* the canyon instead of at its lip. Bo limped to the edge and glanced downward ten stories at a drama made soundless by a warm surface wind sliding over the cooler air mass in the canyon below. Zach was yelling at a man in a suit, the man who, but for his crew cut, might have been the nation's first president. Henderson. Bo watched Zach's mouth moving without sound, watched him raise the .22, watched Henderson turn to run only to realize there was nowhere *to* run. He was trapped.

Then from a fall of rock on the canyon's western slope, still lost in morning shadow, something moved. A figure, nearly as big as Zach, flinging itself from a rock to land on the black man.

For a moment the figure seemed suspended, floating below like a dark bottle on a river, seen from a bridge. Then it crashed into Zach, a shot exploded, and the man in the suit flung his arms over his face as if he were weeping. The rifle lay on parched rock, and Bo could hear nothing but a sound like a huge pellet spinning in a metal can. A throb that hummed. The sound of the rifle shot, she realized, trapped between the canyon walls. Then something behind her, a crunch of dry gravel, made her turn and move away from the precipice just as a long arm pushed hard through the space where she'd just stood. Above it two flat blue eyes regarded her with distaste.

"Come here," the man told her in a voice used to address children by people who hate children. "You're going to die now."

"You're going to hell now," Bo answered as events began to shine with speed.

He grabbed her arm in lean, wiry fingers and she fell, only to be dragged toward the canyon lip a few feet away.

"A suicide," he pronounced in cultured tones. "You've been depressed." The humorless chuckle that followed was familiar. Bo had heard it inside fog, and panicked. But not this time.

"Hadamar," a voice chanted in her head, over and over. Beneath the word she felt clear and certain as the wind she could actually see as she wrapped her right hand around the only weapon available, a single cholla growing feebly between slabs of granite. The pain made everything dark, slammed up her arm and into the base of her brain as she let him pull her upright. Then she smashed the agony in her hand against his face. Into his eyes.

Later she would remember that he clawed at his face, that

he reeled away from her into singing air. She would remember that his scream as he fell was weak, like a bit of fence wire whining in a breeze. But at the moment all she could remember was to fall backward onto warming granite as the pain made her vomit, and then lose consciousness.

Chapter 35

Someone had placed two boulders in a small blue room. Bo
blinked as the image refused to go away. She knew she was in a
hospital; she could remember parts of the drive down from the
desert. A man named Bob had driven her to the hospital in a
rental car that smelled like licorice. He'd been strangely cheerful, she recalled. As if the drive were a social event. But after that
things were a blur.

Shock, they said in the emergency room. She was in shock.
No sedation then, but maybe a little local anesthesia for that
hand? They had bustled about as she lay on a gurney under
white flannel blankets. Occasionally a nurse or emergency
room tech would pause over the blood pressure cuff and whisper, "You *grabbed* a cholla?"

Eventually Andrew had arrived accompanied by an Arab
sheik with the most spectacular eyelashes Bo had ever seen. A
hand surgeon, Andy said. Dr. Something-Or-Other. He
would be, she thought as the boulders moved slightly, the one
responsible for the gauze balloon full of tubes swathing her
right hand. The balloon was swelling and deflating regularly,
pushing her hand against a Ping-Pong paddle to which it was
taped. The sound was oddly reassuring, and it didn't hurt.
Nothing hurt.

"Why are there rocks in here?" she said aloud, causing both

rocks to stand and move toward her bed. They were both Zach Crooked Owl, except that one of them was a woman. Zach had lost weight, Bo noticed, and the woman was wearing a dramatic ensemble with a cape. And scarves. Bo recognized the use of scarves.

"Ayma!" Bo greeted her. "I thought you were dead!"

"Bo, I'd like to introduce my mother," Zach said proudly.

"Mother?" Bo hauled out of memory the story of a woman who left the Neji Reservation thirty years ago and never came back. A woman who might or might not have killed her brother, who'd been her pimp. "How can you be Zach's mother? You're Old Ayma. What's going on?"

"Let's just say my line of work requires discretion," the woman said in a voice like rustling silk. "When I read in the papers about this MedNet thing trying to rip off my son, I did some checkin' around, found out somethin' else was goin' down out there as well. Rich white dude campin' out there, watchin'. Thought I'd watch him back."

Bo's head was clearing, but not fast enough to make sense of the information. "Rich white dude?" she said.

"*Dead* rich white dude," Zach answered with satisfaction. "Randolph Mead, Jr. He got the other end of what they just dug out of your hand. Long fall, too."

"I knew who it was. But *why* . . . ?"

"A sick man," the female Crooked Owl noted with distaste. "I knew he was up to somethin', just wasn't sure what. Best way to keep an eye on him, watch out for Zachary and all those beautiful grandchildren of mine was to get myself in the place, right? So I got crazy."

Bo wiggled her nose to clear the fuzz from her brain. "You put on a terrific act," she said. The fuzz was tenacious.

"My line of work *is* acting, honey. But I didn't act fast enough. If I'd known he was gonna kill that young man, I would've made sure he didn't. I went lookin' for him later, after I knew what he done. Went to his dumbass little tent the morning after Zach found that young man's body, but the sucker wasn't there. Left my crazy clothes on his bed so he'd know somebody'd been there."

"Hopper Mead's brother killed Mort," Bo pronounced slowly. "He camped out in the desert and killed Mort after he'd sliced open his sister's femoral artery and thrown her to the sharks. And he named his camp Hadamar, even had a sign made. Why?"

Zach sighed. "You're right on all counts. Mead's alibi for the time of his sister's death was the word of a clerk in his office, old guy named Anselm Tucker. Tucker panicked and took off over the weekend with some of Mead's millions, leaving a condo as collateral. When the cops found him someplace in Tennessee, he told them everything. Seems it started when Hopper Mead met Mort at some fund-raiser up in L.A. last year. They began dating; it got serious; Randolph couldn't handle it. Looks like he killed them both."

"But *why* . . . ?" Bo spluttered as Bird, Ann Lee Keith, Estrella, and Andrew hurried into the suddenly crowded room.

"Our plane leaves in an hour, but I had to see you," Ann Keith said through tears as Zach and his mother politely left. "Thank you for everything you've done. What a courageous friend my son found out there in the desert!"

Bo nodded. "Hey, Moonmuffin," she grinned at the raven-haired boy inspecting the lid of a plastic pitcher on her nightstand, "which bird are you today?"

"Moonbird," he announced, spilling ice water into a box of tissues. "I'm Moonbird, like the Indians said. Moonbird is the son of Raven, and that's my dad. I'm going to go to his same school, Bo, and take some medicine so I can learn to read like the other kids. Then I'm going to write down my poems, like Baudelaire!"

"And I want to see every single poem," Bo told him as Estrella rattled car keys and shook her head fondly.

"Madge is furious about that case you closed yesterday," she said. "Thinks you should have thrown the mother in jail for having a spider tattoo. She told me to tell you she's ordered a plant as a get-well gift. A cactus."

"Great," Bo grinned. "I can make it into jelly and spill it in her procedures manual."

"She'll just get another one. Hey, I've gotta get your friends to the airport. Try to stay out of trouble until I can get back, Bo: I want to hear all about this later."

In minutes no one was left in the room but Andrew LaMarche, pensive in a three-piece suit.

"Molly's at my apartment, and I've phoned Dr. Broussard," he said. "She wants you to call her as soon as you can. As soon as the anesthesia wears off."

His gray eyes were tired and shadowed with worry.

"Bo, that man nearly killed you."

"Do you know why?" she asked softly.

"The police were able to go through his home and office before his lawyer knew he was dead. They found some things . . . literature, the rifle he used to kill Mort, and a list, Bo. I have a copy."

From his jacket he took a folded sheet of paper and handed it to her.

Bo shook it open with her left hand and read four names. "Hopper, Mort Wagman, Bird Wagman, Bo Bradley."

"Life unworthy of life," Randolph Mead had written beneath the names. "Exterminate."

"Ann Keith was right when she said Bird's life was in danger," Bo wept. "But she had the wrong perpetrator. Why, Andy? Mead was the one trying to drive me crazy as well, the one with the tape of the barking dog, Tucker's dog. And then he was going to kill me. Why?"

"We'll know more later," Andrew sighed, "but it appears that he became obsessed with the idea that his sister would marry Mort and produce 'defective' children. He was always a loser, Bo. Failed at everything he tried and thought the world owed him a parade anyway. This think tank he funded was a sham, nothing but a forum for his own half-baked social theories. About a year ago when his sister began seeing Mort Wagman, he went off the deep end into the old Nazi eugenics thing. 'Genetically defective people,' all that. When he heard there might actually be a marriage, he apparently knifed Hopper on her yacht and threw her into the water. The blood would draw sharks. It *did*."

Bo watched the gauze balloon over her right hand inflating and deflating, pushing blood around the multiple incisions necessary to extract more cholla spines than she wanted to count.

"I found his wetsuit buried in a canyon," she nodded. "And a diver's knife. He must have swum to shore after killing his sister and then taken the evidence out to the desert for hiding."

"The police have the wetsuit and knife. They'll run tests . . . "

"All this because Mort had a psychiatric illness," Bo interrupted, incredulous. "The Hadamar sign, stalking me, two murders . . . "

"There are always people who thrive on an imagined sense of superiority to others, Bo. Randolph Mead was one of them. When his deluded beliefs reached obsessive proportions he felt justified in his decision to kill. I'm afraid our society is full of people just like him."

Bo remembered a vicious chuckle lurking in fog. "But why the dog tapes, Andy? Why did he do all that to me?"

Andrew LaMarche pressed his palms together under his chin and looked out the room's curtained window. "I discussed that with Eva," he said. "It's her guess that Mead became aware of you as he watched you and Mort during your walks to Yucca Canyon. He had no twisted personal resentment of you as he did of Mort and the boy, but he became curious about you, about what it would take to . . . to . . . "

"To break my back psychologically, reduce me to the quivering mess he thought I was anyway," Bo finished the sentence, noticing Andrew's fingertips turning white from the force with which he was pushing his hands together. "He was *experimenting* with me, is that it?" Inside its gauze balloon her own right hand twitched jubilantly.

"Eva suspects it was something like that, at least in the beginning. But then when you denied him the pleasure of that power over you, when he lost at a game built on his fantasied superiority, he added your name to the list. He had to obliterate you as well. It became personal."

"I'm only going to say this to you and to Eva," Bo whispered through clenched teeth. "I'm glad that cholla was there! Now, what about Ghost Flower? How does this affect what's happening to the Neji? Since MedNet wasn't behind Mort's death after all, nothing's changed, right? They're still taking over?"

Andrew LaMarche relaxed and grinned, showing even white teeth under his trim mustache. It was a handsome grin, Bo thought. Magical.

"Well, I don't quite understand what's happened, but MedNet's PR man, this Bob Thompson, seems to know Zach's mother from somewhere. Neither one of them will say anything about it except how meaningful they found the singing of some monks. Then they laugh. It's difficult to imagine a less likely pair in the company of singing monks, but they clearly have a mutual history. She's, umm, a sort of businesswoman. Escort services. It may be that Thompson has met her in that capacity."

"Oh dear," Bo replied, knitting her brow, "I thought she got away from that life years ago when she left San Diego with Zach's father."

"In a way," Andrew hedged. "She owns a number of escort services, *manages* them."

"She's a madam?"

"Obsolete term, Bo. The point is, Thompson's hiring her to manage the PR for MedNet's interests in the Ghost Flower program until the Neji's attorney can untangle the legalities of Mead's loan. Mort's offer of financial help still stands, according to *his* attorney. The legal mess will take months, but meanwhile the proceeds remain with the Indians. Thompson's not playing hardball with them, Bo. He actually seems to want to help."

"And Henderson?"

"Thompson sent him packing. Henderson didn't think it was a battle worth fighting and backed off. The Neji are throwing a powwow this weekend to celebrate. Would you like to be my date?"

"I'd be honored," Bo replied, extending a swollen wad of gauze for him to kiss. "I really would."